Chapter 1

Jake Stewart thought he had seen it all in his two decades as a big-city journalist. But, he had never seen a 200-foot tall naked woman.

But, there she stood, just across the road from him.

At least in his mind's eye.

The play of light and shadows created by the late afternoon sun's rays sliding across the bumps and dips of a towering butte in the Superstition Mountains "revealed" the silhouette of a curvaceous woman — at least to a person with sufficient imagination.

And Jake had that imagination.

Oh, brother, you've been alone too long, Jake laughed to himself.

This was John Wayne country of stark rock buttes, turning red in the glow of the evening sun, towering independently high above the desert floor populated with giant saguaro and other cactus. Where when the sun disappeared, the coyotes came out to howl into the black — interrupted only by a million stars and a moon so bright it lit the imagination.

All that was needed now was for a 200-foot "Duke" to come riding by on a giant horse, sweep up the naked woman, and say, "A man's gotta do what a man's gotta do, pardner."

Popping the top on another can of beer he had pulled from a cooler beside his camp chair, Jake let his brain roam over the mirage in the butte rising on the other side of a gully from his RV.

The nakedness of a woman — whether in real life or an image — was such a beautiful, breathtaking sight when seen for the first time … or anytime, really.

Yet, women who Jake had been with had been quick to turn off the lights.

What were they thinking in their fits of modesty?

But of course, whether here in this Arizona state park campground or near his birthplace of western Washington, that was the question for Jake. He had never known what women were thinking, even when he was with his wife for a dozen turbulent years.

Maybe his cluelessness was the reason he was traveling alone through the Southwest in his aging RV he fondly called the Beast.

Built in the mid-1980s, when dollar-a-gallon gas was still a fresh memory, the Beast looked like a sheet metal box with its non-aerodynamic square corners and flat windshield and drove like a box on wheels, shuddering when hit by wind gusts from passing semi-trucks.

Inside though, she was a tiny home. She packed a sink, stove, fridge, and dinette that could seat four — but better two — in the front and a toilet plus shower and queen-sized bed squeezed into the rear, all in less than 250 square feet.

Jake picked it up for $4,000 from a retired couple who had kept it immaculate but were getting too old for motor homing. Just the price, he figured, if it gave out alongside the road, he could walk away and feel no pain.

Small, snug, best for just one person, the Beast offered an ever-changing view out the three-foot picture window and was Jake's ticket to one giant road trip.

Now, sitting out in the fall rays of a warm setting sun on the eastern edge of the great Sonoran desert — far from rainy Seattle — the decision felt so right.

Jake picked up his camera resting on the side tray of his camp chair to capture the image of the illusion of the naked woman before the setting sun changed it — maybe a shot to chuckle at later when reviewing his trip photos.

"Help! Help! Help me!"

Jake bolted upright. The voice seemingly came from the red cliffs — what the hell, could the imaginary woman talk? — then Jake realized the cry came from a large split between two spires to the right of where he was photographing.

"Help! Somebody!"

Grabbing his camera in his left hand, Jake ran across the campground road, dropped down a gully then worked his way up the other side, where he saw a stunning, real, young woman in a black sports bra and pink running shorts deep in the crack that cuts through the cliffs. She was bracing herself against the two sides, standing on rubble. Long dark hair spilled from her head in waves of curls.

"Don't look up here," she said, dropping her arm reflexively over her chest while nodding her head downward, "look down there."

Looking down, Jake saw two hairy legs in white tennis shoes sticking out of a pile of sharp-edged rocks.

He did what anyone would do in that situation: He froze.

His brain whirled and crackled as it tried to catch up.

"Who is he?" Jake dropped to his knees, quickly tossing aside rocks covering the body. "Is he alive?"

"I don't know," the woman snapped back. Her words were harsh but her accented voice arrived in Jake's ears like music. "I was taking a shortcut through this crack when I saw his legs. He must have been caught in a rock slide."

In a few seconds, Jake and the woman had uncovered the body's head. It was obvious no first aid was needed.

Retrieving his camera from the gravel next to the boulders, and seeing a mist of fine sand drifting through the fading sunlight maybe foretelling further rock slides, Jake volunteered to go call the police.

"I'm not staying here by myself with the body!" the woman nearly shouted. "I'll go call the police and you stay with him."

And that's how Jake found himself in the local news for finding a body at Beaver Teeth Rocks.

Chapter 2

"Bitch!" fumed the man storming out of the newspaper office, brushing past Jake's shoulder.

"An unhappy reader?" Jake asked the woman at the front counter when he got inside.

"Worse," she replied. "An unhappy potential advertiser."

She gave a rueful smile as she said it though, as no big loss. That came as a surprise to Jake, as he knew newspapers were generally hurting for ads.

Her eyes followed the man to his car parked in

front of the office and watched him slam the driver's door and roar off. "He came in here, Mr. all High and Mighty, and announced in a big voice he had invented a new sure-catch fishing lure.

"He wanted to know how much a full-page ad would be. I told him. He toned his voice down and asked how much a half page would be. I told him. Then, he wanted to know how much an ad about the size of his hand would be. Again, I told him.

"Then, he leans in, gives me what could have passed for a charming look on a different face, and suggests I give him an ad this week for free, and if it works, he would be in next week to buy an ad.

"Which is when I said, how about I go to McDonald's and tell them if they give me a free hamburger today, I'll gladly be in next Tuesday to buy one."

She smiled at Jake. "That really set him off.

"So I told him, get out of the office, you're bothering me. Take your business to the other newspaper in town.

"That's when you came along."

"Huh," said Jake. "I didn't know there was another newspaper in town."

A devilish look came to her eyes. "There's not. Now, what can I do for you? Want a free ad, too?"

Jake laughed. He was taking a liking to this short, rotund woman, who looked to be about 50 and had some pizazz.

"No," said Jake. "I'm the one who found the body yesterday up by the campground. I took a couple of photos I thought the paper might be interested in."

"Oh, I am so sorry. My name is Suzanne McPhee, and the man you found was our editor, Gus Noise. Ahhh…" she said, looking around at the otherwise empty office, "There is no one here to take your story at the moment. I'm the paper's owner, but certainly not a reporter."

"I have some news writing experience," replied Jake. "How about you log me into a computer, I'll write what I saw, and the reporter can blend that into a story."

"News writing experience? Are you a reporter?"

Jake paused and then said up until recently he had been the metro editor at the oldest newspaper in Seattle, but when it slashed the newsroom payroll by half — replacing the highly-paid veterans with kids who could get clicks online — he took his severance, bought a 30-year-old RV and was slowly traveling the Southwest, well away from deadlines, ringing telephones and complaining readers.

When he was finished, Suzanne brightened. "I need an editor. You're an editor. Can you help us out for a few weeks until I can hire someone? Otherwise, I may have to fold the *Gazette* — 'The Light of the Desert.' It's 120 years old… a shame to let it die."

Jake had spent all of his working life at newspapers, but big-city newspapers with dozen of reporters, a troupe of editors, and a squad of photographers all hurrying about in a constant state of an uproar trying to get tomorrow's newspaper out.

As he looked over Suzanne's shoulder, he saw nothing like that.

The office itself was one large room in a corner of

a building remodeled from what looked to have been a former car dealership into separate offices, with large show windows looking onto a sleepy main street.

Three wooden desks with well-used chairs took up the front area. One desk had stacks of last week's newspapers alongside, with orange paper tubes stenciled with the *Gazette's* name. Probably the entire circulation department in one sitting.

A computer monitor a few generations past its prime dominated another smaller desk. Coke cans snuggled up against the keyboard. A stack of reporter's notebooks teetered along the edge.

Further back, against a window with a massive shade was likely the editor's desk — larger but no neater, piled with papers, notepads, coffee cups jammed with mismatched pens, and its own monitor.

Shoved back from the desk as if the occupant had just stepped out for a coffee break was an antique wooden office chair on wheels, stuffing breaking through the seams of a seat cushion. This must have been the editor's — Gus's — desk. He wasn't coming back.

The rest of the office was given over to glass-topped layout tables along the back, another desk and computer where likely the ad designer worked, and the front counter where Suzanne was standing, waiting for Jake's decision.

Jake didn't need a job. He still had a bank account fat with his severance pay — 52 weeks at his previous salary.

Before coming in, out of professional curiosity, he had picked up a copy of the *Gazette* someone had tossed away at the campground. The school lunch menu, a dry recitation of last week's town council meeting, and a recycled press release from the local electric company on conservation made up the front page — this was a newspaper like a child's drawing was to a Picasso. All the lines, none of the art.

Still, as his first boss had said, once you get ink in your blood, it's hard to find anything else as satisfying. And this would just be temporary. He would be like a mercy worker, coming to the rescue of a country newspaper, putting out a couple of issues, then getting back to lazy travels. Like "editors without borders."

He could continue staying at the RV campground. Along with the towering, start buttes unmatched by anything in his native Pacific Northwest, there were trails, a pool, pickleball courts, plus showers. If he paid by the month, he would get a discounted rate.

And editing a weekly? That only comes out once a week? He was used to the high pressure of a city daily, where every minute counted in the race to beat the cruel deadlines. How hard could one issue a week be? How would he fill up his days?

Although as he had that thought, he also remembered another editor who had worked his way up from small-town weeklies to metros, and who had told Jake: "At a weekly, you work six days a week and come in on Sundays to straighten up your desk."

But that's oldtimers for you, Jake smiled inwardly. They loved to talk about how hard they had it in the old days.

"Sure, I could help out." Jake extended his right hand to make the universal handshake agreement.

Which is how Jake went from being the metro editor of a 150,000-circulation big-city daily newspaper where none of the public paid any attention to his name to the editor at a 1,625-circulation weekly in a rural desert country where shortly, every reader would know him by his first name.

Chapter 3

Jake was nursing a late afternoon Wednesday beer at Lester's Whiskey Saloon, the town's watering hole, that had a dozen swivel stools along a well-nicked but highly lacquered wooden bar, a couple of pool tables, round tables, and mismatched chairs along the walls and a closet-sized kitchen.

Waiting for his order of a BBQ Cowboy Burger and tater tots to come up, he was feeling proud for getting his first edition of the *Gazette* out.

And sure, he mostly followed the lead of the paper's staff, but he had stepped in and as the owner, Suzanne, wished, had kept the paper alive for another week.

He was surprised Suzanne herself wasn't around the office or had even come by to see how he was doing. Once she had announced to the staff that Jake was a temporary editor, she had disappeared.

The bell over the bar-room door jingled, and like the other half dozen patrons in the bar, he automatically pivoted his head to see who was coming in.

Rodney. Oh good grief thought Jake, turning his head back so as not to catch Rodney's eye, I've been in town only a few days and I'm getting to know the town characters.

Rodney looked around, getting used to the bar's dark and cool interior when he noticed a couple of guys sitting at the bar. Maybe they were tourist fishermen, as one of the men had on a well-worn t-shirt, sporting the witticism, "Big Mouth Bass..." and in smaller letters, "...Liar."

"Hey, one of you guys like to shoot some pool?" Rodney asked.

"Sure," said the smaller of the two men, sliding off his barstool.

"I'll roll you for the break," said Rodney, and then suddenly slid one arm under the guy's butt, another behind his shoulders, lifted him up, and rolled him across a green felt pool table.

"I rolled you, I break," announced Rodney, who had run around the pool table to pick up the shocked man on the other side.

"Rodney! Put the little fella down!" yelled an exasperated bartender from her position working behind the bar. "I've told you, that ain't funny."

Rodney apologized to the still dazed little guy, offered to buy him and his buddy a beer, and started racking up the pool balls.

"So Jake, any word on how Gus ended up beneath a pile of rocks at Beaver Teeth Cliffs?" asked the bartender, sliding a plate of burger and cheesy tots in his direction.

An image of the rock spires near his campsite in the shape of a curvaceous naked woman, captioned with "Beaver Teeth," quickly ran through Jake's mind, proving a man's lizard brain is always at work.

However, out loud, he replied, "No. The sheriff is being real tight-lipped. Maybe he is holding back some clues, but I think he has no real idea either.

"He is also searching for the woman who first found Gus's body. I guess she just disappeared after making the 9-1-1 call."

The bartender was wearing a faded blue t-shirt with the words, "Not today... and probably not tomorrow, either."

To Jake, she could have been 30 to 50 years old, that mid-range where women can linger so long. A clue to her age may have been the frosted blonde hairdo, now out of date by a couple of decades. Or maybe it was her small-town hairdresser who was a couple of decades out of date.

She looked friendly enough, but still, her face matched her t-shirt, she didn't look like she took any guff. She had introduced herself as Bonny when sliding Jake his first beer. She already knew who he was. Such is the notoriety of a small-town newspaper editor.

"Gus was probably another victim of the Moser's hoax," said Bonny, sliding off to pour a couple of beers for two women down the bar.

She returned in a few minutes with another beer for Jake.

"Thanks," he said, "and what do you mean by the Moser's hoax?"

"The legend is that a few miners were returning to Phoenix from the 1899 Klondike gold rush with a haul of gold, but a local Indian uprising scared the bejesus out of them. So, the Army assigned Major Pat

Moser and a small troop of soldiers to escort them through the hills. Well... just a minute, I got to cash out an order," said Bonny, leaving Jake alone.

Coming back with another beer, she continued: "But what really got the story stuck in people's minds, a couple of women 'retired' from their jobs in Vegas in the '50s, came to town and opened a pie shop. An idea of their former profession might be in the double entendre names of their pies, like 'Poppin' cherry pie,' 'Cream me coconut,' and of course, 'Hard as a berry fruit pie.' Kids came for the pies and parents chuckled at the names.

"One of the women heard about the legend of Major Moses, and to add color to their restaurant, printed paper placemats telling the story of how Major Moser and the miners hid out in the hills to avoid the Indians, but only the major came out. In a couple of months, he had resigned from the Army, returned to this area, bought a couple of burros, and headed back up into the hills.

"And then... Rodney! Quit bothering the ladies and get back to your pool game! So...," turning her attention back to Jake, "one more?"

"Sure. So there are missing miners, stories of gold and then the major goes into the hills? What does he bring out?" asked Jake, taking the first draw off the fresh beer.

"That's the thing," said Bonny. "No one ever saw the major again. His belongings were left in his hotel room just like he disappeared from the face of the earth."

"That is strange," said Jake.

"Augh, it's a bunch of hooey," snorted Bonny. "First of all, the Indian uprisings were well past by the time of the Alaskan Gold Rush and why would miners bring gold home when they could have sold it in Alaska for dollars and transferred the money home?"

"Yeah, makes sense. So, why did you say Gus was a victim of the Moser hoax?"

"Gus was not the bubbliest beer in the six-pack," said Bonny, "and the last year or so, he had been in here cornering any old-timer he could find asking about the Moser gold. He had the idea the major either didn't come out of the hills alive or only brought out some of the gold.

"Then I heard he bought a fancy drone airplane with a camera and on weekends was flying it at different locations in the backcountry. I think he believed he could find where the gold was stashed."

"So the newspaper editor dreamed of getting rich off a fable," grinned Jake.

"Well," said Bonny walking away, "money is being made off the Moser gold."

"What?" asked Jake, "How do you mean?"

"You came in here for one beer, and stayed for four while I told the story. And Lester's cash register went cha-ching, cha-ching, cha-ching." And she laughed all the way down to the other end of the bar.

Chapter 4

"Robbie has done it again!" Jamie announced to the office on Thursday morning, holding the freshly printed *Gazette*.

"She has Jean Martin married to Dean Turnbull, and taking a vacation together in Mexico."

The young reporter looked over at Jake at the editor's desk and clarified, "The Martin's Silver Eagle Market is our biggest advertiser. And Dean Turnbull is the president of the bank. Oh, this is not good! We're doomed!"

Susan, the bookkeeper and circulation guru, looked up from the phone she was holding, "Jake, Jean Martin is on the phone for you. And, she sounds mad."

In a big city newspaper, the newsroom takes pride in tweaking the nose of advertisers. Once, a full-page advertiser called Jake at the city desk, asking that an arrest of his son for drunk driving be left out of the paper.

"We're putting that on the front page, and if you don't like it, go advertise in the other paper," shouted Jake.

The whole newsroom of nearly 100 broke out in applause at Jake's show of independence.

But here at the *Gazette*, there's only the ad designer Barbara, who worked three jobs around town including 20 hours a week at the *Gazette* to support her disabled husband, Jamie trying to get a foothold in journalism, Susan the bookkeeper, circulation director and ad sales rep still living with her mom, and then Robbie supplementing her meager nurse's retirement with her weekly Heard On the Street column.

And, the owner, Suzanne, who according to Jamie, wrote checks from money earned by Patrick, her husband, who brokered frozen chickens to keep the paper alive.

How do you measure the weekly paychecks of three real people against the freedom of the press? Would a woman reported — wrongly — of being unfaithful to her husband accept a First Amendment argument? Would she even listen?

"Hi, this is Jake, the new editor, can I help you?"

*****

"Well, that went better than expected," said Jake after a long conversation where he mostly said, "Un-uh," and "I see," and "Yes, of course not," and finally, "That's very nice of you."

Looking around at Susan, Barbara, and Jamie, who had not even pretended to be working while listening to Jake on the phone, he said, "She was naturally angry at first, but as she talked, she calmed down and ended up saying, 'Robbie is Robbie. We all love her.'

"And then she said something strange. She said Robbie was the only one who got the child sex scandal right. And that the whole town was so grateful that she gets a free pass.

"Weird."

Jake watched the entire staff of the *Gazette* exhale in relief.

Even better than applause, realized Jake.

*****

"The crows are chasing me!"

Robbie came bustling in the front door and

around the counter to where Barbara was working on the largest monitor in the office, crafting ads for next week's issue.

Robbie was well past 60, probably more likely 70 and maybe even 80. Short, white hair tightly curled on top of her head, dressed in a plaid jumper and hand-knitted sweater, holding tightly to a spiral notebook she used to record what people told her on the street.

Most of the time, she wore a bemused expression but not today. "The crows started cawing at me as I passed the Catholic Church, then chased me down the street. What do they want? Caw, caw, caw. What do they want?"

"The crows are big in this town all right," said Jake, "but Robbie, we have to talk about something in your column this week."

"OK, but let me give you a back massage. You look tense."

"That's not necessary, Robbie," Jake started to say, but the former nurse was already working her fingers into his lower neck. Jake thought in the modern workplace, it really wasn't right for a female employee to be rubbing her boss's back, but damn it felt good. Her 50 years of nursing taught Robbie how to relieve the sore spots.

"Has anyone seen Suzanne around?" wondered Robbie, switching to her elbows to hit pain spots Jake didn't even know he had. "Patrick is out of town and when he goes on a sales trip, she usually treats me to an ice cream sundae at Sweet Williams."

Leaning forward on his desk, head bowed to offer up as much of his back as possible, Jake made efforts to engage Robbie about the error in her column. Each time, Robbie deflected his questions with non sequitur comments about what people are saying about Gus's death, or who had just returned from a vacation.

Giving up, Jake wondered what's to be gained in criticizing a grandmother-aged rookie reporter. You'd just hurt her feelings. Who wants to make your grandmother cry? Anyway, it's unrealistic to expect an octogenarian to learn a new job skill set.

It's his job to keep errors out of the newspaper. He would have to watch her column more closely, maybe run it by Jamie before placing it on the page.

Robbie rubbed her hands together in tight circles to create heat from the friction, then held one warm hand near each of Jake's ears.

Robbie is more like a goodwill ambassador for the paper, rationalized Jake, and after that massage, anything she does was all right with him.

Chapter 5

"So, Rose, your husband suddenly returned home after going missing 16 years ago?"

Jake had learned the story from Robbie — in his first conversation with the "Heard on the Street" columnist since he became editor — about a local man, Frank Pflugrath, who had walked out of his home more than a decade ago with no hint or word why, and then returned just as abruptly.

Rose was the scorekeeper for the high school Wildcats football team and called in the team's stats on the Friday nights if the 'Cats lost — the coach wouldn't talk about defeats. She also worked as a candy maker at Arizona Dark Chocolate ("We're high on chocolate") the local chocolate factory started by a couple of hippies in the '60s, and Jake had asked her to drop by the newspaper office after her shift so he could get the story.

Still, in her white smock smeared with dashes of both light and dark chocolate, the woman in her early 50s twisted her free-chocolate-in-the-breakroom-sized backside on the hard wooden chair Jake kept beside his desk for in-person interviews. Jake had learned years ago a too-comfortable chair would just encourage people to talk, talk and talk well after their stories were told.

Another woman could have been embarrassed by the question, or angry at the newspaperman's invasion of family business, but Rose wasn't showing either of these emotions.

"I suppose Robbie told you that," she said, looking at Jake through a few strands of loose hair straying out from a purple scrunchie. "Well, it's true.

"I asked Frank to get off his lazy ass, and go to the store and get some milk for tomorrow's breakfast. I think he was watching some silly sports show. Anyway, he muttered something like, 'Yeah, I'll go get your milk,' and out the door he went. I saw his pickup backing out of the driveway, and that was the last I heard or saw Frank."

"But he came home again last week?" asked Jake, trying to slow down her retelling so his note-taking could keep up.

"Yeah, on Thursday, I was in the kitchen making my

dinner when I heard the door open, and in walked Frank. He dropped a grocery bag on the table, said, 'Here's your milk,' and then went over, plopped into his old lounger, grabbed the flipper, and turned on the TV to another sports show."

"He just walked in and resumed his old life?" asked Jake, who was finding the story incredulous. "After 16 years, how did he know you still lived there, or you hadn't changed the locks or weren't remarried, or that you still had his chair?"

"Yeah, strange, huh?" said Rose, though Jake thought she didn't exactly look like she thought it was strange at all.

"Well, it was my mom's house, she gave it to me in her will, so why should I have moved, and one husband was enough for me," she said, making "enough" sound like "enough nonsense."

"And his chair, I guess I just never got around to getting rid of it. Besides, having only one chair — my chair — in the living room looks unbalanced, don't you think?"

"So Frank is back, and all is right in the Pflugrath home?" inquired Jake.

"Well," said Rose, drawing out the word, "when Frank and I were first married we always drank whole milk because that's what Frank drank growing up on the farm. But just before he left, I had switched us to one percent because a woman's got to look out for her figure, right? Especially if she is working at the chocolate factory." She shifted from one over-stuffed butt globe to the other, leaning in for Jake to see the wiggle set off in the tight front of her smock.

"After he came in like that, I was like in a daze, I didn't know what to do. I drifted from the kitchen to the table, and not knowing what to think I looked into the grocery bag. Whole milk, he bought whole milk.

"And then it hit me: Isn't that just like a husband? You send him to the store for one thing, he takes forever and he still gets the wrong thing."

For a second the newspaper office was silent.

And then, "Hey Jake!" Jamie busted in the front door, "the radio says a body has been found in the caverns. You want me to cover that?"

"Eh, no Jamie, we can both go. But first, can you take a photo of Mrs. Pflugrath here? And Rose, I may have a few follow-up questions. Can you leave me your phone number?"

"Glad to, Mr. Newspaperman, glad to."

*****

In the car, Jake asked Jamie to tell him about the caverns.

"They were discovered about 100 years ago by some old rancher named Hap Brown," said Jamie, who was speeding in his paint-peeling VW Bug from the '80s.

"Old man Brown thought someone was rustling his cattle so he sat out one night in the rocks and sagebrush to keep an eye on his herd. He heard a cow bellow, and thinking a rustler was corralling it, he raced off, gun in hand toward the sound. But just as he arrived, he saw the cow fall into the ground. When he got nearer, he almost fell himself into a hole that later was measured to be about 20 feet across.

"At night, he couldn't see the cow or how deep the hole was but he came back the next day with wire and posts to fence it off. That's when he noticed the hole had no bottom."

Jamie honked twice and then passed a slow-moving motorhome on a curve. Jake was about to object, but Jamie said, "We get lots of tourists and fishermen coming for the reservoir lakes around here. They're gawking, but we have news to get to."

Jamie picked up the caverns story. "The rancher fetched a lantern he lowered into the hole on a rope, but the rope he had was only 50 feet long. Still, the lantern didn't touch the bottom.

"So, he rounded up a couple of brothers and came back the next day. I think the old coot was thinking there could be gold down there, as a couple of big gold rushes were going on elsewhere.

"Anyway, because he wanted to be the one to discover the gold, he tied a rope around his waist and had his brothers lower him. He went down, down, down until finally, at about 200 feet of rope, he touched the bottom.

"He saw, and probably smelled, a couple of his cows, dead from the fall. Looking around, light from his lantern didn't even reach the walls."

"Over the next year," continued Jamie, "he kept going back, each time being lowered by a rope tied around his waist, prospecting around the caverns for gold, silver, or any metals. He didn't find any. The walls sparkled, and for a while, he thought they might be embedded with diamonds, but it turned out to be some worthless crystal stuff that virtually melts in your hand.

"What he did find was some perfectly preserved carcasses of animals. It turned out the caverns were carved out of limestone over millions of years. The limestone draws moisture from any living creature, creating mummified remains. Nothing can live in the caverns — a mouse would die in a day and if you were left down there, you'd be a dead mummy in less than a week.

"Creepy right?" finished Jamie.

"Creepy, yes," replied Jake. "So no gold, no diamonds. What's the deal with the caverns today? Are they still fenced off?

"Oh, no," said Jamie, "they are one of the town's claims to fame.

"While the old rancher didn't find any gold, he did discover people would pay him 25 cents to be tied to a rope and lowered into 'The Hole to Hell,' as they were called for a time. Later, he upped the fee to 50 cents, rented them lanterns, and sold them lunch.

"After a couple of decades, he sold the caverns to a company that installed an elevator, and they offered guided tours at $10 a head. Owners have come and gone, but the caverns still draw the tourists who now pay $25. Probably 10,000 people a year descend into 'The Cowboy Caverns' — the new company thought 'The Hole to Hell' wasn't a very marketable name."

"Hey! Watch it! What the hell!" exclaimed Jake as a semi pulling two trailers nearly sideswiped the Bug.

"It's OK, that's a poop truck," said Jamie, slowing to make a turn onto a broken-up one-lane asphalt road. "They do drive fast."

"A poop truck?"

"Yeah, they bring biosolids from the metro areas to be dumped on farmland here in the rural part of the state. Biosolids, you know, right?" said Jamie. "It's what's left after the liquids and non-organic materials have been extracted at sewage plants."

"They dump that on farmland, where they grow crops for people to eat?" wondered an incredulous Jake.

"Well, technically, no. I think they spread it on fields where they grow alfalfa. And since most of the alfalfa around here is exported to Japan, our poop is fed to Japanese beef cattle. You've heard of Japanese cattle, right, raised with piped-in music and daily massages? Steaks that sell for $800 a pound?"

Warming to his topic, Jamie continued, "I did a story on the poop farm for the *Gazette* when I was still in high school. It's all pretty interesting, I guess, but the best part was the headlines I thought of:

"From crap to cash.

"Poop plops out a profit.

"And the best one — From ass to green grass.

"But Gus had no sense of humor. I think he used, 'Biosolids turn a buck.' Jeeze! How dull that man could be."

Jamie slowed on the paved but bumpy and broken blacktop one-lane road. "We have about a mile of this," he said just as the Bug hit a jarring hole, forcing Jake to grab the "oh hell" handhold.

"Sorry," said Jamie, twisting the wheel to avoid another bump. "After struggling for years, and putting off most maintenance, the current owners went bankrupt earlier this year. Now this place — including the restaurant at the caverns and the campgrounds all around — is up for auction."

"Waaaaaahhhhhhh!" a siren blasted from behind the Bug. "Oh-oh! I got a police car and an ambulance behind me. Hold on!" Jamie veered towards a wide spot where pavement gave way to chunky gravel.

"Just get us there in one piece," urged Jake. "But get us there quickly while the news is still fresh."

"Don't worry," said Jamie, nodding towards a dirt parking lot. "It was probably some tourist on a dirt bike riding at night who fell into the hole."

But that wasn't it at all.

Chapter 6

"Can I get you a cup of coffee while you wait for the sheriff to come up?"

Jake was sitting at the caverns' restaurant counter — now closed for the season — as Jamie ran around snapping photos. Rookie reporters with their junk energy. Sometimes, Jake had learned, you have to wait for life to come to you.

"Sure," he told the 40-ish caverns employee behind the counter, wearing a name tag that simply said, "Just Nell." He had seen her around town once or twice. She had a few extra pounds — but then, don't we all, thought Jake — but still echoed her youthful beauty with her blonde hair and generous curves.

Looking at her face, Jake now saw her real beauty all along was those azure blue eyes and "tell-me-more" smile. When a woman like that looks at you, a guy's libido roars to life.

"So what's the deal with 'Just Nell'?"

Pouring black coffee into a Cowboy Caverns' logo cup in front of Jake, she exhaled and said, "I might as well tell you. It's going to come out anyway now."

This was the moment Jake enjoyed most about his years in the newspaper business — when people let down their guard and told the story of their lives. Jake had found people collectively were pretty much the same world-round, yet individually each person was a different facet on a billion-sided diamond.

As long as they avoided politics and religion, and stuck to facts they had experienced rather than opinions they had borrowed — and kept the stories fairly short, as he was a newspaperman, not a novelist — Jake was the ears these talkers longed for.

"I grew up just outside of Tallahassee," Just Nell started, "and I was the perfect cliché of a trailer trash girl. But I had this body. So when a rich boy offered to marry me, I thought I had struck gold."

She pushed sugar and pods of creamer on a saucer toward Jake.

"But Junior was a weak daddy's boy who jumped when the old man barked. He drank, hit me, and called me filthy names. And then Daddy wanted a piece of me.

"After one particularly bad Saturday night, I was sitting crying behind the country club where the family went to drink and brag to their cronies when I saw a guy changing a tire on his van. I figured he was a hippie, the van was covered in neon psychedelic paint colors.

"But, there was something about his movements in taking off the wheel nuts, rolling over a new tire, bolting it on that spoke of someone who knew how to do things in the world. Junior couldn't open a beer without spilling some on his shirt."

Just Nell had taken a stool a couple of chairs down from Jake and was leaning her face on her arms propped on the counter.

"I don't know what made me do it, but I walked up to the guy and asked, 'Where are you heading?'

"He said he was going to the Northwest for the summer after just spending the winter in Key West.

"And then I said, 'If you'll give me a ride out of here, I'll keep you company.'

"That became our deal. He gave me a ride, and each morning I gave him a ride, and we put my old life miles behind.

"His name was Marv and he was a good guy who was kind to me. I surely didn't mind my part of the bargain, as he was a thoughtful lover. Junior was only after what Junior wanted.

"Marv also was really smart... but not smart in a show-off, 'I'm better than you' way but he opened doors in my brain."

Just Nell told how the couple found piecework across the U.S., sometimes working in the fields, sometimes her waitressing and Marv working as a short-order cook, sometimes working at golf courses that needed maintenance help for tournaments.

"We had been traveling for a couple of months, in no hurry, stopping to work odd jobs for cash, as we made our way up to the Northwest.

"We always took the back roads because that's where the real part of the country was, Marv said. One day, he saw a sign to 'Cowboy Caverns,' and he said,

'Cool, we've got to see that.'

"We had taken the tour and were having lunch here at the restaurant when I saw a help wanted sign.

"I asked an old guy sitting in the office over there," she nodded towards a glassed-in office in the back, "about the job, and he looked at me. And then he looked at Marv, and then back at me.

"A job for just you, or both of you?"

"Just me,' I said. I don't know why, but I felt it was time for me to strike out on my own.

"Marv gave me a surprised and disappointed look, but he had honored our deal, as I had. He turned and walked out to the van.

"Let me get my things,' I told the old guy, who I later found out was the owner and named Roy.

"And then I realized, I didn't have any things, other than the clothes I was wearing and the purse I was carrying.

"Roy sized up my situation pretty quickly, and told me, 'There's a room in the back where I sometimes stay when I'm tired, you can sleep there.'

"'Oh, it's that kind of deal, is it?' I asked him."

"'It's no kind of deal at all,' he replied. 'There's a lock on the inside of the door, and a bathroom — also with a lock — down the hall. This way,' he said, going back to looking at papers on his desk, 'I know you'll be to work on time.'

"I eventually did all of the jobs here. For the last two years of Roy's life, he was sick and I pretty much ran the place.

"When his heirs sold, I went along with the sale and became general manager. And then when that company went bankrupt and sold, I was as much a fixture here as the stuffed animals for sale in the gift shop and rock exhibits by the door. And that's where I'm at today."

Jake nodded, finished his coffee, and again asked: "Just Nell?"

"Oh, that. I told Roy I was running from an abusive husband who I didn't want to find me. He paid me in cash so my name wouldn't get reported on any forms.

"When his bookkeeper insisted on my name, Roy told her: 'Just Nell will do.'

"So 'Just Nell' became my new identity.

"Now, I guess, all my past will come out because I'm probably the first person to be questioned about what happened below."

"What do you mean?" asked Jake, who still didn't have a clue to who died or what was happening in the caverns below.

"Because I'm the only one who has a key to the elevator."

Chapter 7

"She died from dehydration. We'll be bringing her desiccated body up in a few minutes," Sheriff Highkok told Jake and Dave Barns, the owner of K-TUS, the local radio station.

"Dehydration? That doesn't make any sense. I just saw her three days ago when she hired me to fill in at the *Gazette*," said a puzzled Jake. "The human body can go several days without water."

"You don't know about the caverns, do you?" Dave said to Jake. "Sheriff, you better explain to our new editor. I have to go out to the van to do a live remote."

"These caverns are limestone," said Sheriff Curtis Highkok. "Limestone draws moisture. There are no bugs down there, or rats or snakes or any living thing. A rat would be dead in a couple of hours, a human would be dead in two to three days."

The sheriff was a trim man, about 50, who kept his graying hair short, his black boots shined and greenish-brown uniform sharply creased.

His dark eyes bored in on Jake. "One of the exhibits down there is a bear that scientists think fell into the cave a couple of thousand years ago, but it's perfectly preserved. Scientists think it survived the fall but died when limestone sucked out its moisture. It was mummified. You can still see the claw marks on the wall where the bear tried to climb out."

Jake was still trying to resolve the conflict of being hired by Suzanne McPhee on Tuesday and then learning she was dead in the Cowboy Caverns on Friday. And that she had been in the giant, dark caverns long enough to die of thirst.

And even though he tried not to think of her clawing the walls to get out, that image of the bear's claw marks stuck in his brain.

"How did she get down there? And why? Was there any evidence of foul play?" Jake asked the sheriff.

"We don't know at this point. I can confirm we are treating this as a homicide, as her arms and legs were bound.

"The caverns are closed for the season, and as far as we know, she had no business down there. She is the mayor of the town, and as you know, owns the newspaper, but neither of these would give her reason for being down there. As for a toxicology report, we'll leave that up to the coroner."

Hearing a ding, the sheriff moved to one side. "Here's the elevator now. Can you step back and let the ambulance crew bring out her body."

Jamie had sidled up to Jake at this point. "Hey, Jake, let's catch the elevator down and take a look. I'll try to get some photos," he said, leaning into Jake's ear. Lifting his head, he added, "If that's OK, of course, sheriff."

"Go ahead. Just don't disturb the spot where she died, and if you find anything, let me know." The sheriff turned to follow the body outside.

Jake had never been any more underground than the subbasement of the Federal Building in Seattle. But, on the elevator ride down, he told Jamie he had seen pictures of Carlsbad Caverns in New Mexico and Mammoth Caves in Kentucky with its underground river.

"Yeah," replied, Jamie. "You're kind of talking about the Nordstrom of caverns. This is more like the Wal-Mart of deep holes in the ground."

The elevator doors opened to a short man-made tunnel leading to the first natural cavern. Along the walls, tiny crystals sparkled in the brightness of strategically placed floodlights guiding visitors.

"Don't touch the walls," cautioned Jamie. "The moisture and oils from your hands will discolor them.

See those sparkles? The old guy who discovered this place thought they could be diamonds. That was his first disappointment."

Jamie became a walking brochure, telling Jake the caverns were formed millions of years ago in limestone deposits. The deposits themselves were created when the southwestern part of the United States was covered by an ocean, some 345 million years ago. Over time, skeletons of sea life settled, creating a mud high in calcium, which eventually hardened into limestone.

Over more time, the limestone deposits were pushed upward, likely by the collision of tectonic plates moving over the earth's surface. Over eons, as rainwater flowed through cracks in the ground, the limestone was hollowed out, creating massive caverns.

These caverns are classified as dry caverns, which is true for only three percent of the caverns in the world, said Jamie. Because they are dry, they don't have the impressive stalagmites and stalactites associated with more famous caverns, like at Carlsbad.

Since much of the subsurface around the area is limestone, numerous cavernous veins run for miles in all directions. Few have been explored completely.

The biggest cavern, which they were entering, was over 200 feet long and a hundred feet high, with dull white boulders clinging to the ceiling.

"Those rocks up there with the big cracks," said Jake, his eyes roaming the roof, "how often do they fall?"

"According to a tour I took, a big rock hasn't fallen in 50,000 years. Think our luck will hold?" asked Jamie with a smile.

Jake wasn't smiling. He felt suffocated, wondering how long the air would last down here, whether an earthquake might bring down the ceiling, and what would happen if the lights went out. Would he be clawing at the walls, too?

Looking around, he saw round polyps of hardened mud grouped tightly on the dull gray, almost greenish walls in some places, and then smooth walls elsewhere where sloshing and backfilling water over centuries had worn the sandstone smooth.

An oblong mouth of a cave about 20 feet up from the floor branched off into the darkness. In another place was a pit, maybe 30 feet across and 50 feet deep. How in the world did early tourists, holding only a kerosene-fired lantern, avoid stumbling to their deaths?

Two emotions warred in Jake. The spectacle of being inside a massive hole, carved by the forces of nature over a hundred centuries, made his mind reel. Mankind and its accomplishments were just a speck in the life of the planet.

But then, he remembered all around him was sand — true, hardened sand but still sand. He had built numerous sand castles at the beach when his family vacationed along the Pacific Ocean, and he knew it didn't take much for the most carefully crafted castle to be crushed by a foot or a wave. So massive were these caverns, yet, delicate, too.

When Jake brought his eyes down to the floor, any awe he might have had for the natural wonder quickly dissipated.

A shoddily made concrete walkway crookedly

wound through mounds of football-sized mud-colored rocks piled about, reminding him of a construction site. And then off in one hollow was a neon sign for a Subway sandwich shop.

"Subway?" he said aloud.

"Yeah, the previous owner thought it would be clever to have a Subway restaurant down here," said Jamie, from just behind Jake's shoulder "'Subway,' you know, underground. But it failed, too. Who wants to eat a sandwich while stumbling around in the semi-dark 200 feet below ground?"

Jamie pointed out veins in rocks the old rancher who found the caverns thought were gold, but they proved not to be. Jake didn't think they looked anything like gold, nor did he think other colors on the walls looked like a vein of silver. Perhaps the poor light of the lanterns allowed the imagination of the original finder to "see" what he wanted to see.

"So Suzanne," wondered Jake. "What do you think happened? Does she... or did she have any political enemies?"

"Political enemies?" laughed Jamie. "In the last two elections, she ran unopposed. Nobody else wants the thankless job of being mayor."

"How about her husband, Patrick? Aren't spouses the first suspects in a murder?"

"Patrick? Nah. He and Suzanne were high school sweethearts, a few years ahead of my mom. Suzanne was the girl in high school who was class secretary, organized the prom, and took attendance for the teachers. Patrick was always interested in business. He ran the concession stand, and the magazine drives, and had a side business teaching kids how to drive. That was a little on the questionable side, but no one cared in those days, especially if they got their licenses."

"Has the *Gazette* pissed anybody off recently?" asked Jake. "Pissed them off enough to make them want to kill the editor, and now the owner?"

"I know you come from a big city paper where you have scoops, inside sources, and digging up dirt on the powerful," said Jamie. "But here... well, our big front-page story the week before you arrived was the resounding success of the annual chili cook-off that raised $3,000 for scholarships, and the week before that, we had a six-column photo of the Little Miss Sunshine contestants. Now, one of the moms could have been peeved that her little miss was not exactly in the center..."

Jake ducked his shoulders and head to avoid a sharp rock protruding over the trail as he and Jamie wandered through the cavern. He could see slight bloodstains where others had not been so agile.

"I thought you were a news reporter at the *Gazette*," said Jake. "Yet you seem to know a lot about this town."

"I actually grew up here," replied Jamie, nodding his head while giving a sour expression.

"When I graduated from high school and left for college, I thought I would never come back... not even for reunions. High school was not fun for me. I would never want to repeat those years.

"But then, in my junior year at college, my mom got sick. She raised me as a single mom, so I owed her a huge debt. I came back during spring break to care for her. When she didn't get better, I stayed on. Gus knew me, as I used to write sports for the paper in high school, so he offered me a full-time job. And, so, here I am."

"I'm sorry to hear that about your mom. How is she doing?"

"Oh, she has better days and worse days. Doctor Myers doesn't know what is wrong with her. She was fine when I left for school, working in the office out at the poop fields. But then her red blood cells started dying. There's a lot more medical stuff going on, but I'm a bit of a hypochondriac, so if I think too much about an illness, I become ill myself."

Jake and Jamie had reached the end of the cavern, where Suzanne was found, as evidenced by the yellow crime scene tape strung around on orange traffic cones.

"The sheriff said she was found with her back against the wall, hands and feet tied," said Jamie, speaking softly. "What a way to die, in the total, total dark, tied up, without an idea of where you are, with your life slowly being sucked out of you."

And not for the first time when at the scene of a homicide, Jake was saddened by how small a space even the most robust person occupies in death.

Chapter 8

"Jamie, why aren't you using people's names in the police blotter — it's all public record," Jake asked, glasses on, peering at this week's column of police doings on his computer screen.

"Because of Coach Collins," said Jamie, from

behind his computer monitor.

"Coach Collins?"

"Yeah, Gus, the old editor, had me covering high school football last fall. I was in the locker room after a win on a cold November night when Coach Collins called me into his office. He told assistant coach Davis to step out and close the door.

"I thought maybe he has some game quotes for me, but instead he lit into me.

"I think I saw spittle fly out of his mouth as he accused the *Gazette* of having him inside the Little Viking on the previous Saturday night, drinking with the fellas. 'How does that look to my team and their parents' he ranted, 'when I'm telling the players they have to live by a curfew and keep their noses clean?'

"Since I wrote much of that week's paper I knew I said no such thing and told him that.

"That's when the police blotter came up. 'Everybody knows your paper is just a joke,' he said, 'but that police gossip can cause real damage and you need to get your facts right if you're going to keep doing it."

By this time, Jamie has migrated over to Jake's desk and the look on his face told Jake the pain of being pummeled by the coach was being relived in the young reporter's head.

What the police blotter item actually said, Jamie told Jake, was the coach reported his car's fender was dented while in the Little Viking's parking lot.

The coach told Jamie the car was there because the coach took his wife out to dinner at Uncle Bob's Italian House and finding the parking lot full, parked next door at the Little Viking.

"Coach Collins banned me from the locker room for the rest of the season. And Gus decided in a small town, names were too explosive in the police blotter as the police often get these reports wrong.

"So that's why the coach calls in game reports now — when the 'Cats win — and why there are no names in the police blotter."

"Ok, I see," replied Jake, who knew at the big city daily he just came from, such an affront from a high school coach would result in a snow storm of phone calls and letters by the paper's lawyers. But here, considering the uncertain fate of the newspaper, and the fact he was only a temporary editor, maybe the best he could do was to offer up: "So you know what the newspaperman's motto is, don't you?"

"What? 'All the news that's fit to print,' or 'We're here to comfort the afflicted and afflict the comfortable."

Jake grinned and returned to reading his screen. "Those are fine for the general public, but mine is: 'Don't let the bastards get you down.' Now, you have some photos from the caverns for me, right?"

*****

A little later, Jamie brought over a contact sheet of photos from the caverns' crime scene. There were two dozen thumbnail images for Jake to look over.

A couple were of yellow tape around rocks deep in the caverns, another showed Sheriff Highkok talking to bystanders, and then one was of a body, covered by a white sheet on a gurney, being rolled towards the ambulance. Through the haste of attendants, the sheet had hiked up, revealing an orange tennis shoe.

An orange tennis shoe... the same shoes Suzanne was wearing the day she hired Jake, just a week ago. Orange being the color of the *Gazette*'s newspaper tubes, and the color of the masthead on the front page each week.

"This is the money shot," thought Jake, holding the contact sheet in his hand, and staring at Suzanne's shoe.

And yet... in his role at the metro paper, his job was all about trying to impact readers. Words and photos to jar them out of their comfortable apathy — hold up real reality to break through the cynicism of viewing too much pretend reality on TV.

Oh, the big-city newspaper had their rules — no dead bodies, at least of local people, no broken children, no profanities except in quotes, and then nothing beyond hell, damn and screw you.

There, that picture of an orange shoe on a body under a white sheet would be center page one.

But here, in this small town? That orange sneaker seemed too personal. Everyone in town knew Suzanne from her various community and social roles. Everyone knew she was dead, as the story had been well reported in the area daily newspaper and on radio stations.

That orange sneaker photo would be poking a nail into a fresh wound for no good purpose.

"Let's use the one of the sheriff, with a smaller photo of the scene in the caverns," Jake told Jamie.

"Oh, and where is her husband, Patrick?"

"He's flying back from Japan," replied Jamie. "He was there on a sales trip with other poultry brokers. Who knew Japan bought so many frozen chickens?"

Jamie left to create photos for Jake, who paused to think about his own situation.

Two weeks ago, he was jobless but also stress-free, living on severance pay while roaming the Southwest in his aging RV, the Beast, with nothing to worry about other than what to fix for dinner and whether his beer cooler was getting low.

Then, a week ago, after finding the body of the former editor, he was hired to be a temporary replacement while the publisher, Suzanne McPhee, advertised to find a permanent replacement.

Now, this Tuesday, he was shepherding this week's edition to the press, and the main story was the death — apparently by homicide — of the paper's owner. And a most bizarre killing it was.

He had no idea if he would be paid for his work — he and Suzanne had never really talked salary — and he had never met her husband, Patrick. Would Patrick want to keep him on?

Hell, would Patrick even want to keep the *Gazette* going? From the mumblings he heard around the office, while just about everybody in town subscribed to the little weekly, the number of ads had fallen off in recent years. Suzanne had an active community streak and didn't mind writing support checks, but Patrick? A broker of frozen dead birds? Would he have a sentimental streak for the *Gazette*?

Why am I even thinking about this? Jake

admonished himself. Two weeks ago, I didn't even know the *Gazette* existed. Two weeks from now, I could well be in a different state, or a couple of states away.

Let's get this edition out, and see what happens, he said to himself, and then, not for the first time, wondered who exactly he was talking to when he talked to himself. Were there two Jakes inside his head?

Chapter 9

"I wouldn't want a beautiful woman," came a voice from down the bar, rising above the click of pool balls and a half dozen other conversations going on at Lester's.

"A beautiful woman thinks showing up is all she had to do. She's like Cleopatra." Rodney raised his voice to a falsetto, "'I'm here to be pleased, you're here to please me.' Pfff. Give me a homely, but eager woman every time."

"Shut up, Rodney!" broke in Bonny the bartender, standing across the wooden bar from Jake and Jamie. "She might be homely, but she would have to be blind, too."

Turning to the two men, she asked, "You two ready for another one?"

Jake looked down at his glass, surprised it was empty.

"Er... I'm not so sure. I have to drive back to the campground tonight. I don't want to get pulled over."

"No problem. The sheriff left a little while ago to take a prisoner to the regional jail, and that's the deputy over there, behind the pitcher of beer, playing liar's poker with the fellows. There'll be no patrolling the roads tonight."

As Bonny pulled the tap for two more beers, Jake took a quick look around.

Rodney, probably mid-30s and wearing a dull red horizontally striped t-shirt that did his stout-going-to-tubby body no favors, was talking at a thin man in a dirty cowboy hat sitting a couple of stools away. The thin man didn't look pleased as he opened pull-tab tickets, then tossed each one away.

A couple of men sat at the bar down from Jamie, talking to each other about fishing. Probably tourists, guessed Jake, here to try their luck at the reservoirs around. For a desert, the reservoirs — created mostly for irrigation — became popular with fishing tourists when the state started stocking them with fish every year.

The four liars poker players in the back were slapping down cards and laughing a little louder after each round.

Three couples were spread out at the tables, all eating the greasy fried chicken special of the day. Maybe "greasy" wasn't an actual part of the name, but considering the thick smell of cooking oil, maybe it should have been.

A sign above the mirror in the back of the bar was proud that Lester's was founded in 1867, well before Arizona even became a state. The sign, like the rest of the bar, sparkled. The saloon was clean, and the beer cold, fast and cheap. Better than most small-town bars Jake had been in.

Taking his fresh beer in hand, he twisted his bar

stool towards Jamie. "So, what was this child sex scandal Mrs. Martin was talking about? And how did Robbie get it right?"

"Oh, that was terrible," replied Jamie. "It started about four years ago, while I was a freshman at State. For a while, nobody at my school wanted to admit they were from here. Time magazine even sent in a reporter and did a piece.

"I think close to 30 people were arrested, and it turned neighbor against neighbor. Parents were afraid to let their kids out of their sight.

"The *Gazette* got caught up in the hysteria, running big stories each week for months, quoting the sheriff and the local prosecutor as they detailed the accusations, the gist of which was a local pastor and most of the adults in his church were sexually abusing kids in the church. The paper stoked the fires."

Jamie's voice had started not much above a whisper as he leaned towards Jake, but it had steadily risen in volume, until the fishermen were listening, along with the thin man. Rodney was staring down at his beer.

"Jamie, hon, that's no story for here," said Bonny, laying one of her hands onto his on the bar. "You'll drive away my customers.

"Let me get you one more on me and then I'll send you on your way."

"Sure, Bonny, you're right. Sorry."

As she turned to draw two more beers, Jake silently gestured a question with his hands and mouthed to Jamie, "And Robbie?"

"Later," mouthed Jamie.

Chapter 10

"So Jamie, tell me about Robbie and the child sex ring." Jake and the young reporter were killing time, waiting for the press to print this week's edition of the *Gazette*.

The newspaper itself was too small to have its own press, so early each Wednesday, someone had to drive the page flats to the big commercial press 45 miles away, wait for the paper to be printed then drive it home.

This week, Jake went along with Jamie to see that end of the operation.

In all the years Jake had worked at metro newspapers, he had never set foot into the pressroom. First of all, the printers were a different union, and not welcoming of "white-collar types," even though no one in the newsroom had worn a white-collar since the millennium, and secondly, the big press made so much noise it shook the entire building when running.

Here, the press was much smaller and made a ker-chunk sound each time it printed a copy of the paper.

Ker-chunk, ker-chunk, ker-chunk. Some 1,625 of these ker-chunks, plus a few more in case some proud parent with their pride and joy in the paper wanted to purchase extra copies, and Jake and Jamie would load up the office Suburban and return home.

Stepping away from the noise of the press, Jamie started telling the story about the child sex ring, repeating what he had said the afternoon before at Lester's and told of meetings the sheriff and prosecutor had held around town detailing activities and names of the parents swapping their children around for sexual abuse.

"Everyone was afraid," said Jamie, no one would allow their kids to stay overnight, even at their best friends' homes. Adults that had gone to high school together avoided each other on the street.

"At one briefing my mom attended at the Chamber of Commerce, the sheriff told how the church was just a front for these pedophiles. He said when deputies went to search the church, they found the kitchen dirty, with pots and pans scattered all around, dirty dishtowels thrown in the corners, and food crumbs littering the tables.

"My mom quoted the sheriff as saying, 'My grandmother was a good Christian lady, and she and her friends made sure their church was spotless after every Sunday service. Spotless. You wonder what kind of Christians these people were, and what really went on at that so-called church.'

"It was anecdotes like that that found their way into the paper, and into the minds of residents," said Jamie.

"All of this was happening right around football season, and parents pulled their sons off the squad when a few of the kids said to be involved were allowed to be on the team.

"It was also election time, and the sheriff was running hard on the platform to make the county safe again for kids, although he didn't have any serious competition," added Jamie.

Ker-chunk, ker-chunk, ker-chunk.

"Then Robbie wrote this column. And instead of her usual around town items, she told of the time she was in the South Pacific, a nurse on a medical ship that had docked on a small island to help natives who had hacked each other half to death.

It all started with a rumor, Robbie wrote. An older woman thought she had seen a young boy playing with a crow, a known demon creature in that culture, and she told a few friends.

In a short while, those friends told others, and as the story spread, it grew to encompass the boy's whole family as possessed. Soon, the "good" people of the village were hunting down the "bad" people, who thought of themselves as good and the others bad. Out came the machetes and the hacking began.

Only later — by the time the medical ship had docked — was it discovered the boy wasn't playing with a crow, rather a kite a sailor had taught him how to make. The old lady just had bad eyesight.

"All of that hacking, over a failure to see clearly," wrote Robbie. "I wonder if the same thing could be happening here?"

Ker-chunk, ker-chunk, ker-chunk.

"Once her column was out and read, the hysteria over the alleged child sex ring collapsed. People in the community started having second thoughts.

"The next week, a well-respected elementary school teacher wrote in of seeing the sheriff berating his stepdaughter in his sheriff's car, and the stepdaughter crying. It had been the stepdaughter who — according to the sheriff — first reported the sex crimes against minors.

"'If this is the way the sheriff treats a child witness, I wonder how we can expect a fair investigation,' asked the teacher."

Then the following week, three local pastors plus the Catholic priest wrote a letter jointly saying they knew the accused pastor for years as a pious man who always was there to help the community.

Ker-chunk, ker-chunk, ker-chunk.

"The following week, Suzanne wrote one of her rare editorials, attacking the sheriff for a shoddy investigation and using the sensationalism of child sex crimes in his campaign."

Her editorial came out on Wednesday, but the election was on Tuesday, too late to affect the outcome. "Still, the sheriff was incensed," said Jamie, "and a shouting match broke out at that week's town council meeting, with Suzanne calling the sheriff a child abuser for the way he rode roughshod over the kids in this case, and the sheriff labeling Suzanne a sad, barren woman with no kids of her own to care about."

Shortly afterward, the investigation fell apart when the sheriff's stepdaughter recanted her accusations. The town felt ashamed, and since, people have spoken very little about the episode.

The ker-chunking noise came to a stop. "That's it, gentlemen," the head press operator called out to Jake and Jamie, wiping his ink-stained hands on a blue rag.

The pair began loading bundles of this week's news into the Suburban.

Chapter 11

There are famous newspaper editors of fact and fiction: Ben Bradlee who directed the Watergate coverage for the Washington Post, Perry White who yelled at Clark Kent and Lois Lane, "Great Caesar's ghost, get me the story on Superman!" and even Mark Twain who for a short time edited a weekly in a dusty western town.

But likely, none of them had to do what Jake did this afternoon.

Each Wednesday when copies of the *Gazette* were delivered to the office, a gaggle of young boys and girls stuffed bundles of papers into cloth shoulder bags and then went out to deliver the papers door to door.

Just like big-time newspapers in the old days.

Except, since these kids were paid a nickel per delivered paper — $5 per hundred papers dropped on doorsteps — the kids and their moms would sometimes blow off their routes. And that meant a responsible adult — in this case, Jake — had to make deliveries.

This afternoon, two kids didn't show up. One was sick and the other had soccer practice. Which meant Jake after a long week of reporting, writing, editing, laying out pages, and taking calls from readers placing classified ads, walked a portion of the town, bringing fresh news to the doorsteps.

If at first walking in a crisp fall afternoon with its bright leaves from non-native trees changing color brought relief to his congested brain, after the first 50 or so front porches and several suspicious dogs, the joy had evaporated.

Now he was at Sweet Williams, awaiting his

reward of a large peanut parfait being prepared by the girl behind the counter.

"Why can't the newspaper ever get anything right?" complained a voice from a nearby table occupied by two young women and a man.

Jake recognized the man as a teacher in the middle school, so guessed the other two were also teachers. The man saw Jake and shook his head at the woman who was talking.

She didn't get the signal. "I mean really, I got my degree from Northern Arizona University, not the University of Arizona. There's a big difference."

Ah, guessed Jake. She was Robbie's man — or in her case, woman — in the street interview this week. And Robbie being Robbie, her writings sometimes floated away from the facts.

Jake knew he could lean into the teachers' table and say reporting was Robbie's second career, after 50 years of being a nurse. That Robbie served aboard a hospital ship in two wars, where she tended broken, burned, and shot men. Where her gentle voice and soft hands reminded them of mom back home, and in too many cases, hers was the last female face these dying men ever saw.

Maybe getting the exact college a newbie middle school teacher graduated from was not exactly the high point of Robbie's contribution to mankind.

"Mr. Stewart, your parfait is ready." This saved Jake from saying any of this. Likely a good thing considering his state of mind.

"Let me get you a straw," said the girl, who Jake recognized as a cute redhead from the volleyball squad.

And holding up the straw, she used the thumb and forefinger of each hand to slowly tear the paper covering from the end, all the while peering up at Jake with a sly look in her green eyes.

It was a deja-vu moment for when Jake was 17, his first serious girlfriend had used the same thumbs and forefingers to slowly tear open a condom package, saying: "This is the only one, so make it last."

But, of course, he hadn't.

And when the moment was over and the girlfriend rolled away, for the first time but not the last, Jake wondered what women saw in men.

Why bother with us when we disappoint in so many ways? he thought.

Chapter 12

"What made you suspect there was something wrong in the trailer next to you?" asked Jake of a mismatched couple of RV'ers standing in the gravel campsite lot.

Ed was probably in his early 60s, with a lean bicyclist body and a quick handshake, while Evy displayed long fingernails — a catty person might call them an inch long, but they were not quite — heavy makeup, poofed up hair and giving off an aura of perfume. In her arms she held a tiny white dog she called Baby that had barked at Jake furiously when he had first approached.

"When we were hooking up to utilities after arriving yesterday, I noticed the rooftop air was on," said Ed, tilting his head towards the 35-foot Airstream trailer now surrounded by yellow police tape.

"I thought that was odd because here in mid-October, the days don't get much warmer than 70 while the nights are below 40.

"When the air didn't go off all night — the noise kept Evy awake — we complained to the campground manager the next morning. When he didn't seem to be doing anything about it, Evy went over to knock on the trailer's door.

"That's when Baby went off. She hardly ever barks," said Ed.

Jake doubted that, but asked, "Do you think she smelled something?

"I did too," inserted Evy. "Gross!"

"We went back to the campground manager, he came down for a look, smelled something rotten too, and called the police. That's how all of this happened," said Ed.

"This" was three police cars, an ambulance, the yellow tape, and a small group of RV'ers standing around whispering among themselves.

Jake had already talked to Sheriff Highkok and got the basics: a dead woman was in the trailer, a bloody toaster next to her head, and a missing husband.

Chief Highkok guessed the husband left on the air-conditioning to keep the body cool to give him time to flee in the Ford 350 pick-up he used to tow the trailer.

"Good front-page story for the *Gazette* this week, right?" Jamie leaned into Jake's ear as the young reporter/photographer was raising his camera to shoot Ed and Evy.

"Oh no, I'm a fright!" said Evy. "Let me put my face on."

While Jamie tried to soothe her, Ed stepped up to speak to Jake.

"You know, some couples think taking off in an RV would be the good life, but living with a spouse in less than 200 square feet of space 24 hours a day can drive both of you into a rage. In this case, I guess a killing rage."

Chapter 13

"Rodney had been pestering me to take him fishing, so I told him, 'OK, we'll go this Saturday.' But, I told him, I wanted to be on the lake early, I mean early. I'll pick you up at 4 a.m."

Jake was only half-listening to the fishing story being told by the red-haired man — called, appropriately enough Red — to half a dozen buddies at the end of the bar, while paying more attention to Arizona State's football game on the bar's TV.

The campground had terrible reception. If Jake wanted to watch college football, Lester's was the place. Plus, cold beer was delivered by Bonny right to his waiting hand.

"So when I got to Rodney's at 5:30, he was in the house, taking a whiz, as I guessed he had drunk his entire thermos of coffee while sitting on the steps waiting for me," continued Red.

"Anyway, we made a quick stop at Murphy's Grub and Go for bait and a sandwich for me, and then gassed up the boat. Rodney had to hit the john again.

'Goddammit Rodney,' I told him, 'I said I wanted to be on the lake early before all the tourists get there.'

"So, we get the boat on the lake by 8:30 and immediately hightailed it to my favorite spot down around the bend. When we get there, there is only one other boat nearby, with a man and woman. It's kind of bobbing around and I don't see any poles in the water.

"Then, the guy in the boat starts waving his arms at me.

"'Damn it,'" I said to Rodney, 'no fishing is getting done this way.'"

"Hey, it wasn't my fault," piped up Rodney.

"So when we get over to the boat, the guy says they had run out of gas, that his brother-in-law promised he had refilled the tank when he had borrowed the boat, but of course, the brother-in-law is a worthless liar, and then the guy gives the woman — who I am guessing is the sister to the brother-in-law — a dirty look."

"I wouldn't have given her a dirty look — as she was pretty good-looking," added Rodney, with a big grin. "Wait until you hear the rest of the story."

"What the hell, I think," continued Red over the top of Rodney. "Fishing today is pretty much a dead issue. So I siphon some gas out of my tank into his. He offers to pay, and I say Nah, it's fine. And then he turns and glares at his wife again.

"And that's when the most amazing thing happened... you won't believe it."

At this point, Jake swung his head around to the storyteller who has most of the men in the bar enthralled.

"She says, 'Thanks fellas,' reaches down and pulls her bikini top up... and out they flop."

"They were nice ones, too!" added Rodney, holding his hands well in front of his man boobs. "That was my best day fishing ever!"

"Rodney, shut up!" yelled Bonnie from down the bar. Then, looking around and seeing the same dumb look on every guy's face in the bar busy imagining the topless woman on the boat, she slammed down her bar towel, exclaiming, "Men!" and stormed out the back door for a sanity break.

Chapter 14

Jake had stepped out of his rig into the brisk morning to clear his head from the night before when he saw a man about 60, slender, maybe a little shorter than Jake's five-ten, long white-gray hair tied back with a band, wearing a black leather jacket — not the kind motorcyclists wear, a little more fashionable, maybe something he bought second-hand at a thrift shop — walking his way.

"Good morning," the man said to Jake, stopping on the campground road, "I'm Daniel."

"A beautiful morning, too," he added, looking around at the soaring Ponderosa Pines, the giant saguaro cactus the area was famous for, and the 200-foot vertical towering rock cliffs. A small creek, so small that Jake had failed to notice earlier, flowed without making a sound.

Beyond, up the narrow asphalt road winding around pines, Jake could see a Cruise America rental RV parked in a visitor's slot. Daniel had been heading that way.

"We are spending so much money on gas," he said, noticing Jake's gaze. "Sometimes, $400 to $600 a day. We make it up, however, by dry camping in the country and avoiding the cities. We've been staying just outside the Cowboy Caverns in a little grove by a dried-up creek bed."

Without prompting, Daniel continued with his story. "We've been all over around here and throughout the Southwest. Do you know Area 51? We overnighted there on a small service road for maintenance workers."

"Did anything eerie happen?" Jake wondered aloud.

"Strange things always happen on the road, don't they?" Daniel smiled and nodded his head, agreeing with himself.

"I've been traveling all my life. My dad was in the Army and moved around, and for 18 years, I drove cross-country trucks. You can make $100,000 a year if you push it. Me, though, I took three months off each year to winter in Key West.

"Now, for the last four years, three months and seven days, I've been traveling mostly on my own, but sometimes with other people, with no job, no government check, no income whatsoever, living on just the little savings I have.

"You want to know how I do it?" He leaned in closer to Jake while dropping his voice, "God provides."

Straightening back up, he added: "I keep a Bible on my dashboard for all to see. You might say I'm a missionary for Jesus Christ."

A bark followed by another came from the Cruise America RV, causing Daniel to look away. "There's four of us in the camper, plus a dog that is already this big," he indicated by holding out a flat palm about at his knee.

Another bark and Daniel took a step towards the RV, but he had one more tidbit: "There's a resort where you can stay 100 days in your own cabin, and they offer gourmet meals. You know how much it costs?" He held up a hand, making a zero with his thumb and forefinger.

"It's a place for meditation, and at the end, they ask for a donation, which you can give but don't have to. Rich folks go there and their donations keep it going. They have 300 sites around the world... Check it out on the internet, the name is V-A-..." but a series of barks drowned out the last few letters.

Daniel hurried up the road, and Jake returned to his RV.

"Who was that character?" asked Wil, who had stayed the night.

"He was a guy trying to tell me the secret to paradise, but as usual in my life, the message was scrambled."

Wil was the dictionary definition of "getting lucky" in Jake's eyes.

He had met her just the day before in the county courthouse when he had dropped in to see the sheriff... who was conveniently out.

As Jake hung out in the common foyer on the second floor of the massive, old stone building, Wil —

who according to the name badge riding high on her left breast, was the county clerk — had come up to him and the two started chatting. Before long, she was asking questions about how Jake found Gus's body, about the missing woman who had also found the body, and if there were any new details about the case.

Seeing no ring on her finger, and tired of talking about the case, Jake had said, "Bring a bottle of wine over to my RV tonight, I'll make you dinner and tell you what I know."

Now, a line like that never works in Jake's experience. But it is a way to change the subject.

Surprise. Surprise. And one thing led to another… and another.

Now, the fully dressed Wil was sliding her phone into her oversized purse.

"Whatever. I just got a call and I have to get down to the courthouse. Judge Hockiss is having a shit fit over some missing file."

"That's too bad. I was hoping to make breakfast for you. You know, last night was fun. Maybe we can do it again?" asked Jake, in his soft, hopeful voice.

"It was great," agreed Wil, "but probably not. You know…" the last bit came with a shrug of her shoulders as she zipped up her purse.

"Sure," replied Jake, giving his got-it face. But actually, Jake didn't get it at all. If something was fun, why wouldn't you want to do it again? And again?

If going to an Indian casino and winning $500 was fun, why wouldn't you go again? If attending an outdoor winery rock concert was a blast, why not attend another? If driving to a lakeside café and finding the fish and chips tasty, why wouldn't you do it again sometime soon?

Wil wasn't the first woman who had said something similar to Jake the following morning.

Once when they had been married for a few years and Jake was feeling confident Anne wasn't going to pack her purse and leave in the morning, he asked why since women appeared to have fun during sex, what held them back from engaging in it all the time.

"If I were a woman," he said while lying in bed during a lazy Sunday morning, drawing slow circles with his finger around an erect nipple on her breast, "I'd be the biggest slut in the world."

"No you wouldn't!" shot back Anne. "For men, sex is external... it's like someone just gave that finger there the perfect massage. For women, sex is internal. Sure, we can like the massage too, but it's a feeling that comes from deep inside us. We can love the massage, but if the guy or the time isn't right, the sex isn't right. So yes, while it may have been fun, no, I may not want the owner of that particular 'massager' in me again."

"Ooh, look, your talk is making my 'finger' stiff. How about another go?" suggested Jake.

"Rub your own finger, kiddo, I have things to do," said Anne, bouncing out of bed with a flash of her behind, ending any thoughts of the lion roaring again on this Sunday.

Chapter 15

What a week it had been!
First, Mrs. Kennedy had come in demanding the

paper list all 27 little girls taking her Dance with Carolyn fall class. "The old editor did it every year," said Mrs. Kennedy, peering over the top of her glasses at Jake.

Then, the town's newly elected councilman Mac Cheese had stood at the front counter lecturing the entire office on what was wrong with the city government (which was fun for the first 15 minutes as Jamie and Jake exchanged pun-filled text messages by email, such as "Mac's sure in a boil today," and as the rant continued, "Pasta la Vista, Man.")

And then a new parent in town came in to demand the paper investigate the football coach for harsh treatment of the players.

"I've taken this to the school board, and they won't do anything because he won three state championships. Heck, two of the school board members played football for Coach Collins. And they're the guys who drink at games and fire off the cannon when the Wildcats score a touchdown."

When Jake said, "We're not the Washington Post. We don't have the staff to investigate anything," the parent wondered, "you are not very gutsy here, are you?" and then demanded the paper run an unsigned letter accusing the coach of abuse.

When Jake said the paper didn't run unsigned letters, the parent dictated a letter on the spot accusing the coach of unprofessional behavior, which he signed with a flourish.

So now it was Wednesday after work. This week's edition had been printed, thankfully all of the little boys and girls — and their moms — showed up to make deliveries and another week was closed out.

Jake stood at checkout at Martin's Market, a frozen pizza and a six-pack of beer in hand, thoughts of being alone with warm pizza and cold beer, shoes off, feet up, and maybe a ballgame on TV oozed through his head.

There was only one customer ahead of him in line — Mrs. Collins. Mrs. Coach Collins. The wife whose husband the paper had just printed a letter accusing of abusing high school kids.

Oh, damn!

Do you think Woodward and Bernstein of Watergate fame ever stood in a grocery line behind Mrs. Nixon?

It's tough being a bold journalist in a small town.

Chapter 16

Jake couldn't believe on a clear and warm winter Saturday in the southland, away from the rain and fog of Seattle, he was wasting a morning driving a backcountry road to visit the poop farms.

But here he was, and the lush, green poop farms were here, too.

Massive sprinkler systems rolled in circles on both sides of the road in this flat valley.

Elevated aluminum pipes, looking to be three or four inches in diameter, were supported by braces on large, metal wheels. One end of each system was attached to a base — maybe a well or at least a source of the water? Jake didn't know much about the mechanics of farming. The other end of the pipe revolved in large circles, maybe 200 yards across.

On the underside of the aluminum pipes were sprinklers, spraying out water as the entire structure slowly rolled over the field. The result was large rings of green, separated by diamond-shaped pieces of the arid desert where the water didn't reach.

It reminded Jake of when he was a child and his grandmother rolled out dough to make biscuits. She used a round silver-colored mold to create perfectly round biscuits to place on a greased cookie sheet. When she finished, left behind in the sheet of dough were little bits on the edge of the circles.

"Are you going to throw that dough away?" Jake asked his grandmother.

"Oh no, Jake, I'll just roll those bits and pieces together to make another sheet, and cut out more biscuits."

Except out here in poop country, there is no rolling the bits and pieces together. The unwatered edges are where the bunnies, coyotes, and other wildlife got to live — on land man hasn't use for.

Jake had called ahead to schedule a visit so when he braked to a stop in front of the office of the farms — "office" being a grand word for a single wide mobile home that had been new about 15 years ago — Ray Schmidt was waiting for him.

After introductions, Ray said, "I could take you on a tour, but honestly, you can about see it all from here.

"Pull up a chair," he said, sitting on one end of the tailgate of a dusty Dodge pickup with the words "Schmidt Bros. Farms" painted on the door. He pointed to the other half of the tailgate for Jake.

Ray was a man in his 50s, gray hair showing from the bottom edge of a John Deere cap, wearing tan Carhartt overalls over a pair of jeans and a plaid work shirt. He hadn't shaved this morning, and perhaps yesterday morning either and in his hand he held a large, stained insulated coffee mug.

"What you see around you was born out of two crying needs," Ray began.

With a farmer's unhurried sense of time, Ray rolled out his story, starting with how his grandfather was the first Schmidt to farm these lands and had about starved to death.

With only a tiny bit of rain — about three days each in January and March on most years — growing crops was a worthless venture. Only raising cattle made sense, and only then if enough land could be cobbled together to make a huge range for livestock to find pickings here and there. Of course, a large ranch meant more ground to patrol, more fences to mend, and more wild critters to make a meal on newborn calves.

"Daddy didn't have much better luck," continued Ray, "however, he did get government VA financing to drill deep water wells. With a steady water source, ranching became more predictable.

"Except there is no predicting beef prices. Some years, we would have huge herds, but the prices were terrible, and other years, after we thinned out the herds and didn't have many head to sell, prices would soar."

When Ray and his brother Frank inherited the farm, they flipped a coin to see who would stay and who would go, as the farm couldn't support two families.

Ray won, or lost "depending on how you looked at it," he said with a short laugh and shake of his head, and Frank left for the growing city of Phoenix.

Then, something stunning happened. Ray was visiting his brother one winter day, and in reading the paper, saw the local sewage plant was running at over capacity because of Phoenix's growth. To make matters worse, biosolids were piling up as new subdivisions were taking up the dumping space.

"They were literally up to their eyeballs in shit," roared Ray. "So much so, they were looking for sites where they could pay to dump the dried crap. Pay to dump crap," he repeated, emphasizing each word in wonder.

Ray had sprung up from the kitchen table, put on his cap, and off he went to the sewage plant. "We signed a contract that day, and since then, poop trucks have been beating a path here."

Ray had to drastically adjust his farming when the trucks started arriving. He needed massive manure spreaders to evenly distribute the biosolids. "I couldn't have them just dump the shit in piles, it would be too much for the thin topsoil that we have here to absorb."

He tried grazing his cattle on the lush green grass that grew after being fertilized, and while the cattle chomped up the delicious, tender blades, when word got out that Ray was feeding his cattle on soil full of human shit, buyers turned away.

For a couple of years, he tried row crops, but they were too labor-intensive plus the same ick factor turned off customers.

"I was really in a pickle," said Ray. "I had land, I

had water, I had better than free fertilizer, but I didn't have a crop I could sell. And while I was doing OK with getting paid to take the crap, I knew I could do so much better."

And then, once again, a story in a newspaper came to the rescue.

"I read that in Eastern Washington, Japanese buyers were grabbing up all the alfalfa hay they could find, and flying it — I mean, flying it — to Japan. Get this: farmers were growing hay, which is one of the bulkiest crops you can have, and not usually worth all that much in comparison to other crops, and selling it to the Japanese who were flying it to Japan. What a strange world we live in!"

A few phone calls and Ray's problems were solved. Alfalfa didn't need fences or a crew of farm workers and the end-users didn't care about what was being added to the soil.

"I did my time in Southeast Asia," said Ray, "and there, human crap has been added to rice paddies for centuries. What we turn our noses up at they accept as natural. You might say I'm doing my bit for the environment by recycling human shit — I'm a greenie."

Listening to Ray, Jake noticed the price of being a green success came with a certain odor. Maybe it was time to be returning to town.

But first, he had a question. Two questions, actually.

"I heard a woman became sick after working here," Jake said. "Are there contaminates in the poop to be worried about?"

"My neighbors and other people ask me that

often," said Ray, sitting down his empty coffee mug in the bed of the pickup. "We don't do any testing here and we don't have to. Believe me, the sewage plants are crawling with state and even federal inspectors. What we get here is the purest poop that can be."

"And then the water," said Jake. "I'm new here, but I get a sense water is in short supply. I've heard wells in the town are going dry. On the way here, I saw a lot of irrigation going on."

"Yes," replied Ray. "Water is an issue. In the past couple of years, we have had to drill deeper.

"But anything the prissy mayor of the town may have told you about robbing the community of water would be a lie," he said, emotions raising his voice.

"She and I have gone around a few times and while — God rest her soul — maybe she should be looking out for the town's interests first, she didn't see I have water rights too, and without the water and the poop, this farm would be just another set of abandoned shacks alongside a forgotten back road.

"She accused me of contaminating the town's water supply, with poop seeping into the water table. Hell, water from the sprinklers doesn't soak way down to the limestone caves we have running underground all around here. I've seen those caves, they are as dry as a bone.

"She was trying to put me out of business. And what about goody-two-shoes' husband, selling frozen chickens? Do you think those chickens are raised on humane farms, you think those farms don't pollute with chemicals and chicken shit? The money I make here is cleaner than the money a chicken broker makes by a damn sight!"

Folding up his reporter's notebook, Jake said his goodbye, got into his car, made sure all the windows were rolled up, checked that the air conditioner was set to not bring in outside air, and promptly left poop country.

Chapter 17

With a big mug of strong coffee in his left hand and keys in his right, Jake unlocked the front door to the *Gazette* at exactly 9 a.m. Sunday.

"Ahhh... peace and quiet. Maybe I can get some work done."

Jake's goal was to finish by early afternoon, then walk to Lester's to watch the Seattle Seahawks play the Arizona Cardinals. Jake would probably be the only Seahawk fan in the bar for the football game, but he wanted to see a new running back the Hawks had picked up. This could, finally, be the Hawks' year.

First, he wanted to edit Jamie's feature about the strange goats of Caxton Canyon. Every week, there were two, three, four, even five, and six calls to the sheriff's department about these goats.

The goats were accused of leaving their owner's property and being general nuisances. One neighbor said they ate laundry off her outside clothesline, another said the goats bullied his chickens so badly they stopped laying eggs, and a third said the goats were eating expensive plantings along his driveway.

When the sheriff's office contended they didn't have the manpower to wrangle wayward billys and nannies, the neighbors decided to pester the hell out of the sheriff's office until they got satisfaction.

Jamie interviewed the goats' owner on Friday and reported he took a laissez-faire approach to the complaints.

"He said, 'We all live up here at the end of the canyon to get away from the rules and regulations of society. I say let goats be goats.'

"And, the most amazing thing," added Jamie, "is these are not your normal goats. These are miniature goats. Cute as hell, but mischievous and aggressive. One of them climbed onto my car, and it took me 10 minutes to get him off. And, not until he had butted me half a dozen times with his little two-inch horns and left scratch marks from his hooves on the roof."

That's when Barbara — designing next week's ads at her desk — started laughing.

"It wasn't funny," responded Jamie. "Those little horns hurt like hell."

Barbara laughed even more.

Jamie hadn't finished writing his story by the time Jake had to leave for a Friday night date — dinner and a movie and maybe something more. This being an editor of a weekly seemed to be sparking something with the ladies.

Once Jake had finished editing Jamie's story, he intended to write next week's editorial laying into the sheriff's department for making no progress on the murders of Gus and Suzanne.

It had been a month since Jake had found Gus's body, and more than three weeks since Suzanne's body was discovered in the caverns.

In that time, they hadn't located the woman in the black sports bra who first discovered Gus. They hadn't even located Gus's family. His body was still lying in the morgue, unclaimed for burial.

Nothing had been discovered — at least nothing the sheriff was willing to talk about — about why Suzanne was in the caverns, how she got down there and who wanted her dead.

Patrick, her husband, was completely broken up, according to Robbie, and was day drinking at home. Jake had no idea if this was true, as he had no conversations with Patrick. Suzanne's body, too, was still in the morgue, awaiting test results from the state crime lab. No funeral date had been set.

Since Jake didn't know what Patrick planned to do with the *Gazette*, he told the bookkeeper Susan to keep selling ads, collecting subscription money, and writing checks for expenses.

It turned out that without the editor's salary — Jake and Suzanne hadn't established his pay before she died — the paper could meet its payroll and pay the press and other bills just fine.

Jake was reading Jamie's suggested headlines: "Goats-b-Gone," or "Rascals on the range," or "Ruminants gone wild," when the phone rang.

"*Gazette*," Jake said automatically.

"Hi, you folks still offer free want ads if the item is under $50?" the person on the other end wanted to know.

When Jake affirmed the deal, the caller said, "Good. I have a fridge I want to sell for $49.95," and proceeded to give Jake the details.

After Jake had read the ad back to the caller, he paused and asked: "Why are you calling this in on a Sunday morning? You're lucky you caught someone."

"Nah, I can see lights on through your big windows all the time. You are always there. Thanks for the free ad."

And when he hung up, Jake had to smile. The old-time editor was correct, working at a weekly meant six-day weeks, and coming in on Sundays to straighten up your desk. And in Jake's case, at no pay.

Chapter 18

The editorial challenging the sheriff's non-progress on the murder investigations had its desired result: a summons to meet the sheriff at 10 a.m. the next day.

Jake showed up at the courthouse that housed the sheriff's office at 9:55 a.m. and then was told by a stern deputy to wait on a hard wooden bench. Well, fine, newspapermen are used to waiting while officials puff up their feathers.

By 10:20, Jake was laughing to himself, remembering the old saying, "Don't offend a newspaper, they buy ink by the barrel." Meaning, newspapers can throw a lot of words — either positive or negative — at opponents. Pissing a reporter off was a short-term pleasure but a long-term pain.

At 10:30, Jake was shown into the office palace of the sheriff — and was surprised.

Expecting the cliché — an ego-filled space of glad-handing photos with other white men, framed awards, American and state flags on poles, and props specially set up to show progress on the murder cases — Jake was greeted by a restrained sheriff in a restrained setting.

Except for the nearly at-attention deputy standing beside the sheriff's desk, the office looked like any other office of a mid-sized company, with a computer on the sheriff's desk — indicating he did some of his own work — a pile of files on one corner, in and out baskets, and a waste paper basket half full. A small table with three nondescript chairs was off to the side where likely casual meetings were held.

The voice of Sheriff Highkok, however, was not casual this morning. "I don't appreciate a civilian, much less someone who just arrived in town, challenging the fine work of my officers," said the sheriff. "You know nothing."

"I do know there have been three murders in the month I have been here," responded Jake, "including the murder in the RV at the campground, apparently by a husband who just drove off into the night.

"According to the *Gazette*'s archives, that's three more murders than happened in the past 10 years."

Shaking his head, the sheriff interrupted Jake: "You don't know that Gus's death was a murder. You found him under a pile of rocks. Maybe he died in a landslide. You know, it is the nature of rocks to roll downhill."

"I do know no arrests have been made. I do know that Gus's body still lies in the morgue, with no next of kin found. I have not heard of any motive for either Gus's or Suzanne's murders, or if they were connected.

And I do know that you and Suzanne have been frequently at odds, even engaging in shouting matches at the town council meetings.

"I don't know," continued Jake, "what progress has been made in any of these investigations, because, unlike other police officers I have worked with in 20 years at newspapers, this office has been ducking any requests for updates. The public has a right to know from their paid civil servants if they are in any further danger."

Jake's session with the sheriff went downhill from there, ending with Jake being escorted from the office by a stern deputy as the sheriff said, "I'll tell you and the rag of a newspaper more when I'm damn good and ready!"

Jake hadn't expected to learn much from the sheriff, he only wanted to poke the sheriff in hopes of getting an interesting tidbit. Sometimes, the role of the media was a dance, thought Jake, and you had to go through the prescribed steps.

He believed the next office to visit in the courthouse would yield better results.

"Hi, Shirley," he said, reading the nametag of the white-haired 60-ish woman working the counter in the county clerk's office. "Is Wil in?"

Jake saw that Wil, working head down in her office fronted by a large window, brown hair falling around her glasses, paused for a second when she saw who was asking for her at the counter.

Then she rose and walked past two other women working at desks on her way to the front. "Hi, Jake," she said in her official voice, meaning, don't bring up anything personal here — especially like the fact we spent the night together a week ago.

"Hi, Wil. Hey, the strangest thing. I was going through Gus's desk at the newspaper office recently, and I found these two files that look like they came from your office." Jake held out two orange file folders.

"See, they each have the County Clerk's stamp. I thought I should return them. Have any idea what he was doing with them?"

"No. Usually, we don't let people take files," she said, reaching out but not quite touching the files.

"They both seem to involve court cases over old land disputes," said Jake. "Are you familiar with the cases or why Gus would be interested? Anything new going on with either?"

When she again said no, Jake explained he found the files together with other files in a metal box at the hard-to-reach very back of the bottom drawer in Gus's desk.

"In one of the files was a topographic map with several circles drawn on it. And, oh yeah, a protractor for drawing the circles. I haven't seen a protractor since ninth-grade geometry. All those little holes pricked in the map by the protractor and overlapping circles."

Wil's voice took on a guarded quality. "Circles?"

"Yeah. Someone mentioned Gus recently started flying a drone in the hills. Maybe he was doing aerial surveys. But I have no idea for what. Or where, since I can't make heads or tails of the map."

Suddenly brightening, Wil replied, "I could take a look, I've lived here all my life. Have the map with you?"

Of course, Jake didn't bring the map with him. His

purpose for the conversation was to gauge Wil's interest. And now he knew. Wil's earlier interest in him came from a desire to learn what Jake might know about Gus's activities.

Jake's lizard brain kicked into gear to wonder if a promise to share the map might be worth another wine and dinner date. After the briefest second, he decided that wouldn't be right. Fun maybe, but not right.

Saying he had another interview he was late for, Jake promised he would try to get together with Wil soon to show her the map.

Pushing his way through the Clerk's glass-paneled wooden doors, he wondered what was Gus up to out in the hills, and what did Wil know about it?

Could she have been involved in Gus's murder? And despite what the sheriff had said about a possible accident, it certainly was murder. Wil didn't look like a killer, but thoughts of easy riches have made killers out of even the nicest people.

Chapter 19

"Hey Jake, I have a great story for next week's front page!" Jamie came flying in through the front doors of the *Gazette*'s office, waving his reporter's notebook.

"We need one, Jamie," said Jake, looking up from his computer monitor. "Right now, the best thing we have going is the schedule for the Thanksgiving community potluck and a grade school 'Color The Turkey' art contest."

"This story is so great," exclaimed Jamie. "It's got

it all — a rogue character, diamonds, foreign intrigue, adventure in the jungle, and — best of all — a local connection!"

"Tell me more," said Jake, smiling at Jamie's enthusiasm.

"Well, you know Jim Daggett, the big realtor in town, right?"

"No, Jamie, because I live in an RV in a 20-by-40 space I pay for by the month in a public campground. But, imagine I do know about local real estate."

"Ok, Daggett has had a real estate office in town forever. He has a daughter who works for him, but he also has a son — which I didn't know about.

"Anyway, according to my mom, who was kind of mysterious about it when I asked her for some background, this son dropped out of college and left town about 20 years ago... I think by the way my mom talked, under some kind of cloud."

By now, Barbara had stopped working on ad designs and was listening intently. Jake took this as a good sign, news should be so compelling you'd stop work to listen.

"So the son, Jimmy, is back in town and I just interviewed him!"

"And the story is..." prompted Jake.

Putting down his camera and notebook on his desk, Jamie remained standing as if holding court, and laid out what he had learned.

Jimmy had indeed dropped out of college — anxious to get on with "real life" — and drifted around a bit before hearing of a diamond rush in the Amazon. "That's Amazon, like the jungle, not the online seller," clarified Jamie, as if anyone needed clarification.

He worked on a freighter going to Brazil, then jumped ship once it got to Rio. From there, he traveled upriver, through swamps, shady frontier towns, and man-eating animals.

For a couple of years, he mucked around in the diamond fields — mostly just staying alive, not making the big find.

"And then it occurred to him — the one thing he learned from his dad is you don't make the real money by owning land, you make money by buying and selling land. Even if he could stay alive in the old west atmosphere of the diamond mines, his chance of getting rich wasn't in finding a diamond, but in buying and selling the diamonds other, luckier men found.

"So, that's what he started to do. Now, imagine this: A guy at a rickety wooden table in a shack along the Amazon, a couple of beefy musclemen at his side, a pistol in a belt around his waist, gazing into the red mud-caked palms of one sweaty worker after another, and seeing the sparkle of diamonds."

"Wow, that is some story," admired Jake.

Buying and selling diamonds comes with its dangers and challenges, continued Jamie. Along with the treachery of bandits and fellow diamond buyers — there were shootings and throat cuttings every week in the minefields — government officials were always there with their hands out.

Finally, when one official noticed Jimmy was in the country illegally and wanted too large a bribe to stay quiet, Jimmy fled downriver. He bought a house in the hills outside of Rio where he had been living since with his beautiful Brazilian wife.

"And now he is back in town?" asked Jake.

"His dad has serious health problems," said Jamie, "so he is visiting for the first time since leaving. I get a sense he and his dad didn't get along when Jimmy was a kid.

"Oh, oh, I left out the best part — or maybe not the best part, but anyway, when the interview was all done and I was setting up to take some photos, Jimmy pulls out a leather pouch, loosens the leather string around the top, and pours half a dozen diamonds into my hand. And you betcha, I got that photo!"

"Get writing kid. The front page awaits," said Jake.

In a city newspaper, Jamie would have to verify his facts, and make a few calls to Brazil and a diamond broker to find out if Jimmy was just spinning a tale. But at the *Gazette*, where most readers likely knew the character of Jim Daggett and probably his son, Jimmy, Jake would leave it to their BS detectors to separate truth from fiction.

Besides, diamond hunting in the wilds of the Amazon sure beat out school kids coloring paper turkeys.

Chapter 20

For Jake, the newspaper business wasn't a calling, it was an accident.

The result of chance supercharged by his smart-ass teenage mouth.

At 16, schoolwork was a breeze, but with his

slight frame and the fact his mother had him skip the sixth grade, he was the smallest and youngest kid in his junior class — thanks, mom.

To compensate for his size, he developed a sassy mouth — although he thought of it as clever — along with enough negotiating skills to keep him from being punched out by the bigger guys.

Having a smart mouth and being a good talker was fine to gain him a few close guy friends, but not good enough to impress girls. Especially cute girls, especially one senior girl named Carol Ann who certainly had an impressive body moving under her shirt.

Like yikes! She smiled once at Jake in the hallway. That one smile occupied his nights for a month.

So, what to do to get Carol Ann to notice him again? Girls draped themselves over the jocks in school, but Jake didn't have a jock body.

Carol Ann was on the school newspaper staff, so Jake joined the Tiger Tales, the paper named after the school mascot. Soon, he discovered his smart mouth translated to the written word, which gained him some attention. While Carol Ann never quite came around, other girls did, and Jake discovered the pen is mighty indeed.

In his senior year, he became the paper's editor — ok, not a lot of competition, but still — where among other duties, he got to write editorials.

One week, bummed by how boring school was, he lamented in the Tiger Tales how he and his fellow seniors couldn't wait to get out of this soulless school with its silly rules and dull teachers.

On the Friday the paper came out, he had taken an early out to hang with friends at a local drive-in hamburger joint. Later, he learned the school superintendent had roamed the halls, looking to expel the smartass editor.

He was saved when the faculty advisor took the blame for allowing the editorial. She demoted him, but when the local daily newspaper called, seeking a stringer to cover Friday night high school football games, she offered up his name. He got the job.

When summer came, the sports editor continued his newspaper stay with a temp job filling in for vacationing reporters.

Right away he discovered these were his people.

Here was a place where a smart mouth was appreciated, the cleverer the better, especially when paired with a lack of respect for the powers-that-be.

Reporters sharpened these skills on each other with puns and witticisms, often at the expense of the people they covered and senior editors, who they regarded as having lost their edge the higher they rose in the newspaper's bureaucracy.

Yet, a smart mouth was only as good as the smart writing that went along with it. A particularly good sentence or quote was read aloud, to the appreciation of reporters around.

And if you did a really good job, snared the perfect interview, found the fresh angle, some editor would put your name at the top of the story. And your byline would be on the breakfast table of 150,000 local homes. Take that, you since-forgotten high school jocks!

Jake continued in the sports department while attending college and became a fast-rising star until, using an unnamed source, he reported the coach of a local pro soccer team had been stopped for drunken driving but then let go by a cop who was a fan. The other reporters loved the story, but the coach called Jake out at a press conference and demanded he provide his source.

For a while, Jake's name was all over local sports radio — and in truth, he loved hearing it. As the old-time politician who understood the value of publicity said, "I don't care what you say about me, just spell my name correctly."

To appease the coach, when Jake stood by his story but wouldn't name his source, he was moved out of sports and to the newsroom — a growing fish moving to a bigger pond.

With newspapering and newspaper people, it was all about finding a good story and then telling it even better later at the bar. And the girls — rather women now — were part of the mix, telling their stories, sopping up their beers, willing to spend drunken nights in strange beds.

Being a reporter was the best job in the world, Jake told anyone who would listen. You only dealt with interesting people — if they weren't interesting, you wouldn't be talking to them.

People would ask Jake which famous people he had interviewed, and while he had stories on some, he preferred the average person who somehow was thrust into the news. That's where the best, most unguarded quotes came from.

Like the mom he interviewed about her famous son who said, "He now thinks he is so great, he doesn't wear pants."

Even when he put that quote into the story, he couldn't say exactly what it meant, but he laughed every time he thought of it.

Then, he was tempted by the promotion ladder — with its extra pay and status — upward. First to the news desk to whip other reporters' copy into a seamless flow, then the city desk where he got to assign stories, to, at the end, running the metro section covering local news and features.

Being a reporter meant interacting with real people and the crazy fireworks of real life.

Working as an editor, though, was all about leaning towards being exact — just the right story at just the right length, with no misspellings, no typos, no shading of opinion.

Editors never gathered at the bar to tell rollicking stories of typos fixed, deadlines met, stories trimmed to fit the exact space.

Part of the fun seeped out of the job.

Only now, in the four-person office of the *Gazette*, did Jake realize what a bad bargain he had made when he started up the newspaper bureaucracy ladder — taking a hint of power in exchange for the joy of the work.

The job at the *Gazette* had found him by chance — but like the first chance that lead him to an ink-stained life, an accident that put him exactly where he should be.

"How did you get onto this story about Jimmy and his diamond exploits in Brazil?" asked Jake, hand on a freshly poured beer at Lester's where he had taken Jamie when his story was written.

"Funny thing, he called me." Jamie took his first sip. "He said I might like a local-boy-makes-good story. During the interview, he also asked a few questions about my mom. They both grew up here, so I suppose they knew each other. Who knows, maybe even dated, although neither of them has said so. I should ask my mom."

A commotion erupted at the other end of the bar. Rodney was grabbing pool balls from a table where two guys Jake didn't recognize were shooting eight ball.

"Rodney, get your hands off his balls!" shouted Bonny.

Today, Bonnie was wearing a kelly green t-shirt saying, "I could be wrong... but I doubt it."

"I should 86 Rodney from the bar," she said, coming up to Jake's and Jamie's end to wipe up a drip, "but I wouldn't want to inflict him on any other business in town. Besides, he does a good job as a fill-in bartender, and god knows, an honest part-time bartender with character is hard to find.

"Rodney, quit playing hide the cue stick!" she said, striding off.

"And Jimmy's back in town because his dad is ill?" said Jake, picking up the conversation.

"He also said he has some old business here," replied Jamie.

"So, a treasure hunter returns to town, just as murders happen and rumors of a treasure lost in the hills resurfaces," mused Jake. "Odd, do you think?"

"What's odd is that my schooner is empty," said Jamie, tilting his glass side to side. "And I am the guy who is filling up next week's front page…"

Chapter 21

"I don't see much difference. The *Gazette* office has always been a mess every time I've been in here."

"How about the broken window in the door behind you, sheriff, or how all of the drawers have been yanked out of my desk?" asked an exasperated Jake.

Sheriff Highkok, trim in his tight-fitting pressed tan uniform and fastidiously neat as usual, surveyed the small newspaper office in front of him, stopping his eyes at the big desk in the back where wooden drawers had been pulled out and turned upside-down, their contents spilling out around the tipped over wheeled captain's chair.

"Anything missing?"

"We haven't done an inventory, but the computers are all here, thank god, and none of the other desks were bothered. We don't usually have cash in the office, except for the jar of quarters from people using the copy machine. It's still here.

"It looks like whoever broke in was looking for something in my desk."

"Any idea what?"

"Maybe some of Gus's papers. I certainly haven't been here long enough to accumulate anything," replied

Jake, suddenly seeing an image of Wil in his mind.

"Well, let us know when you figure it out. We have two — maybe three — murder investigations going on. We could drop them if the newspaper insists..." said the sheriff, giving Jake a dead-eye look.

"Otherwise, call your insurance agent," said the sheriff, turning with his deputy by his side and pushing past Jamie who was just coming into the office. "And get this door fixed. The broken glass could cut someone, and that would be a crime of endangering the public."

Jamie pulled up suddenly when he saw Jake's desk. "Whoa, what happened here?"

When Jake growled, Jamie pulled up his camera. "I was just past Gus's duplex and his front door has been smashed open, too, and yellow crime tape is taped over the frame. Want to see?"

But Jake didn't wait to see.

Instead, he angrily went to his desk and started noisily slamming the wooden drawers back in, all the while thinking the only thing of value in the desk was Gus's files on the legendary Major Moser's treasure and the topographic maps showing Gus's aerial searches. And the only person other than Jake who knew about the maps was the county clerk, Wil.

This did not look like a break-in by a woman. Not to be sexist, but a woman would have used less force, more guile. Could she be working with someone to find the treasure? But what a ridiculous thought — there is very likely no treasure to be found. The whole myth of a treasure was a marketing ploy by a couple of ex-hookers from Las Vegas running a pie shop here.

"Did I catch you at a bad time?"

On his knees picking up loose debris, he swiveled his head toward the counter to see Just Nell standing there. She looked dressed up today compared to when they had first met at the Cowboy Caverns. She was holding a piece of paper in her hands.

"Everyone has been laid off at the caverns as the bankruptcy drags on," she said, "so for the first time in 20 years, I am looking for a job. I'm dropping off my resumé around town, although frankly, it lists only one job. And, I don't think there are any other 'managing the caverns' jobs around."

"Well," said Jake, standing and swiping a hand at his knees, "Susan, our ad sales and circulation person, is talking about moving to Phoenix so she can get a life away from her mother. Oh, and she does bookkeeping, too."

"Bookkeeping is what I did at the caverns, so I should be good there. For ad sales, I've represented the caverns at the Chamber of Commerce for almost 20 years, so I know most of the local business people. Circulation, though, would be new to me."

"Yeah, that's mostly tracking who has paid and who needs to be billed and then working with our little carriers and their moms. You'd learn quickly."

"Of course," said Jake, now standing at the counter opposite Just Nell, suddenly nervous by her physical appeal, "the future of the *Gazette* is anyone's guess because of Suzanne's death. I can't promise a lifetime job."

Just Nell laughed. "For 20 years, the caverns have been a big hole in the ground one owner after another has thrown money into. I know about uncertain business futures."

And the deal was made. Jake said he would confirm that afternoon Susan was leaving. And, he would run her hire past Patrick McPhee, now the owner by default of the *Gazette*.

But in truth, any of Jake's efforts to talk to Patrick these last few weeks had come up empty. And now with the *Gazette* squeaking by in paying its bills — mostly because Jake and Suzanne hadn't discussed pay when she was alive, so Jake wasn't drawing a check — as long as Patrick didn't come into the office to shut down the weekly newspaper, and as long as Jake didn't draw a salary, the paper could continue.

So, while Jake didn't exactly have the authority — really, he didn't have any authority — to make a new hire, who was there to stop him?

Now, if he could just control his lizard brain to keep his eyes above Just Nell's collar line...

Chapter 22

Jake poured beer into a glass at his RV dinette and pulled open the metal box he had found buried in Gus's desk.

"I wonder if this is what the thieves were looking for?" he mused as he carefully started pulling papers out. After discovering the break-in at the *Gazette* this morning, he had been waiting all day to get home to examine the contents of the box.

Good thing he had moved it to the toolbox in the bed of his pickup a couple of days ago, he thought.

First out came the topographic map and

protractors, next came a few pages of hand-written notes, followed by yellowing newspaper clippings and finally a key.

Jake twisted the key back and forth in his hand. He tried it on the metal box lock, but it was too big. He chuckled that in mystery stories, the key was always a clue, but he had no idea what kind of key it was or what it would unlock. Maybe it was just a lost key that had found its way to the bottom of the box. Maybe there was no mystery.

Pushing the map and protractors to one side, Jake unfolded the old clippings — because staying in the playful scenario of a storybook mystery, he was a newspaperman, and that's what a newspaperman would do, right?

He started to read the first clipping.

Gold finding family killed by Indians

Several gold prospectors, including a husband, wife, and their family of six, were reported killed by Indians in the Black Hills gold rush area.

A military patrol led by U.S. Army Major Pat Moser, who had been trying fruitlessly to keep white prospectors out of the territory given to the Black Hills Indians by treaty, discovered the massacred bodies.

All their belongings had been looted, and no gold was found on the prospectors.

However, a recovered letter written by Isaac Stone, the family's father addressed to his brother in Philadelphia, said, "I got all the gold we could carry and I'm heading home a rich man."

The clipping went on to describe the Black Hills as "mountains of gold" attracting hordes of eager miners and prospectors from around the world.

Another clipping spoke to the lawlessness of the gold country.

Deadwood is the deadliest town in America

Deadwood, the instant Dakotas boom town that sprung up in the smack center of the Black Hills Gold rush is well named — with gunshots ringing out at all times day and night.

"We git three killings a day here, and those are only the ones we know about," said Sheriff Otis Keller.

Sheriff Keller is new on the job, with the previous two sheriffs each killed in shoot-outs during the past couple of months.

Thousands have descended on the Black Hills, finding gold in streams and on the hillsides.

Others find gold at the end of a gun.

Road agents frequently attack treasure coaches — armored stagecoaches — hauling as much as $300,000 of the precious metal to Cheyenne, Wyoming where it can be safely put on armed trains for transport east.

In a recent robbery south of Deadwood, robbers bound and gagged the stationmaster at a way stop for the treasure coach, then ambushed the coach when it arrived. The outlaws tied the driver to one of the coach's wheels, opened the safe with sledgehammers and chisels, divided the loot, and rode off in different directions.

Huh, said Jake under his breath. Maybe Gus had determined the Black Hills Gold Rush in the mid-1800s, rather than the Alaskan rush at the turn of the century, was the origins of the local missing gold story.

It would make sense, as the Arizona country was much less settled — and safe — in the mid-1800s.

And since Deadwood was festering in crime, sneaking gold out rather than depositing it in a local bank also made sense.

And this Army Major Pat Moser mentioned in the first story... he was the one who was supposed to be escorting the gold and gold miners south to Phoenix. Could he have been overcome by gold fever and have robbed the men?

Reaching across his RV's narrow aisle to the fridge to grab another beer, Jake saw the dome light flash in his pickup.

"What the...?"

He squirmed out from the tight dinette bench, grabbed a long-handled flashlight sitting on the settee, opened the rig's door, took one step down, then whack! Something smashed into the back of his head.

The blow caused his foot to miss the final step and down he went on his hands, knees, and shoulder.

"Damn, I told you we should have waited for him to go to bed!" came a voice as two sets of footsteps ran across the campsite's gravel.

"Shut up and drive!" said the second voice, followed by the slamming of doors and the gunning of an engine.

Jake rolled over onto his knees and using one

hand to brace himself on his front doorstep, shakily rose. Both of his hands were weeping blood. Pebbles were embedded around the knuckles of the hand that held the flashlight.

The knees in his pants were torn, but he didn't see any blood there. His shoulder didn't feel anything like the time he had broken it flying off a motorcycle. That was good.

A new set of car lights swept over Jake.

"Are they back? I'll show those bastards." Gripping the heavy, long-handled flashlight, he took a staggering step forward, only to be stopped by seeing Just Nell step out of the driver's door.

"What are you doing here?"

"I could give you a dozen innocent answers, but..." she said, shrugging her shoulders. "I did bring wine."

That's when she saw the full picture of Jake, torn pants, blood on his hands, a snarling look. "Oh my god, what happened to you?"

＊ ＊ ＊ ＊ ＊

A full-to-the-rim glass of pinot noir, bandages, and Just Nell's delicate plucking of pebbles from his knuckles had calmed Jake.

Even dazed from the attack, he had decided in an instant upon seeing Just Nell it probably wasn't her who had jumped him. He had also decided her tight jeans and white cowgirl shirt with a couple of buttons undone were reason enough to invite her in.

Still, he had quickly picked up all of Gus's papers,

returned them to the metal box, and then slid the box into a cubbyhole.

When Just Nell asked again what had happened, Jake guessed whoever had broken into the *Gazette*, and Gus's duplex apartment didn't find what they were looking for. So, they came by the campground grounds to check out his pickup.

"What do you suppose they are after?"

Keeping the information about Gus's metal box to himself, Jake shrugged. "Who knows? But I hope this doesn't discourage you from working at the *Gazette*."

She laughed, setting down the tweezers with a pebble still in its teeth. "I do like an exciting man."

By the second glass of wine, Jake was feeling all better — even philosophical on the twists and turns of life, where an angry conk on the head could be followed by a flutter of the heart.

Then, Just Nell reached up and switched off the overhead light.

As the moon came in through the blinds, Jake and Just Nell stood up. "The French say that the best part of an affair is going up the stairs. Desire is almost always more thrilling than fulfillment," said Jake as the two of them moved back to the queen bed fitted in the corner. "And I say the French don't know fuck all about sex."

Just Nell giggled and unsnapped her bra.

Jake didn't do a lot more talking, especially about the French.

Chapter 23

"I want to be a famous novelist so bad!

"The money, the babes, the exotic venues…"

Did he just say "venues," wondered Jake, looking at the kid he guessed would be 19 or 20 sitting in the chair next to the editor's desk, actually wearing rose-colored sunglasses likely lifted from his hippie dad, or more likely, hippie grandfather.

The young man, probably five-foot-six and close to 200 pounds but well-groomed with short blond hair, had launched himself into the *Gazette's* office and over to Jake's desk with a story to tell.

"So, have you written any novels?" wondered Jake.

"Yes, my first one just went live today on Amazon and I'm halfway through my second one. The career of Aaron O'Dell, famous novelist, lifts off…"

"Oh, so Amazon is publishing your novel. Impressive."

"Dude, I'm published on Amazon, not by Amazon. Anybody can get published on Amazon but that's how it starts. Many big-name authors started on Amazon, then were picked up by traditional publishers, then sold movie rights, and then the big money just rolls in. Famous Aaron O'Dell," he said, drawing his hands across the sky as if looking at his name on a theater marquee.

"Did you bring in a copy of your book?"

"Dude, it's all digital these days, not dead trees and smelly ink like the *Gazette*. You know, you should be all online."

"Ok, we'll look into that someday," said Jake, thinking like in never, dude.

"What is the book about?"

"It is so-o-o-o original," said Aaron, getting even more animated.

"It opens with these two young couples — about my age — bombing around Tijuana in a jeep. Three guys — three cartel guys — see them, and one of the guys says to his buddies, 'Hey, amigo, isn't that Carlos's jeep? (Because, you see, inserts Aaron, the cartel runs Tijuana and cartel members with machine guns patrol the Mexican border town in jeeps.)

"So, the cartel guy sprays machine gun bullets over the heads of the young couples and blocks their path.

"Now, at this point, you think the young couples — who are Americans — would be terrified, but no! When a cartel dude reaches in to grab the driver, the driver touches him, and the cartel guy falls backward, melting away like a Dove bar dropped on a hot Mexican sidewalk.

"That's my phrase: ... like a Dove bar dropped on a hot Mexican sidewalk.

"So," said Aaron, now hunching towards Jake, "when the other two cartel guys see that, they start to pull back but the American driver points his fingers at them, and two fingertips fly off his hands like missiles, right into their torsos, and they melt...

"... like a Dove bar dropped on a hot Mexican sidewalk," finished Jake.

When Aaron laughed at Jake's reiteration of his phrase, Jake offered, "Well, that's certainly different."

"Damn right, bro. You don't get rich or famous — or get the luscious babes — by being the same as everybody else. Be different or be dead, I say."

With Aaron's joy in sharing a personal motto, Jake suggested, "Maybe I should read the book before writing a story."

"Nahhh," said Aaron. "Wait until I have completed all three in this series, then you can buy the box set."

* * * * *

After Aaron had left and Jake had entered his story notes into his computer, he had to admit he admired the kid for his moxie.

Aaron O'Dell, maybe that was a perfect name for a famous novelist with a babe on each arm. Although Jake wasn't quite as excited about the book's name: *American Werewolf in Mexico*.

"Jake, phone... now let me see if I can work this transfer button..." said Just Nell, her first day on the job after Susan had indeed left to find a life in Phoenix.

"Jake, this is Patrick, Patrick McPhee. You had better come up to the house."

"Yes, I'm anxious to talk with you. When is a good time?"

"Make it before noon, because that's when I open my bottle of Chivas for the day."

Chapter 24

Noon came early at Patrick McPhee's home.

The widower, dressed in a faded Scotch plaid flannel bathrobe, belt loosely tied around the middle, didn't say a word to Jake when he opened the door.

Rather, he turned and walked into the dark

interior of the house, ice cubes sloshing around inside a glass tumbler, already filled with a couple of inches of smoky liquid.

Jake shut the door behind him and followed Patrick towards what turned out to be his destination of a kitchen table. "I'm so glad you called, we need to talk about the *Gazette*."

"Suzanne. It's Suzanne I want to talk about."

"Yes, of course. I am so sorry for your loss, and with her being the publisher of the paper...

"I need to explain some things to you, and then maybe you can figure out why she was killed."

Patrick sat in a wooden kitchen chair, a padded seat laced to the back and bottom. Probably the same padded chair he occupied when he and Suzanne sat around the table talking about the humdrum minutia of life. People never expect the end to be so near.

Looking at Patrick, it was hard for Jake to imagine him as anything but old. His owl face emphasized by dark-rimmed glasses over bloodshot eyes, a few strands of fly-away gray hair laying hit or miss on the scalp discolored by age spots, trembling hands lifting the Chivas Regal bottle to splash more liquid into his glass, he seemed a perpetually old man.

"Water, that's the thing," began Patrick. "Water has always been hard to come by here.

"The pioneers dug wells by hand as deep as 80, 100 feet. Can you imagine some poor bastard, 100 feet down in a well, digging with a small shovel, and the dirt carried to the surface by a bucket. What did he do when he had to take a shit?

"Anyway. That was then. Now, the town has five

drilled wells, all between 200 and 300 feet deep.

"Except," said Patrick, pausing to add more to the empty tumbler — Jake hadn't even seen him take a drink — "one of those wells is contaminated by nitrates. Not unusual in farming country where nitrate in fertilizer works itself into the water table. Another well has become clogged by sand and is unusable. Three wells, that could be enough.

"But in the past six months, one of the wells started to show a new kind of contamination. Not something natural and not something caused by farming. The town can't make it on two wells."

"I had not heard this," said Jake. "Did Suzanne have some tests done? What was her thinking? Did she hire a company to investigate?"

"Mmmm... you are not from Arizona. Here's how taxes work. The state income tax goes mostly to the state. Property tax goes mainly to the county and special taxing districts like the regional fire departments and libraries. Towns like ours have to survive mainly from the small piece of sales tax we get.

"Now, a little history. In the past few years, the big furniture factory and store closed on main street. Furniture is big-ticket sales, generating big sales tax. Gone. Then a couple of years ago, some graduating high school seniors snuck into the water slide park. One of them drowned. A terrible thing, as we all knew the kid. Anyway, his parents sued, and the waterpark closed.

"Now, with the Cowboy Caverns in bankruptcy, there are three big sales tax generators not spinning off any sales tax.

"This is why Suzanne has been fighting with the

sheriff. The town contracts for police services from the county sheriff. He keeps wanting more money for high-tech geegaws, and the town can't afford it. The town can barely stay in business.

"Likewise, the town can't afford an official investigation of the contamination until more information is unearthed. I believe Suzanne was down in the caverns, doing her own investigation, someone saw her who didn't want her there, and killed her."

Drawn into the story, Jake opened his reporter's notebook and took out a pen. "Why the caverns?"

"Because the contaminated well was the one closest to the caverns.

"Believe me, we sat around this very table, in these chairs, and tossed out dozens of possibilities. Something going on in the caverns was just one of them. But that is where Suzanne died."

"Have you shared your ideas and concerns with the sheriff?"

"Of course. But, as far as I know, as of yet he has not sent anyone down into the caverns to look around."

"I saw crime scene tape. I know officers have been down there," Jake suggested gently.

"The caverns run underground like a spider web for miles. No one has explored all of the possible tunnels or hides-hole."

Patrick reached across to an unoccupied chair to grab a cardboard box full of papers. "Listen, I have papers here from Suzanne's investigations. I would like you to take them. See if you can find out who killed my little Suzie."

Chapter 25

The next afternoon, walking along the main street past Ed's Hardware on the way to Lester's for a drink with Jamie, Jake heard a shout-out.

"Hey, Mr. Editor. I just got my first sales!"

"Congratulations, Aaron. What's that earning you?"

"The amount doesn't matter, dude. Do you think any big-name novelists worried about the size of their first royalty check? No, the river of cash has started. I'm on my way, editor man, and one day, the *Gazette* will be known for running the first interview with famous novelist Aaron O'Dell," he said, fanning his palms across the sky, seeing his name in lights.

"Gotta run man, these pizzas won't deliver themselves," said Aaron, opening the driver's door on a dusty pink van with Rose and Son's Pizza lettering on the side.

"You deliver pizza, too," said Jake, raising his voice at the end, a little sarcastically.

"Yep, gotta help my mom out until I can go full-time famous, eh?" With that, he slammed the door and started the engine.

"Who was that?" asked Jamie as the van roared away.

"Probably a guy who one day we'll say, 'I knew him when...'"

* * * * *

"Midgets with guns? Midgets with guns?

"Are you saying short people shouldn't have guns? Midgets have the same rights as all Americans to own guns!" shouted Rodney, waving his cue stick at a man on a barstool.

Jake had never seen Rodney this indignant. "Don't you wave your hand at me, you tourist. I won't be shushed up!

"My dad was only five-foot-two, and I always considered him one of the little people. I loved my dad, I LOVED my dad and he had the same rights to own a gun as any cross-eyed fisherman!"

"Rodney, shut up. Go back to your pool game. This man didn't say anything about midgets with guns, he said, 'Son of a gun, my arm itches.' You just misheard him," chided Bonny, slapping the bar with a towel.

"Yeah, OK, but I still loved my dad, I don't care what his height was," said Rodney, sulking back to the pool table where it was his turn.

"Jeeze, this place gets nuttier all the time," lamented Bonny, laying down two draughts in front of Jake and Jamie. Today, her t-shirt suggested, "If you're reading this shirt, your phone battery is probably dead."

"Hey, I finally talked to Patrick yesterday," Jake told Jamie. "He wants us to investigate Suzanne's death."

Jake then shared his conversation with Patrick about Suzanne's worries over the town's water supply.

"Patrick also said Suzanne had been in early talks with a company inquiring about — get this — buying the former furniture building to create a factory to 'grow' diamonds. I guess there is a new, high-tech way to create diamonds that are indistinguishable from real diamonds. Some Hollywood types are involved who want to put an end to blood diamonds."

"Growing real diamonds here? Wow, that would be so cool!" exclaimed Jamie. "Would it create a lot of jobs?"

"Probably a couple of hundred. A couple of hundred local people spending money locally, is how Suzanne looked at it.

"But, any questions about water quality would spook the company away. That's partially why Suzanne was investigating quietly and on her own. Patrick thinks she was seen down in the caverns looking for the source of the contamination and was killed to keep her quiet."

"So the mayor went down into the caverns by herself — that violates the first rule of every scary movie," said Jamie, swirling the remaining beer in his glass.

"Yeah. But now, I'm at a loss for how to proceed. Newspaper investigations are just conveying quotes from experts or insiders. We don't go down into a dark hole ourselves, looking for wrongdoing."

"We do have Suzanne's notes and water samples. I took chemistry classes at college — if you can believe that — maybe one of my old professors might run some tests for us on the quiet.

"And with Just Nell's help, we might be able to get into the caverns and look around ourselves."

"Another one, gentlemen?" asked Bonny, appearing just as Jake's and Jamie's glasses were empty.

"Might as well," said Jake, "another one might make this plan seem sensible."

Chapter 26

"I told him all day he should go see the doctor, that his doctor had said to come in immediately if these symptoms continued.

"But you know men. He delayed and said if he didn't feel better in the morning, he would go in.

"About two o'clock at night, he woke me up and said he needed to go to the emergency room."

"I got him into the car and just as I was turning into the parking lot for the emergency room — with the lit-up canopy just ahead — he leaned into my shoulder and died right there."

The thin, plain woman, well into her 60s in a flowered blouse with her gray hair tied back by a silver barrette — the only frill on her unadorned body — stopped talking for a minute and Jake didn't prompt her. He had met her a few days before at a campground barbecue and thought her story of a woman traveling the U.S. alone in an RV would be a nice feature for the paper.

"That was 2012 and we had been living for a year in our 25-foot rig after selling our house. We were roaming the country looking for the perfect place to settle.

"After he died," she continued, "I was a basket case, of course. My daughter had me come up to Minnesota to stay with her — that's where she lives now — and that was good for about six months. But she had a busy job, her husband, who was perfectly nice to me, worked long hours, her two boys were in school and in every sport you could name. They were my family, but I came to realize, not my 'family.'

"When winter was coming, I made the excuse that my bones wanted a warmer climate. I got the RV out of storage and headed south to Arizona.

"As I pulled into the senior RV resort just north of Phoenix, a gray-haired woman out walking with her husband waved and smiled and me. I was home among my people."

"And you're OK with driving your 'home' down the freeway," asked Jake.

"It doesn't take a man's muscles to steer," she said with a smile, "and anyway, I stick mainly to the smaller roads. The views are more interesting there."

The woman talking, whose first name was Dottie, said when spring came, she headed west to California and followed 101 north to Washington State. She eventually arrived near Blaine, the last town in the U.S. before Canada, then turned right and kept going.

She sometimes worked odd jobs in towns and at the campgrounds for extra money to supplement her Social Security, and had learned to do every job on the RV — including changing the oil — to afford her travels.

"I'm still looking for that perfect spot to settle," she told Jake, then smiled and added, "meanwhile, I'm loving having an ever-changing view out of my front window."

* * * * *

It had been a couple of weeks since Jake's conversation with Patrick and Jamie sending off water samples to a chemistry professor.

No one had been murdered in town since, that was good.

Jake had fallen into justifying Robbie's frequent back massages in the office, and Just Nell's frequent nighttime visits to the RV, by pretending he wasn't really their boss, since he still wasn't being paid.

Whenever he brought up the future of the *Gazette* — and his future at the *Gazette* — Patrick would turn the conversation to Suzanne, and what was she doing down in the caverns. "She must have known something, or seen something," Patrick said over and over. "But what?"

And for a man who wasn't being paid, Jake discovered he was awfully happy at the *Gazette*. He enjoyed returning to the early days of his career when he was always astonished by the variety of the human experience.

Doing interviews, like the one this morning with Dottie, the full-time RV'ing widow, reopened his eyes to the vast variety life could offer, if a person chose to go down a byway instead of the freeway.

He found a love for crafting the presentation of the weekly, with big photos, headlines that didn't scream but were compelling, and stories built around local names.

An editor once told him a place needed three things to be a community: "One, a school, to show a commitment to the future, two, a bank to show financial wherewithal, and three, a newspaper to weave people together."

It was odd to say, but editing a paper with 1,600 circulation — actually, now almost 1,700 as Just Nell found her groove as circulation director — was more appealing to Jake than his toiling at the 150,000-circulation metro newspaper.

And, he was sure the town would miss the *Gazette* more if it were to fold than Seattle missed the second-largest newspaper when it closed a decade before.

Jake was so comfortable here that he was thinking about having business cards printed up. "Editor, the Desert *Gazette*" was his byway to happiness.

Chapter 27

"Hey, I bet you know these mountains and valleys pretty well."

"You mean these mountains and valleys?" asked Just Nell, who with a twitch, sent a jiggle through her naked body lying atop Jake's bed.

"Hey, you made me lose my thought," laughed Jake, as he went exploring her landscape.

* * * * *

"Ok, back to my earlier subject."

"I thought I was your earlier subject, silly."

"I mean before that. I never told you what I found in Gus's desk. And before you give me that sweet wiggle again — because I am a man of a certain age and my time outs are longer these days — let me tell you something that has been puzzling me."

Jake then told of the map with the overlying circles, the old newspaper articles about the Black Hills gold rush, and cryptic handwritten notes from Gus.

"I am thinking Gus believed he was on the trail of the Moser gold and was using a drone to fly over the backcountry terrain looking for some kind of sign of where it could be."

Just Nell sat up and slipped on a t-shirt. "I've seen a book with lore about lost treasures in the West, and the Moser Gold was a chapter. We sold the book for a while at the caverns gift shop. But I thought the whole thing was a hoax, just put out there to make money off gullible tourists."

Crawling on his knees to the bottom of the bed — it was impossible to look graceful exiting an RV corner bed — Jake bent over, slid open a drawer below the fridge, and pulled out the metal box he had found in Gus's desk.

Placing the topographic map on the dinette, he said, "See these circles? Do you recognize any of this terrain?"

"Is the dangle there marking the secret spot," laughed Just Nell.

"Oh damn it. Let me put some shorts on."

Just Nell traced elevation lines on Gus's map with her fingers, then followed lines indicating streams.

"Yeah, I think this is out by the old military zone. About 20 miles out of town."

"Want to go with me up there this weekend?"

"Would it be a clothes-optional sort of trip?" she said, snapping the waistband on his boxers.

* * * * *

"This Tacoma is just made for this kind of trip," Jake said, holding onto the wheel steady to keep the small Toyota pickup out of the deep ruts in the red clay road.

"It won't be made that way much longer if you don't slow down over these washboards. The gold isn't going anywhere."

"I wonder how much gold we are talking about?" mused Jake.

"Even a pound or two would be worth quite a lot these days." Just Nell bounced off her seat as the pickup found another pothole.

"That's true, a pound of gold in the mid-1800s probably made you a rich man. Heck, I've seen old newspaper ads. Flour went for a nickel for 10 pounds, a good horse could be had for $10. Cowboys would work all month for $5 plus board and room."

"What would a pound of gold be worth today?"

"The price is around $1,800 to $2,000 per ounce. So, a pound would be 16 times that, or roughly $30,000."

"That's something, but not a lot. What if they were carrying two pounds or even five pounds?

"Two pounds would be $60,000, five pounds $150,000. Now that's worth spending weekends trampling over these hills."

Another bump, another cloud of red dust flying

around the cab. Just Nell coughed. "Didn't the old newspaper article say they had 'all the gold they could carry?' I'm not a horse person, but I would think a horse could likely carry, oh, I don't know, maybe 20 pounds. How much would that be?"

"Well, 20 pounds, at $3,000 a pound, would be $600,000. And yeah, we're getting into numbers worth killing for, as a pack horse, without a rider, could carry much more than that."

Just Nell pointed to a parking spot under a tree, saying they were in the area where Gus was flying his drone. They stopped, got out, and then climbed up a little knoll to get a good observation point.

"Ok, it looks like Gus meticulously circled over the rises to our right, and was working his way to our left," said Just Nell, one hand on the map, the other raised, pointing left.

"Ow! Did you hit me!" she cried, glaring at Jake, and stumbling a few steps ahead while grabbing at her left shoulder.

"Just Nell, that was a shot! Are you hurt?" And then Jake saw the blood spreading through the shirt on her left shoulder.

Zing, zing, zing, three more bullets ripped past.

Chapter 28

"Get down, get down!"

Just Nell fell to the ground, Jake collapsed to her side.

"You've been shot, Just Nell, you've been shot!" Jake loudly whispered, as if there was a point in keeping his voice low.

After a minute that seemed like an hour, and hearing no more shots, Jake half rose to look at Just Nell's wound. Her shirt was mostly red. Blood seeped down her left front and side.

"Shit! Shit! Shit! We got to get you to a hospital. Can you stand?"

"Oh Jake, I don't feel so good. Call an ambulance."

"There is no reception out here. I can't carry you, so you are going to have to walk down to the pickup."

"Just let me lay here for a moment."

"No, no! We have to get you to a hospital. Buck up, Just Nell, you have to stand up. You have to fight to live."

Rising to his knees, Jake rolled the wounded woman over onto her back, then taking hold of her right hand and elbow, pulled her upright to a sitting position, and then all the way up.

"Come on, just a step at a time."

"It's not feeling so bad now, I think I can make it."

"Maybe you're going into shock, lean on me, the pickup is just ahead."

The two staggered down the twisting trail of the knoll, slipping and sliding on the loose pebbles, falling once.

"Leave me here, Jake, go get a doctor."

"No, no, get back up. You're tough. You can do it."

Just Nell gamely allowed Jake to help her up again, and they stumbled toward the Toyota until Jake's foot caught in a root of a shrub and they tumbled and then rolled once.

"God damn it, Jake!"

"Sorry! Let's get back up," apologized Jake, looking around for the shooter.

Reaching the pickup, Jake wrenched open the passenger door, helped Just Nell in, ran around to the driver's side, started up, quickly reversed, and gunned it.

"Ow, Jake, ow! You're going too fast!" Just Nell slipped off the seat down into the foot well.

Jake slammed on the brakes, ran around to the other side, lifted Just Nell back into her seat, and this time, he tried going slower and hugging the side of the dirt roadway where the ruts were smaller.

"Bourbon," she whispered.

"Bourbon? You want a shot of whiskey? I'll get you a whole bottle when we get to the doctor's. Just hold on."

"Bourbon. My last name is Bourbon, in case you have to notify anyone back in Florida." She was barely whispering now. "And they knew me by Nellie. Nellie Bourbon."

Reaching the pavement, Jake concentrated on the road, speeding just under reckless.

'Oh, Jake..." she said, leaning her head onto his shoulder, passing out.

"Oh, no, no, no!" Jake said while flashing on Dottie — the full-time RV'er — and her story of her husband dying with his head slumped on her shoulder.

He stepped on the gas, and the pickup bounced wildly. At least with Just Nell — Nellie — out, she couldn't complain.

* * * * *

"So show me on the map where exactly the alleged shooting was." Sheriff Highkok unfolded a detailed county map on the reception desk of the medical center.

"Alleged! There's nothing 'alleged' about it!" Jake said, still jacked up from the shooting and the 30-minute race to the medical center. "She has a bullet hole in her shoulder. The doctor said she was lucky the bullet went through as all the battering she took on the drive in it could have killed her."

"Ok, the site of the shooting then."

Jake traced the road that barely showed on the map. "About here."

"Hmmm... I don't think that's in this county. You're going to have to report it to the sheriff of that county."

"What!" Jake exploded. "A person gets almost killed and you can't take the report because you 'think' the shooting may have happened in a different county? So nobody is going to do anything?"

The sheriff breathed out a sigh. "Ok, I can take the report and forward it to the other sheriff. I'm doing it for Just Nell, as, in my opinion, she was the only reason to go out to the caverns. She certainly lifted my day."

Leveling a skeptical gaze at Jake, he asked, "What were you two doing out there?"

"Doing out there? What kind of question is that? It's public land, we can be out there if we want," replied Jake, suddenly realizing maybe the shooting had something to do with their hunting the Moser gold, a fact he wanted to keep quiet.

'Huh. Well, you newspaper people certainly are getting yourselves in trouble lately. I'm trying to learn if there could be a connection between this shooting and the deaths of Gus and Suzanne.

"I'll take the report, and then try to get a deputy up there to look around. It may just have been a hunter, who from a long way off, mistook you two for deer."

"Deer? What the fuck…" and Jake would have said more but a nurse yanked on his sleeve.

"She is asking for you."

Chapter 29

"How is Just Nell doing?"

"Amazing. She is doing amazing," Jake told Jerry of Jerry's Men's Boutique as they stood on opposite sides of the store's cash register counter.

"The doctor said she was lucky the bullet was likely from a .22 rifle, so it didn't tear a big hole. And, it didn't hit any vital organs or bone. And," laughed Jake, "that my driving down the hill didn't kill her."

"I'm so glad to hear that. She was always a breath of fresh air when she attended Chamber meetings for the caverns, and I was delighted you hired her to sell ads for the *Gazette*."

"Ads is just why I am here," said Jake, jumping on an easy segue.

"Just Nell will likely be out for a couple of weeks, so I am picking up the slack by making her ad calls. I haven't seen your ads in the *Gazette* while I've been here, I thought I would stop in and see if you are interested in an ad this week."

"An ad? Hmmm… I tried some ads when I opened 10 years ago, and I don't know, but I'm not sure I saw a lot of results," said Jerry, crossing his arms and standing back from the register.

"Jerry, you have one of the nicest businesses in town. Yet, you must know more people are buying from Amazon, and others go into the big cities. To compete, you need to constantly give people reasons for coming in."

"Ah, word-of-mouth seems to work for me. That's the best advertising." Jerry mouthed the words like a well-worn answer to pesky ad salespeople.

"Of course," replied Jake, "but word-of-mouth can't be depended on. Word-of-mouth isn't going to say you have a sale on…" looking around, Jake saw a sales rack of men's summer shirts "… those shirts or the pants to go with them."

"I don't make any money on sales items, I wouldn't want to spend money on advertising money-losing merchandise."

"Of course not, Jerry. But, if you are having people come for sales items, isn't the idea they will buy the regularly priced items, too? Getting them into the store is what an ad can do, getting them to buy is up to you."

"Yeah, not today. But when Just Nell gets back, send her in. I sure enjoy talking with her. And, when it comes to ads, I'm always willing to sign on for those community ads when the Wildcats go to the state football tournament."

"Those ads we charge $25 for? Thanks, Jerry. It doesn't look like the 'Cats are going to State in football this year, but the girls' volleyball team is sharp. I think they are bound for State, should I add your name as an advertiser on their congratulations page?"

"Girls? This is a men's store, I don't know about a girls' team."

"Jerry, aren't most of your shoppers women, buying items for men? And, men have daughters. Supporting a girls' team would be a winning spike shot."

"Ok, ok. Just $25, right? I guess I could do it. Be sure to check back with me when and if you decide to do a page. Have Just Nell come by."

* * * * *

The next sales call after Jerry's was Rose and Son's Pizza, where Aaron was at the counter, adding up receipts.

"Hey, soon-to-be-famous-novelist, how are you doing?" said Jake.

"My hand is poised by the phone, waiting for fame's call. What's-up?"

Jake went through the discussion about Just Nell's health for about the 10th time today as his explanation for why he was making ad calls.

"I see pizza ads in all of the little papers, so I'm wondering how we can get Rose and Son's into the *Gazette*."

"Hmmm, pizza, especially delivery pizza is kinda a spur-of-the-moment decision," said Aaron, a dark look coming to his face. "I don't know an ad in a once-a-week newspaper would work."

Brightening, he added, "But, you did do the first

interview on me, so I suppose I should throw some business your way. How about this: We trade pizzas for a weekly ad. That way, you get something to eat, and we get exposure. Can't hurt, right?"

"You mean every week, say for a $50 ad, we would get five pizzas?"

"Five seems like a lot. Maybe three. However, basically, yes."

"What would we do with three pizzas a week?" wondered Jake.

"Have weekly contests where you give them to readers, eat them yourself, give them to staff members as a bonus, I don't care. You're the creative guy, think of something."

"Our staff members seem to like being paid with cash," said Jake. "I think trading an ad for cash would be the best choice."

"Yeah, well, let me talk to my mom. She may have some ideas. Speaking of checks, I got to get yesterday's checks and cash to the bank. Talk at you later."

* * * * *

Jake's last ad call of the morning was on Murphy's Farm Implements at the edge of town.

Once he navigated the rows of tools, parts, and other farm-related gewgaws and got in front of the owner, Sam Murphy, he went through the spiel about Just Nell and why Jake was in the store today.

"I see you have been running half-page ads in the *Gazette* these past few weeks. Thanks. I am here to hopefully pick up ad copy for next week."

Lately, Murphy's had been the second-largest advertiser in the *Gazette*, right behind the full page the grocery store ran.

Sam didn't say a word, he just stared at Jake.

Finally, he said, "Look around you."

Jake surveyed the store, seeing two counter employees behind large parts manuals conferring with customers, other men in Carhartts and stripped overalls picking up and putting down items from wire shelves lining the aisles, a man behind a glass window in the back, working an adding machine spitting out paper tape.

Shit, is this a test about my knowledge of farming? thought Jake, and have I already flunked it. He raised his hands in the universal I-don't-know gesture.

"This store is filled with Billy-Bobs all day long, who needed a bath yesterday, and can't talk about anything but machinery and the terrible things the government is doing to screw up farm prices," offered Sam.

"When your Just Nell bounces into the store — and she does bounce when she walks — she is like dawn breaking on a fresh green field. I quickly learned that if I say 'Yes' to an ad, she stays longer. She will put her notebook on this counter right here and bend over to make notes. I tell you honestly, my heart stops.

"Now, the cost of the ads themselves, or what they promote doesn't matter. I get co-op dollars, that is, the manufacturers themselves will pay for the ads. To get co-op, Just Nell brings in tear sheets of the ads to prove they have run. That means, two times a week, she bounces into the store."

The farm store owner stopped talking, a far away look in his eye. Jake was equally at a loss for words. Just Nell was both his girlfriend and an employee, should he be verbally indignant over the comments just made? He would as a newsman, but maybe ad salespeople play by a different set of ground rules.

The moment for saying anything passed, then Sam asked: "How soon is she going to be out of the hospital and making her ad calls again?"

When Jake said probably a few weeks, Sam looked disappointed. "That's too bad. I guess just rerun the last couple of ads, but save up the tear sheets for Just Nell to deliver."

* * * * *

When a brooding Jake pushed his way through the *Gazette's* repaired glass front doors a few minutes later, a smiling Jamie met him.

"Hey boss, how did the mighty ad salesman do?"

Jake slammed the sales notebook down. "The next time, I'm taking a gun with me."

Jamie and Barbara broke into knowing laughter.

Chapter 30

"All right, Jamie, I can see you are dying to tell me something."

Jake had finished entering the half-page from Murphy's onto next week's ad run list, along with a couple of smaller ads he had somehow bumbled into selling during the morning.

He had sketched the design for the smaller ads for Barbara to create and wrote out the ad copy. Both had far too many words — fitting 10 gallons of shit into a five-gallon bucket, he grumbled to himself.

All along, he had noticed Jamie hopping around the office, fiddling with his camera, twice sharpening a pencil — although no one used pencils anymore — straightening the backside of the front counter.

Once Jake offered the invitation to talk, he happily obliged.

"I have good news and bad news, Jake. The good news is my old chemistry professor got back to me with the results from the town's water sample I sent him, although that could be actually bad news..."

"Whoa. Let's start with the bad news bad news, and then maybe end on a high note."

"Yeah, OK." Jamie was leaning his back on the front counter, looking down at his hands.

"You remember Jimmy Daggett, the local guy who was a diamond hunter in Brazil?"

"I remember he was on the front page a few weeks ago, but we had no confirmation that anything he said was true. Has it turned out to be a big lie?"

"Oh no, nothing like that! Well, the deal is, and I don't quite know why he has called me up and taken me to lunch a couple of times. Most of his old classmates have either moved away, or my mom says, he was considered a BS'er in school, so maybe his old friends are either jealous or still consider his stories BS.

"Anyway, his dad is still bedridden, so I guess he, uh, wanted someone to talk with to take his mind off the old man, and he thought of me because I am such a good listener — a professional listener, you might say."

Jake started making a rolling motion with his hand. "We only have a week to get the next edition out, Jamie, get on with it."

"Well, the thing is, I guess I may have told him about the diamond factory and Suzanne's investigation into the water supply."

"What! Why on earth did you do that? First of all, it's virtually second-hand gossip. Plus, we don't want the town to know about the story before it's in the paper, if there is a story. And then, you should keep the details quiet in a murder investigation."

Jamie walked to his desk and slumped down in his chair. Not making eye contact with Jake, he told how Jimmy shared one fantastic story after another about sleuthing out diamonds in the rough and tumble Amazon outback until Jamie couldn't take it anymore and had to blurt out his own stories. And the diamond factory and Suzanne's mysterious death were the best he had.

"Ah jeez, Jamie. You had it all backward. It's the reporter who is supposed to establish rapport with the subject by revealing personal anecdotes, and then having the subject top with his own, even better newsworthy stories."

"Yeah boss, I knew I had screwed up as soon as the words were out of my mouth. I did beg Jimmy to keep it all a secret, though. And he said he would."

"You asked a world-class BS'er not to repeat the most interesting story he has likely ever heard about this town? Good luck with that."

Seeing Jamie wasn't far from tears, and not

wishing to abuse the young journalist, Jake softened his voice. "Tell me about the chemistry professor's findings."

Jamie instantly brightened. The mercurial temperament of youth, thought Jake.

Jamie looked off in the middle distance as he related the findings. "You've heard of PCBs, right, that were used so broadly as coolants in transformers, fluorescent light fixtures, even copy machines? They, of course, were banned decades ago because they caused cancer.

"But, the need PCBs were created for still exists. So companies have experimented around with several cousins to PCBs.

"In some cases, these cousins at first appeared not to be harmful — or at least, they were not specifically banned by the EPA, and so went into general use."

Over time, though, according to the professor, their toxicity became apparent and they, too, were banned. Most companies went in a different direction. However, a few researchers tinkered with the formula, trying to find something safe and useful. Or at least tried to stay one step ahead of EPA bans.

While some companies produced the new, non-banned formulas, a few devious companies simply produced the banned cousins, and using bribes and subterfuge, sold these products into the marketplace.

When legitimate buyers discovered the ruse, they disposed of the toxic cousins through legal environmentally clean disposal services.

However, in a cosmic twist, the devious

companies that first produced the chemicals offered to take them back from the buyers — for a price of course.

"They made money selling these deadly chemicals, and then were paid to take them back," said Jamie. "Cute."

While there are ways to render these chemicals harmless, that costs money. It's so much cheaper to dump them, on the sly, in some big, dark hole.

"The caverns," deduced Jake.

"That's what the professor thinks. And from there, the toxins leached into the water supply. And now the town has one poisoned well with maybe more to come," summed up Jamie.

Suzanne, without knowing any of the science, had figured out what was happening, and she paid for it with her life.

Chapter 31

"Momma, it's me, Nellie."

Hearing that sentence from Just Nell, phoning her mother from her back deck of Gus's — now Just Nell's — duplex apartment, froze Jake at the kitchen counter as he was carrying in two sacks of groceries.

Jake had been covering Just Nell's jobs of ad sales, circulation, and bookkeeping while she was in the hospital and now recovering at home. In paying bills, Jake discovered Suzanne owned the duplex where Gus had lived. The newspaper paid Gus's modest rent as part of his salary.

Making an executive decision — unpaid editors are allowed to do that, Jake had kidded to himself — he had cleaned up the mess from the break-in at Gus's and moved Just Nell from her backroom bedroom at the caverns into the duplex. The *Gazette* continued to pick up the rent.

Moving day came with a Cowboy Special from Rose and Son's Pizza — "coupon discount for my favorite editor... so far," said pizza maker and soon-to-be-famous novelist Aaron O'Dell — and two trips in Jake's Tacoma. Just Nell didn't own many possessions.

All of his working life, Jake has been a newspaperman, eavesdropping on other people's lives, but hearing Just Nell's voice talking to her mother felt too raw, too personal. He put down the sacks and returned to the pickup for the rest of the groceries.

He dawdled, checking his phone, opening a bag of nacho chips, gazing around at the winter warm scene and arid climate so different from what he knew in rainy Seattle.

"Jake, do you need a hand. And I mean one hand," said Just Nell at the duplex's door, waving her right arm. Her left arm was in a sling.

Jake laughed and brought in the rest of the groceries.

He made coffee and the two of them sat at the kitchen table — the only table in the small duplex.

"That was the first time I've spoken to my mother since I left home more than 20 years ago," she said, looking off.

"When I was young, I blamed her for everything wrong in my life, for not having a daddy, for not having any money, for living in a dumpy trailer in a trashy part of town.

"And I especially blamed her for bringing home one loser man after another. I'd see men working in an office, or the pharmacist at the drug store, or even the mailman, and say why can't she be with a man like that instead of these bums who would move in for a few days, weeks, months.

"I just didn't know how hard life was when you're poor and uneducated.

"I got this from her," said Just Nell, waving her right arm in front of her chest, "and I thought it was my doorway to heaven. I didn't realize bastards can walk through that door, too."

Just Nell pushed around her coffee cup. "And then Junior came along. Momma always said, 'You can fall in love with a rich man as easily as a poor man,' and while I didn't feel love for Junior, I thought I could learn to love him. Until he became one of the bastards."

Emotionally spent, Just Nell went quiet.

When she started talking again, she said her mother had finally found someone to be with who seems decent and had moved from the trailer to a little house in a small town where the husband worked.

"Talking with her was easier than I feared it might be. I told her I was proud of her and I told her my life was the best it had been in some time — except for being shot of course." She laughed and touched Jake's hand from across the table.

* * * * *

Jake made a coming home celebration dinner of jumbo shrimp and feta cheese over spaghetti noodles with sun-dried tomatoes, all sautéed in virgin olive oil. Light, tasty, and best of all, within his cooking wheelhouse.

"I heard you on the phone where you said 'this is Nellie.' That's a pretty name. Can I call you Nellie, too?"

"Honestly, Jake, I know Just Nell is a silly name. I laugh every time I introduce myself. But Nellie is a girl who lived in a trailer with a dead-end life. Just Nell is the woman I invented, the woman I'm comfortable with. I would like to be that woman with you."

"Settled, Just Nell. Any interest in seeing how comfortable life in bed is?"

"Ha, ha. Looking for your own doorway to heaven are you?"

* * * * *

"Can't sleep either?" Jake asked as the dawn's light crept in through the bedroom window.

"No, but it's too early and too cold to get up."

"Hey, something that is stuck in my head is when we first met at the caverns, on the day Suzanne's body was discovered, you told me you were the only one who had a key to the elevator. Did the sheriff ever talk to you about that?"

"Ah, so you are wondering if you might be sleeping with a murderer, is that right?" Just Nell propped herself up on her one good shoulder to peer down at Jake.

"If I am, the sex sure has been fantastic. I hope you will hold off on doing me in until we do it at least a hundred more times," he said, bending his head up for a morning kiss.

"Ow! Ow!" said Just Nell after a few minutes of snuggling. "My shoulder is aching this morning. I need a couple of Ibuprofen."

Rolling out of bed, she added, "To answer your earlier question, yes the sheriff talked to me about the elevator key. But, as Suzanne weighed about 200 pounds, and I weigh... well, quite a bit less than that, he couldn't see me wrestling her down the elevator to the back of the cavern. Everyone knows there are unexplored tunnels and entrances to the caverns. Whoever did this must have found a back way in."

Jake followed Just Nell out of bed. "Another question that bothers me is who found Suzanne. I thought the caverns were closed for the season."

"Yeah, I am guilty there." Just Nell gulped down two Ibuprofen tablets with a swallow of water at the kitchen counter.

"I loaned the key to one of the summer help kids. He wanted to take his girlfriend down there for a little... well, exploring of his own. They found the body. I think it put them right out of the mood."

Pulling down a bag of coffee beans from a cupboard, she added, "If they had not found Suzanne, probably no one would have found her until the caverns opened for tourists in the spring."

Chapter 32

"Jake, we have got to go down into the caverns to see what we can find."

Jamie was leaning on his palms into Jake's desk,

containing such an earnest look in his eyes Jake almost had to laugh.

Except… "No, no, no. The last time I went exploring, Just Nell got shot. And crawling around a big dark hole in the ground gives me the willies."

"Jake, it's now been three months since Suzanne was killed, and the sheriff is making no progress. I think he is waiting for the murderer to walk in off the street and confess."

Straightening up, he started ticking off points on his fingers.

"Just Nell can get us into the caverns. We'll take powerful flashlights, even wear miner's headlamps, and search around looking for other entrances or clues about the illegal dumping of chemicals, and then, if we find anything at all, we'll have a great story for next week's edition."

Jake knew every bit of that idea was wrong. He also knew he didn't want to get Just Nell involved in anything that smacked of being even quasi-illegal. And he especially knew he never wanted to be 200 feet below ground again, in a pitch-dark cavern, looking for a murderer, depending on the whims of a flashlight for safety.

Do three wrongs make a right? No, never.

Still, Jamie's enthusiasm was infectious. Jake was once a young reporter and he did some crazy shit. Once, he stole the high school graduation photo of a victim in a traffic accident off her parent's fireplace mantle to go with a story he was writing.

True, his editor made him return the photo without running it. Maybe crossing the ethics line a few times taught him where the line should be.

No question about it. Going down into the caverns was a line not to be crossed. Jamie's idea was all-around bad, and wrong at the same time.

And that's exactly what Jake was about to tell the bright-faced Jamie. Instead, these words came out of his mouth: "We have to get this edition out before we can go. Maybe Saturday?"

* * * * *

So, Saturday it became.

Just Nell didn't out and out nix the idea — as Jake had hoped — but said since the electricity was turned off at the caverns during the off-season, Jake and Jamie would have to climb down a 200-foot emergency ladder, rather than descend in the elevator.

"Two hundred feet! What kind of emergency ladder?"

"You know the metal fire escapes you see on inner-city apartment houses? They've welded several of those together to make a 200-foot ladder in the elevator shaft. I believe it's a tight fit... you don't have to worry about falling as you'll be squeezed into a tight space."

"Falling! Tight space! Damn it. This is sounding worse all the time."

"It could be an adventure. I would go with you, but..." Just Nell wiggled her left arm around in the sling.

Jake said they could wait until the arm healed, but Just Nell gave him a look. The kind of look that said Jake was shrinking in her eyes. The kind of look no man wants to see in a lover's eyes. The kind of look that sent men off to war, to scale great mountains, to descend a ladder to hell.

The kind of look that told Jake he had no choice: He was going to descend a haphazardly-made emergency ladder 200 feet down into a cold, dark space that was once called, "The Hole to Hell."

Chapter 33

"Are you sure you won't have any problem driving?"

"Jake, this is an automatic. I can certainly drive it one-handed." To emphasize her point, Just Nell swerved the Tacoma back and forth across the lanes while shaking her left arm still in a sling.

"And say, what kind of real man buys a little pickup, and what kind of real man buys an automatic little pickup?"

"You've had your laugh, now, keep us on the road, damn it."

Jake could have told her the light pickup towed easily behind his RV, but he was in no mood for conversation.

All morning he had regretted agreeing to explore the caverns with Jamie. He regretted it while Just Nell drew a map of the caverns, detailing the main chamber and little side caves. He regretted it when Jamie showed up at the door with two hand-held rechargeable spotlights — "the internet says they are the brightest flashlights on the market" — along with wearing a miners' helmet with a headlamp.

And he regretted it now as Just Nell swung off the main highway to the access road to the caverns.

"You are sure no one is there?" he asked for the tenth time since the plan of exploring the caverns with Jamie, looking into Suzanne's death and clues why she was down there, was hatched.

"You are perfectly safe, little pickup man. The place is closed and I'm not even sure there is an owner these days, as the place has been in bankruptcy for a while."

Jake's hope that someone — a guard or caretaker or someone — would be at the entrance evaporated when Just Nell turned into the vacant dirt parking lot.

"Good luck, boys!" she shouted and smiled through the open passenger window. Peeling out, the spinning wheels tossed dust toward Jake and Jamie.

Following her instructions, they walked around to a side door where Jake inserted a flat blade screwdriver into the cheap lock. "Click" went the lock and Jake's last chance for the adventure to be scuttled evaporated.

They walked quietly on rubber-soles shoes — Jamie's advice from watching cop shows on TV — past the lunch counter and into the gift shop towards the elevator.

On the walls were photos of original cavern finder Hap Brown being hoisted down on a rope. For some reason, Hap was wearing a white cowboy hat, although there was no sun 200 feet down.

Another wall had a mounted head of a black bear, its mouth in a roaring pose, next to an elk's head full of antlers — for Wild West atmosphere, guessed Jake.

Most of the shop, however, was given over to trinkets: belt buckles with "Cowboy Caverns," sepia-tone postcards from the 1920s, tiny replicas of dinosaurs — playing off the fact the caverns were created during the age of dinosaurs — t-shirts, caps and in one corner a machine where a person could stamp their name on a penny. A parent could even buy a Hap Brown lunchbox (a caricature of a grinning Hap on one side and a drawing of the caverns on the reverse side) and a set of Cowboy Caverns cap pistols. The girls' set had pink tassels dangling from the holster.

Jake inserted the blade of the screwdriver into a door beside the elevator and it popped open. One step in, and a black hole opened up, swallowing a metal ladder disappearing down into the darkness.

"You first." Jake semi-bowed like he was being gracious, but, if there were falling to be done, he didn't want Jamie to fall on him.

Two hundred rungs, Just Nell had said. Jake started counting, one, two, three... By the time he got to 20, his mind wandered.

When he was a kid, he had a daydream about hunting treasure in a cave, but when he came out, all of the people on the planet had died. Maybe a mysterious meteor exploded in the atmosphere. He couldn't remember.

He hadn't thought about that daydream in years, but now was a perfect time for a revisit. He imagined himself driving his RV down traffic-free freeways, going anywhere he wanted. Living in a mansion on the beach, frolicking in the warm ocean, never shaving or getting a haircut, walking about nude if he liked.

And maybe getting a dog. A big dog, like a chocolate lab with a happy, wagging tail... man and dog living the good life, unfettered and unbothered by other people.

"One hundred," shouted Jamie, his voice sounding distance down the hole. "Oh, and watch out for step 90, the rung is loose."

Jake's foot suddenly lost traction. His hands desperately grabbing the iron railing kept him from falling, but his face smashed into the ladder as his footing was lost.

"Ow, damn it!"

"We're halfway there," Jamie offered hopefully.

Jake felt a trickle of blood from his nose. And I'm all the way out of my mind, he thought.

Jake finally felt his foot hit hard ground.

"I think we should only turn on one light at a time," said Jamie, bouncing the beam around. "Keep one light in reserve. I can use my light. I know the way, follow me."

Peering into the cone of light Jamie sprayed over the walls, Jake suddenly understood the old man Hap Brown's belief that there were riches down here. The walls sparkled more like diamonds in the flashlight beam than they had in the flood lighting left on during the guided tours. And veins that looked ordinary then now did resemble gold. Other veins took on a silver coloring.

"Ow, damn it!"

"Jake, you got to watch out for outcroppings from the walls. You are not supposed to touch them, your body oils discolor the sensitive minerals."

"Why don't they chisel those off?" complained Jake, running fingers through the dampness of blood in his hair, flicking off a few specks of crystals.

"These are natural-made caverns," said Jamie, a little too much like a schoolmarm for Jake's mood. "They can't be chiseling to sculpt the walls down here."

Jake held one arm up for protection and kept his eyes on the barely-lit path as he followed Jamie.

"What the hell!" he exclaimed in a loud whisper. "Eyes, I saw eyes!"

"Where?"

"Right there," said Jake, pointing in the dark. "No, no, over to your left!"

The two men were both crouching, looking intently into the dark faintly laminated by Jamie's light.

"There, there, see that? See that bouncing white spot?"

"Oh," said Jamie, standing erect, "that's the tail of a jackrabbit."

"I thought you said nothing could live in this limestone pit. What's a bunny doing here?"

"Watch this." He switched off his light.

"What did you do?"

"Let our eyes adjust. Just watch."

In a few minutes, claustrophobia nearly overpowering him, Jake started to see narrow beams of light, individual rays not thicker than string, stretching from the top of the cavern to the floor 20 feet in front of Jamie.

"Wow!" was all Jake could muster.

"That's the original hole old man Brown found. When the sun is just right, rays of light reach all the way down here.

"A fence keeps people and bigger animals away from the hole, but bunnies, snakes, and sometimes birds will fall or fly down into the caverns, only to die in a few hours.

"I have a friend who in high school worked here during the summer. One of his jobs was to make a loop of the caverns each morning to collect dead animals before the tours begin. Wouldn't want to spook the tourists, right?

"Oh, and you've heard of the 'mile high club,' right?"

Jake would have just glared at Jamie, but since Jamie still had the light off, the effect would have been lost.

"There is the 'Caverns Club.' A couple joins a tour group, works their way to the back, ducks down one of the dead-end tunnels, and then they 'join the club.' My friend found panties, condom wrappers, and other stuff."

"Can we just turn the light on and get back on task?" asked Jake, who no longer was surprised by humans and the ways and places they find to have sex.

"Let's see if I can rescue the bunny, or he'll be dead in a few hours. He went into that cave," said Jamie, light back on and leaving Jake literally in the dark.

"Hey... ow!"

"Jake, remember, be careful not to hit the walls. Protect the pristineness of the caverns."

Picking himself up after stumbling to his knees, Jake could see Jamie swinging his light around in the dead-end cave, then suddenly stopping to focus on a spot on the ground.

"Jake, look at this!"

"Yeah, looks like a wet spot. Maybe your precious bunny took a whiz there."

"Jake, there are no wet spots in the caverns. That's not water, that's something else."

Jamie bent down on one knee and started digging through his backpack. "My mom made us sandwiches, want one? I want to use the plastic bag to collect a sample of this liquid."

One moment, Jamie was holding up a sandwich in the quickly fading light of the flashlight, and then complete darkness. Jake felt his chest tighten and his mouth go dry.

"No problem, let me turn on the other flashlight," said Jamie, followed by sounds of him digging through the pack, and then the snap, snap of the switch moving back and forth. Still dark.

"Hmmm... my mom said she was going to charge this. I guess she didn't get around to it."

"She made sandwiches for when we break into the caverns but didn't charge the flashlight?" anger rose in Jake's voice.

"Not a problem. I still have my miner's helmet, remember. Too bad I didn't find one for you."

Switching on his headlamp, Jamie turned the plastic bag inside out, and as a pet owner might clean up a dog's dump, grabbed a handful of soil and the liquid, reversed the bag again, and sealed it.

"Let's go. Follow me and stay close. This light isn't very strong."

Chapter 34

"Rodney is like a blister — he shows up after the work is done."

"Hey, I helped out," yelped Rodney amid half a dozen drinkers at the end of the bar in Lester's.

"Yeah, you helped drink the beer and eat the pizza," replied the first man, causing an outburst of laughter.

"Jake, you drinking alone today?" Bonny slid a heady beer in front of him.

Today, she was wearing a crimson t-shirt saying, "You know nothing, Jon Snow."

"I like your Game of Thrones reference, Bonny," said Jake with a nod towards her shirt.

"You're the first one today that's gotten the reference. That earns you the right to buy a second beer. Drink up because winter is coming," she tossed over her shoulder, heading down to see what Rodney and the fellas needed.

Alone time was just what Jake needed. Four months into his stay in this desert oasis, he had found a dead body, been offered a temp job — at apparently no pay — then had his boss killed, reported on another murder at his RV campground, and found the newspaper office broken into and his desk ransacked.

There had been good things, Just Nell topped that list by far, followed by rediscovering the simple joy of newspaper work.

And then there was the finding of Gus's aerial maps and cache of information about lost gold. Wouldn't that be a hoot to find?

But what was this craziness about exploring the dark caverns with Jamie? Sure, Jamie had found a sample of "something" that he was driving today to a chemistry professor at a nearby university. Maybe a vital clue, or maybe just the piss from a bunny rabbit.

And, what were the two journalists doing down there anyway? Actual newspaper "investigations" are not like the movies of daring escapades, high-speed car chases, and narrow escapes from gunmen.

Rather they are taking a photo with a telephoto lens of a county commissioner in the car with a local hoodlum, or, more likely, quoting an "unnamed source" via a telephone conversation.

Reporters do not put themselves in harm's way for a story. Unless it's the wrath of an editor when a deadline is missed.

"Hey, Jake…" Jake jumped, slopping his beer when he suddenly felt a hand on his shoulder.

"Didn't mean to startle you," said Verne, a local deputy who was attached to the hand. "The sheriff asked me to make a traffic stop for a DWI if I should see you in Lester's."

"You're stopping me now?" Jake was reeling from the jarring interruption.

"No, I'm going to have a burger now. But, I'll be back on patrol…" Verne looked at his wristwatch, "in about 25 minutes. You might want to be back to the campground by then."

Too startled to respond, Jake watched the deputy walk down the bar, then stop and turn.

"Oh, by the way, that was a nice story you did on my sister's son, Aaron. Would have been easy to make fun of him and his goofy vampire novel. Drive safe, now."

The sliding sound of a fresh glass of beer heading his way made Jake jump again.

"A quick one for the road, and I say quick," said Bonny, wiping up beer slop, and staying in the Game of Thrones theme, added: "And remember, 'A Lannister always pays his debts.' Get your money out."

Standing up from his bar stool to pull out his wallet, Jake bumped into one of three women passing by.

"Wil? Sorry. I haven't seen you since the *Gazette's* office was broken into."

Motioning for her friends to find a table, the county clerk grimaced. "I am so embarrassed by that."

"Embarrassed? That the day I told you about Gus's maps and his search for the treasure of gold, someone looted my desk? Embarrassed is an odd word."

"Yeah. Well, after you talked to me, I went to a Lions service club lunch at noon. People are always asking me about cop stuff because my office is right next to the sheriff's and they think I have some juicy inside dirt.

"Anyway, put on the spot for a good story, I kinda mentioned our conversation. I feel bad if anything I said led to the break-in. I am so sorry. Please don't think I had anything to do with it. Well, rather than maybe saying something I shouldn't have."

When Jake didn't say anything, she added, "Gotta go. Bye."

As Bonny swung by to scoop up bills Jake had

laid out, he asked, "Say, have you seen anyone strange in the bar lately?"

"Strange? You're all strange to me," she replied, tilting her head toward the far end of the bar where for some reason, Rodney was flapping his hands by his ears and braying like a donkey.

"I meant some new, suspicious characters in town."

"Over the past six months or so, there have been a couple of out-of-town truck drivers who came in, sat over at that far table, had a beer and lunch, and kept all to themselves."

"How do you know they're truck drivers?"

"I've seen them parking their rig in the lot across the street."

"Maybe they were poop truck drivers. If I were a poop truck driver, I'd certainly keep to myself too."

Looking off into her memory, Bonny replied, "They have a smaller tanker truck, like the poop trucks, but with no markings."

"How do you know they are from out of town?" Jake stood up and took his last swallow.

"Because one of them orders the seafood platter. And the locals know you don't order seafood this far from the ocean."

Chapter 35

"Take me on a picnic."

"On a picnic? It's April, that's no picnic weather, Just Nell, that's still hunkering-under-a-blanket-with-another-warm-body weather. Which gives me an idea..."

"Jake, Jake. First of all, April in the desert is the perfect time for a picnic. That's when the saguaro cactus flowers bloom after the winter rains as the days get longer and warmer.

"Have you ever seen a blooming saguaro? The blossom is the state flower of Arizona. The desert is so beautiful when they and the other cactus are blooming, color as far as the eye can see. The rusty soil, the green cacti, orange, pinks, whites, reds, and yellows of the blooms... It's a desert Garden of Eden."

Winding a hand through Jake's thick hair, she continued: "And, a picnic involves a blanket, doesn't it? A blanket has more uses than only a picnic tablecloth..."

Just Nell went to a closet off the front room, rummaged around for a bit, pulled out a fluffy blanket, and shook it out a few times, a devilish smile on her face.

Jake immediately saw the wisdom of a picnic, in the red hills miles away from any other human, a blanket, and Just Nell. Plus, food was also involved. Maybe Just Nell's fried chicken and potato salad.

It had been a tough winter. Maybe a picnic is just what the couple needed.

Jamie had heard back from the chemistry professor that the sample taken at the caverns was indeed some kind of toxic substance, related to the deadly and banned PCBs.

But, by then, Jamie's mother was showing signs of melanomas and further tests revealed cancer in her liver and gall bladder. Mother and son had moved to

Phoenix temporarily for treatment. Word was she was getting better, but still not out of the woods.

The sheriff had made no arrests in any of the three murders, nor had he given any indication the crimes were any closer to being solved.

And while Just Nell's shoulder had healed and she had full use of her left arm now, just like in the other crimes, no arrests had been made in the shooting.

The *Gazette* was limping along. Actually, better than limping. Just Nell had a magic touch in selling ads — Jake didn't like to think too much about her interaction with local male business owners that created the sales, but now the paper was firmly running in the black.

Famous novelist-to-be Aaron O'Dell was filling in for Jamie. It turned out the kid actually could write and write well. Plus, his days as a pizza delivery driver meant he knew just about everybody in town.

Jake had squeezed out a promise from Patrick McPhee — now the paper's owner — to decide by spring what to do about the *Gazette*. Patrick didn't want to close the paper, in deference to his wife's memory, but didn't care one way or another if the weekly continued to publish. Except for one fact: "Find out who killed Suzie" was his constant refrain.

On that front, Jake had made only the tiniest bit of progress. When he had told Just Nell about the strange liquid in the cavern, she said the most recent owners were a suspicious lot.

"They edged me out of the bookkeeping job," she had said, "and made me the manager of the restaurant and had me work the gift shop counter."

One day, when the new bookkeeper was in the gift shop looking over the day's receipts, Just Nell said she saw his ledger showing over $1,000 in cash sales the previous day.

"I knew exactly how much we sold, and it wasn't over $50. When I asked him about it, he slammed the ledger shut, said I wasn't a CPA and I wouldn't understand."

From that point on, said Just Nell, she felt actual operating the caverns as a business wasn't the main point of the owners.

"I wouldn't be surprised at all by any criminal activity by those people," she said. "If you told me they were illegally dumping toxins in the caverns, I would believe you."

When Jake took out the map Just Nell had drawn of the caverns and pointed out the cave where Jamie found the strange liquid, she thought for a moment and said that was below the maintenance garage. A convenient spot to dump in secret thought Jake.

Still, he hadn't gone back out to the caverns to snoop around more.

He did ask Bonny if she had recently seen the tanker and drivers who ordered seafood too far from the ocean, and she said she had not.

Just Nell took up most of Jake's brain, followed by the *Gazette*. The small portion left, he — secretly because he didn't want Just Nell to think he was being foolish — devoted to dreaming about Major Moser's lost gold.

Jake had never been a rich man or particularly wanted to be rich until the idea of finding a treasure of gold — pounds and pounds of gold — entered his thoughts.

Just Nell would catch him staring off into space and ask what he was meditating about. "Oh, next week's editorial or front page," he might say. But actually, he was envisioning his hands digging into saddlebags filled with gold, streams of gold flakes running through his fingers, gold nuggets lodging under his fingernails and in wrinkles of his knuckles.

The phrase, "all the gold they could carry" ran on a loop through his brain.

Once grocery shopping with Just Nell, he paused behind in the baking supplies aisle and picked up five-pound sacks of sugar. One, two, three sacks went into his arms... eight, nine, ten. He could carry 50 pounds of sugar — 50 pounds of gold.

"Have a sweet tooth, do you?" asked a heavyset woman trying to get past him in the aisle. He hurriedly put the sugar back and caught up with Just Nell, a silly grin on his face.

* * * * *

"This picnic," he asked Just Nell, "where should we go to see the cactus in bloom?"

Folding the blanket she found in the closet, she looked at him for a moment. "Let's go back to where we were last fall looking at Gus's map. I know you still have the idea of finding gold on your mind."

Jake could only laugh at how transparent he was.

Chapter 36

"You sure this doesn't feel weird, aren't you scared?"

"Jake, I don't think whoever shot me has been lying in wait all winter long in case we came back. We'll be fine. And, maybe the sheriff was right, maybe it was hunters poaching deer. You call me 'dear' all the time."

Just Nell leaned across the pickup seat, kissed Jake on the cheek, then stepped out into an overcast day.

She had told Jake they could resume their hunt for the gold treasure, and combine it with a spring picnic during the bloom time for saguaro, but this outing was really for her.

Being shot terrified her, even more so as in the hospital she realized how close the bullet had come to ending her life. Just a couple of inches said the doctor, and the bullet would have pierced her heart. Just a couple of inches, from a bullet fired up to a quarter of a mile away.

While she pretended to Jake and everyone who asked she was fine, grateful to be alive, and though the shooting was most likely an accident, in her core, she was angry with herself.

Since escaping her controlling husband in Florida, she had been the boss of her own life.

"I'm not going to let a stranger with a rifle reduce me to being a victim," she affirmed to herself. "If I get shot again, so be it. But I am not going to cower in fear and dread."

Following her out of the pickup, Jake grabbed the basket of food — and the fluffy blanket — from the bed of the truck, and the pair climbed a knoll bordering the road.

"Where should we go?" he asked, huffing at the top.

"Let's go out there." Just Nell pointed with her left arm towards a flat area populated with multi-armed saguaros, daring the invisible rifleman to take another shot.

"I want to go someplace that's never been stepped on by a human before."

Walking across the open desert, Jake marveled at the different cacti, the saguaros with their twisted arms — right out of the Road Runner cartoons he used to watch as a kid — the paddled-leaf prickly pears and the Hedgehogs with their fishhook needles that at a distance appeared to be new growth.

"Feel this flower." Just Nell rubbed her forefinger and thumb over the petals of a white and orange blossom. "It looks delicate but feels waxy and sturdy. Life in the desert has to be hardy.

"Oh, look! It's a wild bunny!" she said, startled by a gray ball of fur darting from under a Silver cholla cactus near Jake's feet.

"I hear coyotes every night at the campground, I guess this guy is a mobile meal."

"Yes, but I hear they have their fun while alive," she laughed.

Just Nell was almost dancing ahead as she veered from one cactus to another, looking at the flowers, lightly feeling the textures of the rugged desert dwellers, displaying a free-flowing joy Jake hadn't seen since she was wounded.

"Hey, what is this? Graffiti?" Jake pointed to a dark boulder about the size of a VW Bug, covered in etchings.

"No, those are petroglyphs, made by early Indians," said Just Nell, coming over to look at the rock. "The early people carved their dreams, visions, and everyday sights into these rocks.

"Look, there's a lizard." She pointed out a stylistic figure of a reptile. "Oh, and that wiggly one looks like a snake."

"Here's something that looks like a target, with rings inside of rings." Damn. As soon as the words were out of Jake's mouth, he regretted bringing up anything that could be associated with the shooting.

Just Nell didn't look fazed. "Sometimes, the artists made designs. No one knows why or what they mean. They made these by picking away with a harder rock on the surface of this boulder. Imagine how careful and dedicated they must have been."

"Hey, here's a human, wearing something on his head and holding something in his hand. Only this guy has three legs."

Just Nell stepped closer for her look. "Silly, I see that third leg all the time."

"Yes, but when you see it, it's usually pointed up."

She playfully punched him in the shoulder and continued studying the figures on the rock.

Scanning around, looking for more boulders with petroglyphs, Jake glanced skyward, where the clouds were darkening. Maybe they should choose a spot for the picnic now, in case it rains later, he worried out loud.

"Nonsense," she replied. "It doesn't rain in Arizona in April. The monsoons don't begin until June or July."

"Monsoons?" questioned Jake. "Monsoons here?"

"I think you are just anxious for the appetizer," smiled Just Nell. "How about that spot over there between the folds of the hills, where we will have this entire vista as our picture window."

A few minutes later, flat on his back enjoying the appetizer, the first drops hit his face.

"Are you crying?" he asked, looking at her inches above him.

"No, I feel them too." She quickly rolled over and rose. "I think we are getting some rain."

A jagged flash of lightning followed by a boom of thunder made them both jump to their feet to start dressing.

Rain exploded all around them, huge drops driving into the ground sending up clumps of wet soil.

"My lunch!" shouted Just Nell in dismay, as a stream suddenly appeared, driving its way across the picnic blanket, tipping over the basket of her homemade food.

Ka-boom! More lightning lit up the sky.

"We have to find shelter!" Jake bent over to grab the basket in one hand and the soggy blanket in the other, but his right foot slipped on the suddenly slippery rocks. He fell face-first into the rapidly growing stream.

"Jake, get up! A flash flood is coming off these hills!"

The roiling water was now a foot deep, rolling a

stunned Jake into a prickly pear.

"Ow, damn it!" The shock of the needles cleared his mind. He jumped up and quickly looked around.

"Over there!"

Jake snatched Just Nell's hand and pulled her towards a crease in the hillside. At the end of a twisty canyon, barely wide enough for one person was a narrow, dark slot. "We need to get into there!" shouted Jake over the pulverizing rain.

"It'll flood, we'll be trapped!"

"No, this area is dry, see?" Another flash and ka-boom ended the discussion.

Jake went first, with a twist to the right, followed by a twist to the left.

"Look at this!"

The slot opened to a large dry room, lit by a dim light from a small hole in the rock roof. But the other end was swallowed in darkness.

Strong gusting wind blew huge drops through the spaces in rocks. "Let's get over to that dry corner, and wait out the storm," said Jake, throwing an arm around Just Nell.

"Hey, you're all wet." Then she realized she was all wet too, and laughed.

"This place in the desert is not my lucky spot," she added, nuzzling into Jake's side.

He was about to answer with a clever retort when his foot stumbled, and — one arm around Just Nell — he fell into a wall, smashing his face on the way down.

"You are not very coordinated, are you?" Just Nell bent over to wipe the blood weeping out of Jake's cheek with the arm of her wet shirt.

"Ow!" Jake jerked his right hand from the muddy cave floor, blood mushrooming from a slit.

"What the hell?"

"Jake, what happened? How did you get cut?"

"Can you see anything down there? Use the light from your phone."

"My phone is back in the truck. Where's yours?"

"I took it out of my pants pocket when we laid down. It's still on the blanket... in the middle of the stream."

Just Nell felt gingerly around the ground. "What's this?"

After a few seconds of digging, she held up a long object. With wonder in her voice, she asked, "Could this be a sword?"

"I'm no expert, but it looks like a military sword."

A realization as thunderous as the storm that was raging above hit them. They both instantly understood what the sword meant.

"We have to look around," said Jake, followed by a painful, "Ow! My ankle!"

Running her fingers over Jake's ankle, Just Nell discovered it was already starting to swell, likely twisted in his latest fall.

"Look. We have to get back to the truck before your ankle gets worse and you can't walk. We'll pick up the blanket and picnic stuff outside, leaving not a trace. And when your ankle is healed, and the weather is better, we'll come back with lights to explore this cave."

"This is like a bad movie," sighed Jake. "And I suppose we will come back at night, while the coyotes howl."

Chapter 37

"My company had scheduled me for training in New York," said the man leaning against the wire fence at the campground's pickleball court.

"Shortly before I was due to go, I called down to verify arrangements and discovered nobody had seen my travel paperwork. I wasn't going anywhere.

"On the day the training was supposed to happen, I was talking on the phone with a woman at the New York office when she said, 'Oh my god, a plane hit one of the Twin Towers!'"

Jake flashed back to that moment, and like just about every American, could remember exactly where he was on that morning. He was coming down for coffee and rounded the bend to the kitchen when he saw his wife, Anne, glued to the TV, which was showing a massive column of smoke pouring out of a building.

But this wasn't his story, it was the story of the man who had introduced himself as Mike.

"We both thought at first it was likely a small plane, and the pilot just had an accident," continued Mike.

"When our conversation was over, I turned on the TV in the office just in time to see the second plane hit. That's when I knew — we all knew — it was no accident.

"I watched the news all day, but it wasn't until several hours later I realized I was supposed to be in one of the towers for the training. I was supposed to be there."

Mike took off his sweat-stained cowboy hat and waved it in front of his face. Even though it was technically winter, the temperature could still get to the mid-70s here at the Arizona RV park.

"It took a few years to hit me — that death could come out of the sky for you at any moment. That's when I started watching the Weather Channel and that's when I told my wife when our youngest was out of college, we were selling the house, buying a big-ass fifth-wheel, and traveling.

"So that's what we did, and now we're in our sixth year of being full-timers," said Mike.

"You travel all the time?" asked Jake.

"No. In watching the Weather Channel, I saw that winters are best spent in Arizona. We spend about six months here, and then six months on the road, going wherever the weather is the best."

"This is my first year living in an RV," replied Jake, "so I'm envious of you. Can I ask, I seem to be spending money more than I expected. You living on savings…?"

"My wife was worried about that at first, too. But, then I started writing a travel blog. You noticed that I am Black, right?"

"Yeah," said Jake, smiling, "I noticed that."

"A lot of RV full-timers write travel blogs, but I am the only Black one. You don't think of Black folks as RV'ers, do you? Admit it, do you?"

"Fair point," replied Jake.

"There are plenty of Black folks getting to retirement age who have the resources and desire to travel, just like white folks. When they see my wife and me, they have a bit more confidence that this lifestyle could be for them. My blog has developed a real niche audience that advertisers are hungry to reach.

"I can't say I'm making more money now than when I worked, but I can say I don't worry about paying for that next tank of gas, or campground stay, or steak dinner at a famous roadside restaurant."

"Thanks, Mike. I think this will be a fun story for next week's edition."

"No problem. I have to get on with my daily walk around the park now — I do 4.8 miles a day — and get back to the rig. Thelma is cooking an Easter ham and I have to video her for the blog."

Sliding his reporter's notebook into his back pocket, Jake thought that everybody has a piece of the truth, a piece of the flame. It's what they do with it that makes all the difference in their lives.

Chapter 38

"Can I buy you a beer?"

"There's probably no newspaperman in the history of time who has said 'No' to that question."

Sliding onto a bar stool, Jimmy Daggett held up two fingers to Bonny a ways down the bar.

"I see you're wearing a boot. What happened to your foot?"

"We got caught in last week's rainstorm in the desert." Jake went on to explain about the picnic, the cloudburst, lightning, and thunder. And about falling, severely twisting his ankle. He left out the part about the slot canyon and the sword that hinted at the lost gold treasure.

"How's your dad?" asked Jake, to change the subject.

"You know, I can't remember a time when the old man has exercised. He never played tennis, or any high school sports, lifted weights, or even golfed with clients. He's always been overweight. And a drinker. Yet, he's rallying, after the doctors said he was on his deathbed.

"In fact, he insisted on going to the office today. Incredible."

"So, are you going to stay around?"

"That's why I'm investing a beer in you." Jimmy smiled and laughed. Jake had observed the best BS'ers had an easy manner of somehow letting the conversation come to their purpose.

"Jamie tells me some Hollywood types are nosing around, looking to build a factory that grows diamonds indistinguishable from the real thing. They want to end the wars and killings over diamonds."

When Jake gave a slight nod, he continued: "Since coming back to town, I've discovered I like it here. I feel a connection I didn't realize before. Maybe my travel itch has been scratched. Anyway, a diamond factory, I know diamonds, maybe there is an opportunity for me."

Jake thought for a moment. The diamond factory wasn't any more than a second or third-hand rumor. He hadn't heard more since Patrick McPhee said his wife, the late mayor Suzanne, had exploratory talks.

Still, Jimmy's dad, Jim Daggett, was a longtime

local realtor, likely he would be a great source should diamond people be sniffing around for a factory site.

If he could unearth one solid lead, it could turn into a great story.

And, somewhat surprisingly, Jimmy the BS'er hadn't been blabbing all over town about it after he heard the rumor from Jamie. Maybe they could exchange info for their mutual benefit. The story could still be a scoop by the *Gazette*.

After talking for a while, Jimmy finished his beer and announced he had to leave.

"I'm taking Jamie and his mother out for a bite, a welcome home dinner."

"I thought you were married in Brazil."

"Yeah... maybe not for much longer. Let's talk again, see ya."

* * * * *

Jake was about to finish his beer and get on the road when two large guys settled on each side of him.

"Hey, mister treasurer hunter," said the one with a dirty John Deere cap. "I hear you've been out looking for our gold."

"What are you talking about?"

"Yeah, that gold belongs to people in this town," said the other one, wearing a work shirt with the sleeves ripped off at the shoulders. "Only someone local is going to get it. Not some fella from the big city."

"First of all, that 'treasure' was a fable on a local pie shop's placemat. There is no gold. But if there were, then it belongs to whoever finds it. Being born here gives you no more rights than anyone else." Jake's voice went up, hoping to snag Bonny's attention.

"That's so, huh?" said the one in the cap. "Look at me, slim, I would be careful, very careful, seeing how you live in a home that a strong wind could topple over."

"Or maybe a strong winch," said the other, and they both laughed at the weak joke.

Doing the eye thing with their hands — two fingers from their eyes to Jake's body — the comedy brothers slid away, leaving Jake to think maybe he would have to hunt the gold during the night... when the coyotes were howling.

Chapter 39

"Jake, you're not what I thought a real newspaperman would be like."

"What?"

They were laying in the RV's bed on a sleepy Sunday.

Jake has been mentally bouncing back and forth, plotting how to get the gold treasure without being attacked by Dumb and Dumber (his names for the two guys who accosted him at Lester's) and what to write for next week's editorial.

The more he tried to focus on an editorial — whether to urge commissioners to allow more money to the fall county fair or applaud the Chamber of Commerce for the spring cleanup campaign — the more his mind would jump to schemes for scooping up the gold on the quiet.

And then once he had the gold, how to keep it a secret, yet sell it. Perhaps he would rent two — no, make that three — of the bank's largest safe deposit boxes to put the gold in and then slowly, over time, take a pound or so to Phoenix to sell on a gold exchange. Surely, they had a gold buyer in Phoenix? Maybe he would have to alternate between buyers in Phoenix and Los Angeles.

Would he get cash or checks? And, if checks, how could he deposit the money in his account without paying taxes? Would he have to get half a dozen or more bank accounts, cash checks for cash, and then deposit small amounts in each account? How does the government track deposits anyway?

Maybe he should get cash, and then replace the gold for cash in the safe deposit boxes and then spend the cash over time. But several hundred thousand, maybe a million dollars in cash? How would he spend that? No one takes cash for big purchases like a house or a new pickup anymore.

Jake had tossed and turned all night trying to solve that problem.

Just Nell had climbed over Jake getting out of the confined RV bed. "Don't take offense, honey, but I saw a movie where the newspaperman hero said his job was to kick over rocks and see what crawls out. You have told me about several rocks in town, but I don't see any kicking."

"What?"

"Like the poisoning of the town's water? Why haven't you reported on that?

"Or, the rumor about a diamond factory? Or what

about an update on the progress, or lack of, in Gus's murder? Are you thinking so much about finding the gold you've forgotten the previous editor was killed, maybe just because he was looking for the gold?

"And the camel in the room — Suzanne's murder? The caverns could reopen this spring, and whatever evidence is down there will be trampled by thousands of tourists."

Jake opened his mouth to defend himself, but instead said, "I think that's 'elephant in the room.'"

Just like that, Jake's dreams of riches popped.

"You are so right. I guess I got caught up in the gold along with trying to make the *Gazette* survive. I don't own the paper, I've only started to be paid minimum wage, and yet, since I arrived, I've felt I had this mission to get next week's issue out.

"It's a lot of work finding stories, writing stories, getting photos, editing stories, laying out the paper, getting it printed, making sure copies are delivered to readers and the bills are paid."

"I know it is, honey."

"But I have been so caught up in the little stories needed to fill the front page and the other dozen pages or so that I have lost focus on the big issues facing the town.

"What a doofus I've been." Jake collapsed back on his pillow.

"You haven't been a doofus, Jake. You've been a doll to me, especially as I recovered from being shot. But, you have some skills and you should use them."

Seeing her encouragement was having no effect on the deflated Jake, she edged closer and laid a hand on his leg.

"You have some other skills, too. Care to try using them?"

Chapter 40

"You can't write that! You'll kill the town!"

Mayor pro tem Mac Cheese — appointed by the town council after Suzanne's death — slammed his hand down hard on his desk at city hall.

"People need to know the town's water supply is in danger, and perhaps poisoned," shot back Jake.

"The town's water supply is fine," Mayor Cheese huffed. "Work is being done at the moment to ensure that."

"The town has five wells. One is clogged with sand, one is pumping up high levels of nitrates, and there is evidence one has been poisoned by an unknown chemical. That leaves two wells — enough for the winter months but certainly not enough when summer and lawn-watering season rolls around.

"So, what, exactly, is this work that is being done?"

This was Jake's first rock to kick over, and he wasn't going to let the mayor off easy. He asked Jamie to come along with his camera, partially to let the young reporter see how to ask tough questions, and partially as a second pair of ears.

Even though the mayor was the butt of many jokes — and who wouldn't be with a name like his? — Jake could still see Jamie was anxious by the strident exchange between Jake and the Mayor Cheese.

"Different scenarios are being discussed. Nothing has been approved by the council yet but off the record…"

"There is no off the record here," counted Jake, making a point of writing in his reporter's notebook. "Citizens will want to know if they can depend on the town's water."

"You know, the newspaper used to work with us. I'm sure Suzanne when she was mayor, controlled what Gus wrote in the *Gazette*."

"We don't know that and besides, you are not Suzanne and I am not Gus."

Mac made a heavy sigh. "Ok, we have some options, according to engineers.

"We can flush out the well with the sand. We are getting the cost of that now. We may also have to drill it a little deeper to get past the sand layer.

"The nitrate level on the other well is being monitored. Some nitrates are OK. Or, we could dedicate that well to fire control, where the nitrate level won't matter. That would free up water from the two good wells.

"And, we could consider drilling a new well. Costly, but we are looking into government grants."

"See, that wasn't so hard," said Jake. "And it shows the town is on it.

"Now, what about the poisoned well? Suzanne was killed when she was investigating the source of the poison. What are you doing about that?"

"Well. The verdict is still out on the third well. I am certainly not going down into the caverns by myself to investigate," said Mac, sitting back and folding his arms.

Jake felt the same twinge shooting through his body as he saw in Jamie's at the mention of snooping around the caverns.

"I'm sure Patrick McPhee will be glad to hear you will not be taking the same risks as his departed wife, however, since the caverns are within city limits, you do have authority. Have you sent a crew down there?"

Mayor Cheese hesitated by looking out his window that, by coincidence, faced the direction of the caverns.

"Well, uh, as you know, the business that owns the caverns is in bankruptcy now. And, all of the company officials have dispersed, leaving no one on site now. We've made some calls to the court, but have heard nothing back. We're waiting for the bankruptcy to be resolved."

"So, poison could still be leaching into the groundwater, and the town is doing nothing?" Jake was poised over his notebook, a feature he made sure the mayor was aware of.

"Look, this is not the crime of the century. We don't know what or if anything is in the water. We are having it tested, but are getting incomplete results. Suzanne, however, was adamant something was wrong with the one well and she ordered it shut down, and for no one to go near the wellhead for their own safety.

"We are carefully monitoring the other wells. Before too long, there will be new owners at the caverns and then we'll send a crew down there."

The mayor paused. "Please don't use that 'crime of the century' remark. It sounds stupid."

Jake nodded. He had his story. He'll need the mayor for future stories, no point in needlessly making the mayor look ridiculous now.

* * * * *

Walking towards the *Gazette's* office, Jamie regained his composure. "Mac sure was in a boil, wasn't he?"

"He knows he's in hot water, that's for sure," returned Jake.

"He did go limp under your hard questions, though."

"He's probably afraid his political future is crumbling."

Chapter 41

A block from city hall after the interview with Mayor Cheese, a quick siren sound made Jake look over his right shoulder.

A sheriff's car pulled up beside him.

Have I been pulled over for drunk walking? he wondered, recalling the warning from deputy Verne.

"Hey, Jamie, why don't you go back to the office. I'll see what this is about."

"Sure. I have lunch with Jimmy anyway. He promised to show me more diamonds."

"Ask him if he has any leads for me. He'll know what you're talking about."

The driver's side window of the police car rolled down and the sheriff himself was behind the wheel.

"I thought you would want to know the suspect in the RV killing has been arrested," said Sheriff Highkok from behind his sunglasses.

"Where at?" Jake bent over to see eye-to-sun glasses with the sheriff.

"Truth or Consequences, New Mexico."

"Oh, ho, ho, that's funny."

Sheriff Highkok frowned. "I don't know about funny, but once extradition arrangements have been made, we'll be sending a deputy down to bring him back."

Jake asked if the suspect admitted to the crime. The sheriff said the man claimed to have found his wife already dead and fled because he had had some past scrapes with the law.

"That sounds like a line out of a bad movie," said Jake. "Don't criminals learn anything from watching TV?"

Sheriff Highkok frowned again like Jake was making no sense.

"Oh, hey sheriff..." said Jake as the sheriff was rolling up his window. "Can I interview the suspect when he returns? I heard he was a maintenance worker at the caverns. Maybe he has an idea what was going on out there."

"Really? I hadn't heard that. You can make a request. Interviews are up to the prisoner and his lawyer. Except for interviews with me, of course. He will definitely be sitting down in a little room with me."

Chapter 42

"Professor Rhodes, I hear you are interested in gold treasure."

"Ah, my secretary gave me a message you would phone back. I see where you are calling from — do you have a new pie restaurant placemat to show me?"

Jake laughed. What could he expect? Obviously, the professor knew the legend and the pie shop hype.

Once his gold fever broke, and he was no longer obsessed with finding saddlebags of riches, he began looking for experts in lost treasure to share his findings with.

Professor, actually associate professor, Rhodes at Arizona State University just outside of Phoenix came up. Her main work was in anthropological archaeology — studying the social changes in human behavior over time — but what got her more media headlines was her sideline of finding treasure.

She had led digs to find buried Spanish coins in southern California, uncovered lost gold caches in ghost towns that were once mining boom towns, and even located a hidden jewelry horde taken in a famous 1920's heist then lost when all the crooks were killed in a shoot-out.

"No, sorry, I have not discovered a new placemat with X marks the spot," joked Jake, referring to the town's former pie shop that inflamed the local missing gold legend. Jake had since learned the placemat had most of the facts of what was called Major Moser's gold wrong.

But like many legends, there was a kernel of truth to it.

And Jake believed he had more than a kernel.

"I need to run some errands in Phoenix this coming Friday and wonder if I could stop by ASU and show you what I have. I believe you will be intrigued."

"Ah, so many men have told me that, and yet, disappointment reigned," Prof. Rhodes joked. "Sure, I have some time Friday, it's a light class load day.

"And if you are not going to bring me a new placemat, how about bringing me a piece of their banana cream pie. I heard that was especially tasty."

Chapter 43

"We have a great business story for you — and it's really good for the town, too!"

The short, blockish-shaped woman standing on the other side of the *Gazette's* front counter from Jake was bubbling with enthusiasm. Her gray close-cut hairstyle said she was probably in her 50s, and her horizontal stripes said she didn't have a sense of fashion.

The taller, slender woman next to her was a decade younger, with a long blonde ponytail poking out the back of a sports cap. She held a button-less machine knitted full-length sweater she clasped at her chest, covering a body that could still turn heads.

Only their matching bulbous noses gave them away as sisters.

"We got this idea from our aunt, Carol Sweet, you might know her?" said the first woman.

"Sorry, no. But I'm still pretty new in town." Jake, by habit, slid out a reporter's notebook and pen.

"Aunt Carol walks all around town, knows

everybody. She is also one-eighth Indian..."

"Native American," corrected the younger sister.

Giving her sister a "don't interrupt me glance," the first woman continued. "One-eighth Native American. Although no one knows where that one-eighth came from.

"Anyhoo, she is a walking medical encyclopedia on medicinal uses for desert plants."

The younger sister jumped in. "Remember that rain we had several days ago?"

Jake's ankle, still in a boot, twitched at the memory of being caught with Just Nell in the unseasonal cloudburst.

"We were walking with Aunt Carol in the wet desert afterwards," said the older sister, regaining the conversation.

Carol had pointed her two nieces towards a head-high bush she called chaparral. Grabbing some of the green leaves between finger and thumb, she rubbed them roughly, releasing a musky, earthy smell.

"'Do you smell that? That's the smell of the desert after a rain,' said Aunt Carol.

Carol broke off branches of new growth to take home and told her nieces, "I keep it in jars — glass jars because it will eat through plastic jugs — on my kitchen table because I get a feeling of peace when I smell it. You can also keep it in your shower. The water releases the smell."

"But, while the smell is nice, it's not just the smell that makes this bush so special," said the older sister.

"It's the oil on the leaves," inserted the younger sister.

Again with the "don't interrupt me look," the older sister leaned forward into the counter. "Aunt Carol told us she puts the leaves in a jar of water and sits it in the sun for several hours. And with the sun we have here, it gets nicely warm.

"The Indians... Native Americans... knew this and used the tea for all sorts of herbal purposes."

"Aunt Carol said the government was trying to keep this information quiet," inserted the younger sister, now also leaning towards Jake in her eagerness to talk. "But, the tea is a natural cleansing agent, plus a treatment for rheumatism — which Aunt Carol can verify — and diabetes. It will purify your blood and help you even lose weight."

"If you see Aunt Carol, she is reed-thin. And, as anyone knows, when you age it is almost impossible to keep the weight off," said the older sister, who had lost that weight battle a long time ago.

"On our walk in the desert, Aunt Carol told us she had broken a tooth the day before. She was drinking the tea to get rid of any infection the broken tooth may cause," said the younger sister.

"And so," the older sister reached into the huge bag of a purse she was carrying over her shoulder, here's our business." She laid out several baggies of green plant material on the counter.

To Jake, they looked so much like the baggies of marijuana sold in the dorms when he was in school.

"After that walk, we went back and picked a bushel of leaves." The older sister stacked up the baggies.

"My son designed up a web page," said the

younger sister. "He's good at that stuff. He put in photos and a testimonial from Aunt Carol. He even linked us to PayPal so we could accept payment."

"We call it, 'The Healing Power of Chaparral,'" announced the older sister grandly.

"On the first day the site was up, the first day, we got 50 orders! Fifty!" reported the younger sister. "We had to go pick more leaves!"

Turning a baggy over in his hand, Jake agreed. "Wow, that is something. Are there any downsides to chaparral tea?"

The two sisters looked at each other, then the older sister spoke. "Well, Aunt Carol said the government was trying to keep this information off the internet. They said someone who drank the tea had an issue with their liver."

"There is information on the internet, however," added the younger sister. "And just like all the drugs you see advertised on TV from big drug companies, there are possible side effects. There are reports of poisoning, liver and kidney damage, nausea, and weight loss."

"Weight loss is one of the benefits, actually," said the older sister, putting all the baggies but one back into her purse. "Who knows whether reports on the internet are true. Maybe that's just big drug companies and the government trying to scare people."

"Getting back to the business idea," said the younger sister. "Chaparral grows all around here on public land. Nature will provide our raw product. We can hire women like us to pick the leaves and bag them up. We can put lots of local people to work. That's good for the town, and for health-conscious buyers around the world."

Pushing the remaining baggy on the counter across to Jake, she said: "For you, try it. 'The Healing Power of Chaparral.'"

When the sisters left, Jake turned the baggy of chaparral over and over in his hand, wondering what other job in the world would bring a person into contact with such a diverse set of characters, doing what his imagination could scarcely conceive.

That was the joy of journalism.

Chapter 44

"Maybe Jimmy is Jamie's dad."

"What!" Jake turned quickly to look at Just Nell, taking his attention off the dark, curvy road on the way to the campground.

"Think about it, Jake. Ever since Jimmy has returned to town, he has taken an unusual interest in Jamie, taking him out to lunch, showing off his stash of diamonds, and even taking Jamie and his mother out to dinner when she came home from the medical treatments in Phoenix."

"Jamie hasn't said anything about it."

"Think of Jimmy's story. He dropped out of college and left town suddenly in his very early 20s. He says now he wanted to travel the world and seek adventure. But isn't that just like a guy who gets a girl pregnant but doesn't want to take responsibility? He runs away."

Newsrooms are seething pits of gossip, so Jake

was practiced in playing the what-if game.

And he, as much as anyone, enjoyed sitting at a mall food court, making up stories as people walked by, based on their clothes, how they held their faces, the packages in their hands.

That guy buying his wife/girlfriend a present from Fredrick's of Hollywood hoped for an exotic night for himself; two glum-faced women were disappointed by their husbands trailing silently behind; that young teen girl was abused, maybe even sexually abused at home based on low-slung jeans, tight shirt, push-up bra but sad eyes.

"I don't know. Jimmy's story could be straight-ahead honest, although I do wonder about the diamond adventures in Brazil. I don't see him rolling in cash."

"Maybe Jimmy came home to care for his dad, and to get away from his wife in Brazil, who you tell me he may be getting a divorce from, only to discover a sense of fatherhood when he first encountered Jamie. Jimmy/Jamie, sounds pretty close. Maybe Jamie's mother chose that name as a link."

"Hum, I don't know. I do, however, wish that asshole behind me would drop back or pass. His headlights are blinding me."

Jake got his wish when the oversized pickup bellowing diesel fumes roared up alongside on a blind corner.

"Jerk!"

Suddenly a pair of headlights appeared ahead. Jake slammed on his brakes, throwing Just Nell towards the dashboard before her seatbelt caught.

"Ow!"

The passing pickup also slammed on its brakes, then the driver seeing Jake was stopping, quickly sped up. Just as Jake stomped on the gas when he saw the other pickup squealing to a stop.

Now, the two trucks were doing the dance where both drivers, reacting to the other, matched each move. Like two strangers in the street, both stepping the same way, and then the same opposite way, trying to avoid a collision.

And the other headlights kept coming.

Three horns blared through the night air. The passing pickup then shot ahead of Jake, clipping his left fender and jerking back into the right lane.

"Hold on, we're going to crash!" shouted Jake, careening to the right. Jamming the steering wheel to the left, Jake avoided going over the drop-off on the right side of the road but over-corrected. Now the little pickup was aiming mid-center of the on-coming vehicle. The terrified teenage girl driver was caught in Jake's headlights.

Too shocked to make any moves, she luckily continued straight down the road.

Yanking the wheel hard right, Jake felt the pickup tilt up on two wheels.

"We're going to roll!"

The girl's car slid past just by inches, leaving Jake the entire road as the right wheels found pavement.

Jake regained control of his steering and the Tacoma came to a stop.

Dazed, he sat straddling the white line, breathing hard.

"Right before I met you, Jake, I was thinking my

life was becoming too boring." Just Nell adjusted herself in her seat and fetched her purse that had crashed to the floor. "I guess it was a case of be careful of what you wish for.

"Now, maybe you should get us out of the center of the road."

Lightly touching the gas pedal, Jake got going. "I don't know if that asshole was trying to run us off the road or not. At any rate, he sure didn't stick around."

* * * * *

The next day was press day. Jake nervously watched his mirrors on the long drive going and coming to the commercial press that printed the *Gazette*. No one tried to run him off the road.

Back in the office with this week's edition, Just Nell organized the herd of noisy paperboys and papergirls. Across the bedlam of tiny bobbing bodies sliding on cloth bags to carry papers to be tossed on front porches, Jake nodded to Jamie, pointing his head toward Lester's. A beer or two were definitely in order.

"Ah, the nectar of gods." Jake abhorred clichés, but this was one he often repeated on bringing the first beer of the day to his lips. Especially considering the past 24 hours.

After a few minutes of talk about this week's issue, Jake eased into a new line of questions.

"How is Jimmy doing? Any leads for us?"

Nothing new replied Jamie. Although Jimmy was considering staying around town longer, and maybe even joining his family's real estate company. "Certainly safer than digging for diamonds he said."

"I realized the other day I don't know much about your family, like how long they have been in town, if you have any relatives here. You have mentioned your mom, I suppose it's none of my business but is your dad still around?"

Bonny slid a couple more beers their way. Today, she was wearing a black t-shirt with white lettering saying, "A hard man is good to find." Jake had to read it twice to make sure he saw it correctly.

"I was raised by my mom. It's just us in town. I have grandparents in Colorado we usually visit once a year.

"My mom doesn't talk about my dad. When I was little, I was naturally curious. All the other kids had dads, but I didn't. I asked and she gave me non-answers. Finally, when I was about 12, she sat me down and said she wasn't going to lie to me, but that she knew she and my dad had no future together. It would be better for me if she raised me on her own. So, that is what she did.

"Then I looked around again and saw a lot of kids without dads, and other kids who had terrible dads. I decided what I had was fine. I never asked my mom again about my dad.

"Heck, for all I know, you could be my dad."

That sent a shudder through Jake.

"Hey pops, how about another beer?"

Chapter 45

"I'm off in an hour or so to interview the poop

man."

"Ray Schmidt at Schmidt Bros. Farms? He's an advertiser."

"An advertiser?" Jake exaggerated a scared look while flapping his hands around his head. "I don't see any ads for recycled poop in the *Gazette*."

"He has to publish legal ads periodically from his accounts — probably a dozen or so times a year." Just Nell was not humored by Jake's funny face. Instead, she banged together pieces of paper on her desk, making a neat stack.

"You mean those little ads with all those words in the back of the paper that nobody reads?"

"Little ads? Jake, for a guy who is supposed to be running this place, you need to pay more attention to how the money comes in."

She stood up, went to the counter, pulled out this week's issue and flipped to the back pages.

"See this trustee sale ad? Mortgage companies have to run these ads before repossessing a house for lack of payment. It will run three times, bringing in more than $800. And, this notice to creditors ad published when someone dies? It is shorter but will run six times for $500. And the poop notice ads, they run only once but bring in $125 each.

"Remember last month when the county ran the list of properties with tax liens? Six pages. Six full-page ads. That's six times what the full-page grocery store ad brought in that week. In fact, more than six times because we don't discount legal ads as we do with big advertisers.

"And one more thing: legal advertisers have to pay

us before we will issue affidavits as proof the ads ran. We never lose a penny for bad debt on legal ads."

Stung by her comment he didn't understand the newspaper business, Jake retorted, "So, you're telling me the *Gazette* is staying in business by people losing their homes, dying, not paying their taxes, and having poop dumped on their land?"

"It's the law and a public service, Jake." Just Nell carefully folded the newspaper and slipped it back under the counter, picked up her ad sales kit, and walked out to call on her downtown accounts.

In a few moments, after Jake felt the chill in the air dissipate, he turned to Jamie.

"I'll need you to come with me, and bring your camera."

Jamie twisted around in his chair. "Ah, I don't know Jake. You know, my mom works for the Schmidt Bros. Farms, I would feel funny interviewing Mr. Schmidt. It would be like a conflict of interest.

"Besides, Mr. Schmidt has been good to my mom. She has worked there for, like, 20 years. He's been a very understanding employer, with her being a single parent. She could always get time off to come to any of my school events, and extra time off each summer to visit my grandparents.

"And, I never noticed until I started earning a paycheck how hard it is to live on one income. He must pay her well. She owns her own home, always pays all her bills, and never denied me anything I needed. I have never seen her worry about money. She even helped me with my college expenses.

"It must be a good job. I don't want to screw it up

for her, now that she is so close to going back."

* * * * *

By the time he was turning into the office area of Schmidt Bros. Farms — by himself and this time, unannounced — Jake was in a right pissy mood.

Just the correct frame of mind to question a man if deadly chemicals were illegally dumped at the farm where human waste — biosolids — was routinely worked into the soil for fertilizer.

Seeing Ray backing out of the trailer office front door, moving a heavy box on a handcart, Jake called out.

"Hey Ray, have a few minutes?"

Ray looked over his shoulder at Jake, then bounced the hand truck down the front stairs.

"Grab a seat," said Ray, nodding with his head toward his pickup's tailgate. "I'll get an extra cup."

"I hope you like café au lait," he said, returning to sit on the tailgate. He unscrewed the top of his thermos and poured light chocolate-colored coffee into two cups. "I learned to drink it from the French."

Jake remained standing, sending a signal this was no friendly chat.

"The last time we talked, you said Suzanne accused you of poisoning the town's water. You got quite emotional about that."

Ray took a deep breath, then a sip of coffee. "Yes, I should apologize for that. I don't believe I actually said she accused me of poisoning the town's water, rather that she was concerned biosolids would leach into the water supply.

"Now, I have to add, the biosolids are so filtered that if they should get into the water supply, they would not poison the water. But, people don't want to think they are drinking poop water, I understand that."

"How about other chemicals dumped out here? It would be so easy for a tanker truck to pour illegal pollutants of one kind or another onto your farm under cover of a typical biosolids operation."

Tough, brutal questions are a way for a reporter to throw off a comfortable interview subject. When subjects get emotional, the truth can come out.

Jake had been at a bar when the other patrons hissed when a TV reporter asked a tough or dumb question — "How did it feel when you saw the fire truck run over your cat?" — but most of the time, it was the answers, not the questions that made the news.

"I see you came armed for bear," replied Ray, pouring himself a second cup of the creamy coffee.

"Now, I don't object to your question. I've been at this for 20 years, and I've had neighbors point shotguns at me until I explained how biosolids work. Some of them are still not too happy with me to this day.

"But, that's not what you asked."

Sliding off the tailgate to stand up, Ray pointed to three irrigation circles, spraying water on richly green alfalfa. Some 15 other circles were spread out over his farm. It was the color of money growing, he said.

The farm was profitable, very profitable. Cities paid to dump the biosolids and then the Japanese bought the alfalfa to fly to their homeland where it was fed to high-end beef cattle.

"Now, imagine a crook came along and said, 'Hey, farmer Brown, how about my boys dump some god-knows-what poisons on your land for a one-time fistful of cash?' It would be stupid on my part to agree. If the EPA found out, not only would I be fined or maybe go to prison, but I would lose my biosolids deal, and with that, the connection with the Japanese. For a few bucks, I would be broke."

"Greedy people have made bad decisions before for easy money," countered Jake.

Ray tossed the dregs of his coffee on the ground as he let Jake's comment hang in the air.

"Jake, money is a tool, like my hammer or the wire cutters in my toolbox here. It's only good for what you can do with it.

"The money I make here allows me to live a very interesting life. I've been to Japan four times, I've snorkeled off the coast of Belize, I've sat at an outdoor café in Paris and — doing my Hemmingway thing — writing stories by longhand. In all, I've been to 27 countries and stayed long enough in many to be more than a tourist.

"Now, you can write what you are going to write, but for me to accept pollutants and poison my future, my own land, would be in a word, nuts."

Ray closed up the thermos. "Now, how about giving me a hand with this box?"

Slipping his reporter's notebook into his hind pocket, Jake wondered: "What's in it?"

"Something to give you a laugh, Jake, something to give you a laugh."

Ray unfolded a flap, revealing a tightly packed box

of books. He handed one to Jake. A roguish cowboy on the cover was firing a pistol with one hand while wrapping the other arm around the waist of a busty schoolmarm. The title was *Shootout at the School House.*

"I told you I wrote stories," laughed Ray. "They're cowboy stories, with a little romance for the ladies."

Jake chuckled.

"Zane Grey is probably rolling over in his grave, but if the poop business goes down the toilet, I have another horse to saddle up."

Chapter 46

Jake limped up two flights of stairs to the office of Prof. Rhodes, using a makeshift cane he'd brought with him.

Being on the Arizona State University at Tempe campus in the spring — seeing all the fresh-faced kids either hurrying to class or idling under blooming trees brought back memories of his own college life.

He had gone to the University of Washington, where, this time of year, he would have been wearing more clothes than most of the students he saw today.

He had majored in journalism, but most of his education came from working on the Daily, the four-day-a-week student newspaper. Whatever was happening on campus — from sit-ins at the dean's office to the social trends of the moment — the Daily was right in the middle of it. And Jake was right there, reporting on it during his first couple of years, and then directing the reporters as editor in his senior year.

Despite the long hours at the paper, he didn't skip any of the excesses of college life. He inhaled, he cheered great stories with glasses held high and girls completed the scene.

Today, taking one step at a time, the tip of his cane echoing on the concrete steps, he wondered where the intervening years had gone. It wasn't that he peaked in college, but now the peaks had evened out rather than stair-stepping higher.

"Hey, quit being maudlin," he told himself. He knew he had a great woman instead of a girl of the moment, and had rediscovered his joy of newspapering. The visit today should also prove quite interesting.

"Prof. Rhodes should be finishing with her grad class soon," said the secretary at the archeology department. Seeing him leaning on his cane, she suggested he sit in the professor's office to wait.

The wait gave Jake a chance to look at the degrees and news stories framed on the wall, shelves and piles of books, and a photo on her desk showing the professor holding a gold coin in her hand. The trick of the photo was the professor was stretching her arm toward the camera, making the coin appear as large as her smiling face. With her beaten-up leather hat, light-colored hair pulled back, and freckles across her nose, she could be Indiana Jones' younger sister.

"Prof. Dusty Rhodes," Jake said when she came into the office, drawing out the first name he had read on the degrees, adding a question to his voice.

"Stay seated," she replied, seeing the boot on his foot while shaking his hand. "Yes, my father had a sense of humor."

"I suppose you could have changed it or used a middle name."

"And you're supposing my middle name would be better than Dusty?" Her eyes twinkled while moving a couple of books from the seat of her chair onto the crowded desk.

"I have a sense of humor, too. It turns out Dusty Rhodes is not a name people forget, a useful trait in my sideline of tracking down lost treasure.

"Now, I don't see a piece of pie in your lap. I trust what you have in your back pocket is not a pie shop placemat."

Jake laughed, knowing Prof. Rhodes was referring to the cartoonish placemat a pie shop in town had made years ago hyping the legend of Major Pat Moser's lost gold treasure.

"I brought this." Jake lifted his cane into his lap and began peeling off duct tape binding a length of heavy cloth around the object.

Jake slowly unwound the cloth until it fell away, revealing a slightly curved sword.

"A cavalry sword!" exclaimed the professor. "Can I see it?"

Turning it over in her hand, she first looked at the ornate hilt and then tested the sharpness with a thumb. She stopped when her thumb reached halfway down. "This red stain? Is it...?"

"It could be," responded Jake to her question about possible blood residue, "or it could be dirt from the red rock cave where I found it."

"Hmmm..." Prof. Rhodes sounded doubtful of the

dirt explanation. "Ok, this is better than a placemat. Tell me more."

Jake told of finding Gus's cache of papers about the Black Hills Gold Rush and an aerial map, of he and Just Nell being caught in a cloudburst and finding refuge in a hidden slot cave among the red rocks of the desert, of nearly breaking his ankle and stumbling back to the pickup, using the sword found in the cave to keep weight off his foot.

Jake also told of Gus's mysterious death, the break-in at the *Gazette* office when Gus's old desk was searched and the threat at Lester's from Dumb and Dumber. "Although I don't give much credence to that last one. These guys were all bluster, no balls."

Still holding the sword, the professor told Jake she had done some research since he phoned a week ago. "There was a Major Pat Moser, and he was attached to the Gen. George Custer's 7th Cavalry guarding the illegal miners who swarmed into Indian treaty lands upon discovery of gold.

"He wasn't at the Battle of Little Bighorn but disappeared from military records shortly afterward. He very well could have left to escort a gold pack train west, and then double-crossed the miners."

What eventually happened to him is impossible to say, she said. Around this time, the mid-1800s, California was starting to boom. If he took the gold and moved to San Francisco, for example, he would have been one of the new wealthy from the goldfields.

"Once in San Francisco, he could have fallen victim to the violence — manmade or natural — epidemic at that time and disappeared from the records.

"At this point, it's anyone's guess — if he robbed the gold miners — whether he took all the gold with him, took only part but never returned to retrieve the rest later, or whether he never made it out of that cave alive."

Neither spoke for a moment, considering the possibilities. Then Jake asked: "Interesting enough for the aptly named Dusty Rhodes to come, take a look?"

"As Indiana would say, 'If you want to be a good archeologist, you gotta get out of the library.' So, for sure, I want to have a look!"

Putting down the sword, she leaned forward to stare into Jake's eyes. "There is a question I have to ask, though. If we find anything, the state will take half, and my deal with the University is they get the other half. They like to see positive news stories about professors here, true, but they also like the cash.

"I could likely get you a 10 percent finder's fee, but you could have gotten it all had you made the discovery and kept quiet about it. Why come to me?"

Jake knew this question would likely be raised, and he didn't have a good answer.

"Ultimately, I decided, sneaking around to be fabulously wealthy wasn't in my personality. I like my life. Besides, I would rather drink a glass of beer in a friendly bar than the most expensive champagne from France in a fine restaurant. And, I would like to have a meaningful job to go to every day rather than lie around on a beach getting fat.

"Ten percent sounds great to me — and, the Gazette gets to break the story first."

"Of course. Now, what I want to know is will you be printing a photo of the original placemat to go along with the story?"

Chapter 47

"Jake, deputy Verne has been killed!"
"What!"
Jamie was holding up a piece of paper as he burst into the *Gazette*. "I've just come from the sheriff's office with this press release. The deputy was bringing a prisoner home this morning from New Mexico when his patrol car went off the road on U.S. 60, southwest of Albuquerque."

Speed reading the release, Jamie added the patrol car went off an unprotected cliff during the early morning. The car wasn't seen by a passer-by until hours later. When rescuers got down to the car, both the deputy and the prisoner were dead.

"Does the sheriff know exactly what happened?"
"No, not really. He said it's too soon to tell, but an investigation is underway," said Jamie. "He did add there were skid marks on the road and a small amount of debris, like glass from a busted headlight."

"You mean he could have been run off the road?"
"Too soon to know, if we ever will."

It was late Tuesday afternoon, and Jake had just finished laying out this week's paper, to be driven to the press early the next day.

Now, he would have to tear up the front page and one inside page for the jump. Maybe a second inside page, too, for the current front-page story — Jamie's feature on twin local girls who were leading the Wildcats volleyball team to state high school finals.

Stop the press moments like these were just what newspapermen and women lived for.

"Ok, Jamie, you do the accident story. Get quotes from the sheriff, and call the authorities in New Mexico for their version of events. Even though our sheriff has a press release, I want to know what people there are thinking. Oh, and get a photo from the sheriff of the deputy in uniform."

"Just Nell, you can proofread the pages we are not going to change now, but can you stay late to read the front and inside pages later? I don't know how long this is going to take."

"Sure, and why don't I run down to Rose's and get a pizza to keep us all going?"

"A pizza? That gives me an idea."

Jake quickly tapped in a phone number and a famous-novelist-to-be answered.

Jake immediately asked if Aaron had heard the news about his uncle, and when the youth said yes, Jake offered his condolences.

"I know this might be hard, and if you don't want to, say no. But, I don't know deputy Verne's family or local history. You do. Could you craft six to 10 paragraphs on his background? Maybe get something from his widow, if possible?" Jake winced when making that hard ask.

"Everyone's gathering at my mom's house now," said Aaron. "Sure, I can get you something. How soon?"

"Can you do it in two to three hours? We need a story in tomorrow's paper, and I would like it to be as complete as possible."

"Ok. Everyone is saying it's so devastating. He has been looking to leave the sheriff's department. I think he was upset with some of the things going on down there. But, finding a good-paying job in this town is tough. He didn't want to leave a place where both he and his wife grew up."

"Ok, you've had some experience of working here while Jamie was away with his mom. You know what we want. Don't miss the deadline."

* * * * *

Hours later, Jake was sitting at the bar in Lester's, trying to read Bonny's t-shirt.

"Whatever this is is it about over?"

He sounded out the words, and realized a comma was missing: "Whatever this is, is it about over?"

Do tee-shirt designers not have proofreaders, he wondered.

And that brought him to the *Gazette's* proofreader, and why he was waiting for a beer in Lester's all by himself.

Jake had done a speedy job of reformatting the newspaper to include Jamie's breaking news story and a nice sidebar with poignant quotes from Aaron about the deputy. He had been a high school baseball star who played a couple of years at the University of Arizona before marrying his high school sweetheart and having the first of their three children.

Jake called the bank to suggest an account be set up for donations for the family but learned the bank was on it. Money was already coming in for the well-liked family.

Jake also whipped together a story on the dead prisoner, who was being returned to town. The prisoner was the main suspect when his wife was found dead in their RV. It was one of the first stories Jake reported on for the *Gazette*.

Three timely stories on a tragedy. Aaron even brought in a photo of Verne in his high school baseball uniform.

Jamie had left for the night by the time Just Nell finished making corrections to the page proofs, with the keyed-up Jake looking over her shoulder.

"Hey, Nellie, let's go have a beer for a good day of work at Lester's"

As soon as the words had left his lips, he knew he had made a mistake. Yet ever since overhearing Just Nell on the phone to her mother, saying, 'It's me, Nellie," the tenderness of those words rolled around in his brain. Now, in his mind, he found himself more and more thinking of her as Nellie.

She turned a cold look on Jake. "I told you, Nellie is a dead name from the past I don't want to recall."

He went from 60 to zero. A lame attempt at apologizing went nowhere, as did an attempt to rally her around their accomplishment this afternoon at the *Gazette*.

"Why don't you just go to Lester's by yourself. You seem to be spending a lot of time there." She stood up, grabbed her purse, and exited the front door.

What happened?

And, that's what he was trying to puzzle out near

closing time at Lester's.

"Rodney, Rodney, get that horse out of here!" Bonny was frantically waving her hands at Rodney, who had braced open the back door.

"Aw, there's nobody here, it's just the regulars," complained Rodney, who by now had indeed led the head of a horse through the back door.

As odd as the horse's head at the back door was, Jake was even more taken back by being termed a "regular." Had he become just another fly at the bar? Maybe Nellie... Just Nell... had a point.

"Rodney, you can't bring that horse in here! I'm telling you, I'll ban you from the bar!"

"But Bonny..."

"Don't but me. There's a guy in the toilets I haven't seen before. He could be a state liquor inspector. Get the horse out of here before he comes back."

Bringing a draft to Jake, she explained how Rodney had piled up so many drunk-driving citations, he had lost his license. Now, he rode a horse into town. On some nights, he would sneak his horse in for a quick one before the trot home.

"I oughta write a book... if I could spell." She left the beer and headed out the back door to check on Rodney and the horse.

Chapter 48

On Saturday, Jake woke up alone — as was becoming too common.

He laid in his RV queen bed, trying to figure out

what was happening with his relationship with Just Nell. She had been cool to him since he erred and called her Nellie on Tuesday night.

But that really couldn't be all there was to it. During the past month or so, they were still fine "in bed," but afterward when he was prone and caressing her back, whispering end-of-the-day pleasantries to her, she was quiet with her back to him.

He enjoyed touching her, and she seemed to like the touches, stretching her neck so his hands could find the pressure spots, or putting her feet on his lap.

But she never reached out to him. She was friendly, but not affectionate.

He always complimented her looks, cooking, and work because, deep down, Jake sensed a hole of doubt she carried around from a childhood in the trailer park.

And honesty, he wasn't lying. She was a tasty cook, maybe she was too attractive to the businessmen she dealt with on the ad sales rounds, and her work at the *Gazette* was showing great results.

Ad sales were up at the weekly newspaper, but so were subscriptions. Jake liked to think his sparkling writing and tight editing drew in new readers but more likely, it was Just Nell's making sure subscribers actually received the paper.

Jake knew it wasn't hard-hitting editorials that lost readers. More subscribers canceled the paper because too many times the paperboy or papergirl missed the porch and tossed the paper on a wet lawn or in a hard-to-get-to bush.

"Maybe I should bring her flowers now and then," he thought, crawling out of bed to write a note to himself on his phone.

Done pondering, Jake rushed through his morning routine because today Prof. Dusty Rhodes was bringing her team to town to investigate the lost gold treasure. The famed "female Indiana Jones" — as one newspaper account called her — and her college students came Friday night, staying at Dick's Sleep-N-EZ Motel at the edge of town. Now, Jake was to meet up with the team to lead the expedition to the cave.

The motel's usual clientele was visiting hunters and fishermen but it also had a secluded parking lot around back for local folks who just needed an hour or two. It was a bit of a joke in town to rib someone if their pickup was seen behind the EZ-Sex motel.

Jake wondered what Prof. Rhodes would think of the motel, but she would probably think of it as a laugh. She had likely slept in worse places on archeology digs. Far worse places.

Nearing town, Jake saw whiffs of smoke rising from the motel's back parking lot. When he turned in, the smell of burning rubber invaded the pickup's cab along with gas fumes.

Driving around to the back, he saw town volunteer firefighters spraying down three burned hulks of desert ATVs. Prof. Rhodes stood among the small crowd around the scene, as did half a dozen students in ASU sweatshirts. Just Nell was next to the professor.

"What happened?" Jake asked as he came up.

"Someone tried to stop our search this morning by burning up the ATVs," said the professor. "Maybe they were trying to buy time so they could keep looking."

"Wow! So, when do you think you can come back?"

"Come back? Jake, the university has resources. Especially if there is the possibility of a jackpot. I've already called, the cavalry is on the way."

The fire hadn't dampened the spirits of Prof. Rhodes — who insisted on being called Dusty — even though the students seemed unusually quiet.

"Let's go eat breakfast. Got a good spot in town? How about the pie shop, does it serve a hearty first meal of the day?"

Yes, there was a great breakfast place in town, but no, unfortunately, the pie shop had closed years ago.

* * * * *

Breakfast done, they all arrived back at the motel just as three big maroon and gold ASU pickups roared into the parking lot, each towing a trailer with knobbed-tired ATVs. Hanging out the truck windows were young men who were beefier than the students with Dusty.

"We get a lot of football players in archeology," Dusty explained. "I think they like going on digs in the outback with the cute girls who come to our field because of Indiana Jones.

"Thanks, Indy."

Dusty organized the students and trucks, and in a few minutes, with Jake, Just Nell, and Dusty leading in his Tacoma, the caravan left on a gold hunt.

* * * * *

"Did you mark where the slot cave was?" asked Dusty once the ATVs had been off-loaded and were at the top of the knoll looking over the desert valley.

"No," said Just Nell. "When the rain exploded around us, and Jake twisted his ankle, our thoughts focused on getting back to his truck safely. It was a very scary moment."

"Maybe just as well. Someone else is desperate to find the treasure, witness the attempt to stop us today. Had you marked the spot, they would likely already found the treasure and wouldn't have cared about us."

Turning her attention to Jake, she asked: "How do you suppose they knew we were coming today? Did you tell anyone?"

"No, no. Of course not. Well, I told Just Nell, but she already knew."

"Hum... well, let's go find that gold." Dusty hopped aboard the lead ATV, and doing her "Indiana Jones" thing, waved her beat-up leather hat forward. The three machines tore down the knoll, kicking dust into the still morning air.

* * * * *

After an hour of skirting the edge of the red hills pushing into the desert, Jake's enthusiasm was lagging when no cave was found.

"Let's do another lap," said Dusty. "Recognize anything, guys?"

Both Just Nell and Jake shook their heads.

"Well, these slot caves are hollowed out by rain over centuries. Sometimes, the mouths of the caves leading to larger chambers can be small. They can be well hidden in the folds and creases of the hills. We have to keep looking. The harder to see the cave, the better chance the treasure is still there."

She turned her attention to one of the football players sitting on the hood of their ATV who kept squirming around.

"Titus, what's the deal? Can't you sit still so I can see?"

"Sorry, professor, but I gotta take a piss."

"Ok," she said, stopping the ATV. "Go for it."

"Where?"

"Over there, behind that crease." Dusty returned to Jake and Just Nell and said since they got a late start today, they could come back on Sunday. She would send students to walk the hills above to see holes indicating possible chambers.

"Professor, you had better look at this." Titus came out from behind the crease, one hand unconsciously checking his zipper.

Dusty leaped over the side of the ATV, followed closely by Jake and Just Nell. The other students crowded in.

"Yeah, watch out for that." Titus pointed to a large wet spot already drying on a rock. "Just up here." He pointed to a narrow opening.

"That's it!" shouted both Jake and Just Nell in near unison.

"OK, we have a protocol for possible finds. You

two," Dusty waved at Jake and Just Nell, "need to stand back until we establish a safe zone.

"Titus, you Rolf, and Yvette form the ATVs in a semi-circle pointing out in front of this area. The rest of you, start bringing in the gear."

Jake watched the students bring in tall stands, floodlights, cables, and car batteries. Out came canvas bags of short shovels, trowels and brooms, and brushes. One carried a metal detector connected to headgear, while another wheeled in a device looking like a gas lawnmower, but Jake recognized it as a ground-penetrating radar unit.

He noticed they were all now wearing white plastic gloves, with a mask over their noses and goggles hanging from their necks.

As Jake watched the students, Just Nell turned towards him.

"Jake, who did you tell besides me Dusty was coming today to look for the gold?" Just Nell faced Jake head-on.

"No one, no one at all."

"You talked about it in the office."

"No, I didn't. When?"

"You were getting that neck rub from Robbie you like so much. And you told me to plan on an extra four pages this coming week, in case Dusty found the gold," said Just Nell.

"Robbie? You are suspecting Robbie? She's like 80. I don't think she would be burning up ATVs."

"Maybe Robbie told someone. You know she is a gossip."

Jake was processing who Robbie might have

talked to when Dusty emerged from the cave.

"You two better come look at this."

Chapter 49

"What are you going to do with your half of the money?"

"My half?"

"You get half of the finder's fee. That's five percent of the value of the gold in the cave. And from the looks of it, that could be saddlebags full."

Jake was driving back to town with Just Nell. Dusty had stayed at the cave, after calling in more students, supplies, and security.

She intended camping at the site, and from the look on her face, a situation that delighted the "Indiana Jones" side of her almost as much as the find itself.

Jake and Just Nell were stunned when Dusty invited them into the chamber at the end of the slot cave in the red rock cliffs.

The last time the pair had been in the cave, fleeing from the cloudburst in the desert, sunlight on an overcast day only dimly lit the knobby walls in the sandstone, and didn't illuminate the size of the room.

They only found the cavalry sword because when Jake slipped and fell, he cut his hand on its rusty blade half-buried in the soil.

Now, floodlights blazed all along the edges, making the oblong room — which was bigger than Jake's RV — brighter than daylight.

Half a dozen students dug at four different locations using trowels and brushes. Other students with video and still cameras carefully recorded each item painstakingly pulled from the red sand floor before the items were laid on a white cloth on one side of the cave near the entrance where they were again photographed and recorded.

Already on the cloth were a few coins, buttons, two knives, the metal top of a canteen, and a rusty pistol.

"We haven't found any bones so far," said Dusty, seeing Jake take inventory. "If there were bodies here, and I think there were, animals got to them."

The students were moving slowly and carefully, walking only on a tight path between the finds, but the cave hummed with the thrill of the find.

Unearthing thousand-year-old bone fragments was the norm on archeology digs and undoubtedly led to insights into how humans and other creatures lived in the past. But finding lost treasure in a cave, and piecing together the fascinating mystery of how it got there, with the possibility of treachery — maybe even a shoot–out — that was the story worth telling and retelling around dorm rooms and over campfires at future digs.

"We have only begun," said Dusty, "we have days of work ahead of us. What a teaching opportunity! But maybe what is most interesting to you two is over here."

Walking to the back where a little niche was naturally carved out of the wall, Dusty bent down. "The metal detector went wild here."

Reaching into a foot-deep hole, she slid her forefinger under the flap of a dirty saddlebag and flipped it up, revealing sparkling flecks in the bright lights.

"That's gold, my friends, and I believe there is a lot more of it."

* * * * *

Now, on the ride back to town, the thrill of the find was ebbing out of Jake and Just Nell, replaced by wondering what happens next.

"You don't have to give me half the finder's fee, Jake. It was you following up Gus's work that led to the discovery."

"Give you? I'm not giving you anything. You deserve half, at least. You were shot in our first try at finding the gold, and only your desire for a picnic in the desert got us back out here, where the monstrous rain chased us into the cave. Maybe you deserve it all."

"Half, huh?" Just Nell smiled brighter than Jake had seen her smile in weeks. "I have some ideas."

* * * * *

Jake dropped Just Nell off behind the motel where she had parked her car. He had to get to the office to begin work on the treasure story for the coming week's paper, but promised, "Once this issue is out, we'll celebrate!"

Jake reflected on how Just Nell smiled on the ride back. Maybe I am just imagining things, he thought. Maybe everything is OK between us. Every couple has little tiffs, and we're both mature adults with some mileage under our belts. We're not teenagers swooning over each other.

Jake recalled how crazy he and his first girlfriend, Bobbie, were for each other. Cruising around town, she'd snuggle up tightly against him on the bench seat, running her fingers through the hair on the back of his head as he drove.

Oh my god, that was heavenly! If there is a paradise after this life, riding around in a car with a girl lightly scratching the back of your head with her fingernails would be right at the top of the moments to be relived.

"Shit!"

Jake slammed on the brakes as a woman ran in front of him towards the motel. He had been so engrossed in a memory he had almost hit her.

"I'm so sorry!" he shouted out his open window as she turned to flash a pissed-off look, her long black wavy hair flying around.

She turned back towards the motel as a room door opened for her.

Wait, I know her from somewhere, thought Jake. As his brain tried to make a connection, he noticed a man standing at the motel door. It was Jimmy Daggett.

Chapter 50

"Jeeze, Jake, did they teach you in newspapering school to believe everything people told you?"

Jake had just cut himself the perfect bite of eggs Benedict — a sunny-side-up egg sitting on a slice of ham, toasted English muffin on the bottom drenched in creamy Hollandaise sauce — and had raised it to his mouth when Just Nell's challenge came.

The two were eating Sunday breakfast at The Blackberry, the most recent restaurant to inhabit the space of the original pie shop.

Jake called the breakfast an homage to the pie shop's legacy. He had ordered the eggs Benedict — his favorite special breakfast — while Just Nell contented herself with blackberry crepes.

Earlier waiting for their order to come, Jake had told Just Nell about seeing the woman in the motel parking lot who, he later remembered, was the woman who discovered Gus's body in the red cliffs.

"Was she still wearing the skimpy sport's bra?"

Jake didn't know how to react to her catty sarcasm. He plunged ahead.

"And, in the room she was entering was Jimmy Daggett. I think she could have been his wife, who I thought was still in Brazil."

Their food came, and after telling the waitress they had all they needed, both picked up their silverware in silence.

Jake cut himself the first bite, but Just Nell laid down her fork and asked the question about believing everyone.

"What is that supposed to mean?" Jake was getting annoyed at her attitude at what should have been a celebratory breakfast.

"Look, I've told major lies in my life, and I have always been surprised at how easily I've gotten away with them. But, I thought someone like you, who should have an ear for BS, wouldn't be so easily fooled."

The hairs on the back of Jake's neck raised. He sat

his untasted first bite down.

"Is there something you want to tell me?"

"Jake, this isn't about me. It's about you listening to, and believing, the wrong people."

"Who do you have exactly in mind?"

Just Nell took a big breath and exhaled.

"Let's start with Jimmy Daggett and the diamond factory. You're the one who told Jimmy about the Hollywood types nosing around, looking for a factory site to grow natural diamonds."

"Jamie told him first, but yeah, I talked to him about it."

"And you talked to him, thinking you might get a story if a factory site were purchased, a fact he might learn through his father's real estate business. And you think he talked to you because — with his experience with diamonds — with enough information, he might find an angle to make money. Right?"

"Yeah." Jake was recalling a few evenings at Lester's, hashing over the diamond factory with Jimmy.

"And, this is partially my fault because I first suggested it, you think Jimmy might be Jamie's father and that's why he spent so much time with the boy?"

"Yeah." Jake felt like he was on the witness stand with a hostile attorney leading him into a trap.

"And, this whole thing about a diamond factory came from your first meeting with Patrick McPhee, who you thought was grieving for Suzanne's death by retreating into a bottle? You have not a shred of other information about such a factory. Right?"

"Yeah." Jake looked down at the cheesy Hollandaise sauce coalescing around the soggy muffins.

The trap was opening wide.

"Jake, what if you had this all wrong? What if Jimmy wasn't staying in town seeking an opportunity with a new diamond factory? What if Jimmy — the self-described treasure hunter — was after the Major Moser's gold treasure all along? What if he isn't Jamie's dad but spent time with Jamie, and you, hoping to learn what you have found?"

"Yeah, that's a possibility all right. So, what set you off in this direction?"

"I ran into Wil, the county clerk, the other day when I was making my ad sales rounds. She again apologized if anything she said led to the break-in at the *Gazette* and the rifling of your desk. She then said she doesn't usually go to the Lions Service Club lunches, where she blabbed about Gus's aerial survey maps but went that day because of the special speaker. Do you know who the special speaker was?"

"No..."

"Jimmy Daggett, who was seated right next to her."

Trap sprung.

The waitress swung by and seeing not a bite taken off either cold plate, asked if everything was OK. Being aware of the truism that breakups are often done at busy restaurants, she didn't hang around when both Jake and Just Nell silently nodded.

"So, maybe Jimmy came back to town just for the treasure?"

"Jake, you are still not getting it."

Chapter 51

Spring was exploding all around them as Jake and Just Nell walked from the restaurant back to her duplex apartment where Jake had left his pickup.

The after-church crowd from the First Methodist spilled out onto the sidewalk, men shaking hands, women looking bright in their "winter's over" dresses, and kids running back and forth in the glee of being free.

There was no glee, however, hovering around Jake and Just Nell.

"All right, tell me the rest of it."

She took a deep breath. "It all starts with that first meeting you had with Patrick. Think of what you thought at the time, and what he told you."

"Well, along with the bit about the diamond factory, he told me Suzanne had discovered one of the town's wells was contaminated by an unknown substance and as the town couldn't afford an independent investigator, and besides, she didn't want word of the contamination getting out, so started looking into possible sources herself. Patrick added he thought whoever was behind the contamination killed her."

"Does any of that make sense?"

Jake stopped abruptly. After a minute of thinking, he held out three fingers: "Suzanne wasn't a chemist, someone would have had to report the contamination to her. A secret like that isn't possible to keep if two or three people know it in a small place like this.

"Two, the town wouldn't have had to hire anyone, it could have requested help from state or federal environmental officials. They would have raced right in.

"And finally, if she wasn't a chemist, she certainly wasn't a sleuth. I can't see her searching for clues in the caverns. This is a little bigger than a Nancy Drew mystery. Again, why not turn the matter over to the feds who have the experience and manpower?

"So, do I have it?"

Just Nell nodded. "You're getting there. Now, take a step back." When Jake stepped back, she added: "I don't mean literally, silly."

Looking off at a cactus wren noisily pecking on a Sequoia, she was quiet and thoughtful for a moment. "I worked for 20 years at the caverns, with a string of different owners. One of them was a high-functioning alcoholic. In the mornings, he was sharp, decisive, and personable. By the afternoons, he shut himself off in his office, just him and the bottle. In two years, he blew through his finances and lost the business.

"Now, think about Patrick. It's always been assumed Patrick, by brokering frozen chickens, is like all middlemen, fat and comfortable. His income supported Suzanne's do-gooder life in town.

"But, with the internet, buyers and sellers can get together directly. Who needs brokers?

"And maybe Patrick isn't drinking because of Suzanne's death, maybe he has been drinking all along. Maybe he isn't the big earner people think he is."

"You think Patrick and Suzanne might have had money troubles?" asked Jake.

"Well, in my bookkeeping at the *Gazette*, I can see it has been losing money all along — until very recently."

"Thanks for that, super ads saleswoman." Jake was looking for any chance to get back in her good graces.

"Suzanne also owned property around town. But, she was giving Gus free rent, and charging the *Gazette* very little.

"Maybe she was desperate for cash flow."

"What are you saying?" asked Jake.

"What if Suzanne wasn't investigating the contamination, what if she was the cause of the contamination? For a profit?"

Chapter 52

"Are you going to rename the *Gazette*?"

"What? What are you talking about, Robbie?"

Jake was at his editor's desk, melting under a massage from Robbie. She had moved from working her fingers through the back of his scalp to making tight circles with an elbow under his left shoulder blade.

He hadn't even known he was sore there until the elbow ran over a tender spot. All of the tension of the past week — getting out the big edition on the gold treasure find, wondering why Just Nell seemed to be cooler to him, and doubting everything he knew about Suzanne and her murder — dissipated under Robbie's touch. Her long career as a nurse certainly wasn't wasted.

"The town's streets are all going to be renamed. Maybe the *Gazette* should change its name too."

"What renaming?" Jake could hardly think, it was taking all of his conscious effort not to drool or moan in pleasure. That would be unprofessional in the office.

"Greg is talking to the town council about changing the name of streets and parks. He says the chocolate company brings thousands of tourists to town every year. Naming streets after items the candy company makes would help the town by bringing in more people.

"Greg says if the town won't go along, then the factory may have to move to a more tourist-friendly place."

Jake leaned as far forward as he could onto his desk to allow Robbie's elbows to run up and down next to his spine.

When she stopped, he slowly emerged from the daze to remember Greg was the president of Arizona Dark Chocolate and the nephew of the ex-hippies who founded the company in the 1970s. Jake had observed busloads of tourists unloading at the factory, although he couldn't quite get what would be so tourist-enticing watching chocolate being made. Maybe free samples were involved.

The factory was one block off the main street — where the *Gazette* with its huge windows left over from when the building had been a new car showroom in the '60s was located. Jake seldom saw tourists wandering far from the buses, but he supposed some must find their way into local businesses.

He guessed chocolate tourists were a good thing for the town. If tourists who roamed the Northeast in the fall for the change of colors were called leaf-peepers, what would chocolatephiles be called? Candy Andys, bonbon buddies, confection aficionados?

"Jamie reports on the town council meeting every week. He hasn't said anything about renaming streets," Jake told Robbie, straightening up.

"I don't think Greg has gone to the town council meeting. He has talked to them at their Monday lunch." Robbie gathered her notebook held closed with a thick rubber band she used for her person in the street interviews and approached Barbara, ready to give the ad designer her massage.

"Monday lunch? What is that?" Arizona had a public meeting law, meaning anytime a majority of council members got together, they had to alert the public, including the media. The idea behind the law was the public not only had a right to know the decisions of their elected representatives, but they had — with a few exceptions involving personnel and real estate transactions — the right to know the discussions that lead up to the decisions.

Since most of the public didn't care, reporting on these discussions fell to the media. The media, as a rule, were sticklers in holding public officials to the letter of the law.

"Gus used to attend those meetings all the time," said Robbie, digging into the neck of Barbara, who was swiveling her head around slowly. "He never reported on them, though. Suzanne didn't want him to. She said it was just for background."

Jake was about to snap, "That's against the law," when he realized Robbie was not the one he needed to talk to.

"Where's Jamie?" he asked Just Nell, working a tape adding machine at her desk.

"He said he was going to the high school to interview the baseball coach about the upcoming season."

"I wonder if he knew about these Monday lunches?"

"Just now you are wondering about Jamie?" She put her finger on a column of numbers to keep her place.

"What do you mean?"

Just Nell took a deep breath, looked out at the main street as she collected her thoughts, and glanced at Robbie and Barbara, who were in their own massage world. "Jake, what made you think one of the town's wells was contaminated?"

"Patrick told me at our first meeting." Jake was starting to get a bad feeling, as Just Nell already pointed out Suzanne's husband was a drunk and probably a liar.

"And…?"

"Jamie took a sample of water from the well Suzanne had gathered to a chemistry professor he knew at college. The professor reported an unknown toxin was in the water." Jake liked his answer but felt the ground beneath him giving way.

Still, he continued. "Oh, and we also found a mysterious liquid spill when we were searching the caverns. Jamie took that to the chemistry professor, too. And the same report came back: possible toxins."

Just Nell took another look at Barbara and Robbie, still engaged.

"Jake, have you ever talked to Jamie about what he studied at college?"

This was feeling worse and worse to Jake. "I don't

know. I guess I thought he was taking some general courses towards a bachelor of arts."

"Jamie was pursuing a theater major. Does it seem there would be a lot of chemistry classes necessary for a theater major?"

Trying to save himself, Jake replied, "When I was getting my journalism degree at the University of Washington, I had to take some science 101 classes, like basic astrometry."

"Unlike you and Jamie, I have never been to college," said Just Nell. "But I have heard these 101 classes are jammed full of students and often taught by a teaching assistant, rather than a full professor.

"Do you think you could just show up at the office of an astrometry professor, and say you have found a handful of stardust, and ask him to analyze it for you? You think you would have developed that kind of relationship from your 101 class?"

Damn it! Just Nell should have been a prosecutor, thought Jake. She had exposed him for assuming too much again.

What was Jamie's role in all of this? And how did his mother develop cancer, especially the kinds of cancers caused by man-made pollutants? And when is Just Nell going to give him a break?

"Robbie," he silently pleaded. "Please come back."

Chapter 53

It was wonderful to go to bed with Just Nell again. And now nice to be in bed with her.

Sex is a magic eraser, thought Jake, it wiped away

the stains and doubts from the past few weeks.

Listening to the little sleep sounds she was making in the RV's bed — not snores exactly, and he certainly wouldn't tell her that if they were — he wondered if they should come to a more permanent arrangement. How did he get so lucky to find a beautiful, smart woman who liked the physical side of love as much as he did?

What was that quote? "In all the gin joints in all the world, why did she walk into this one?" That's not quite right, but he could look it up tomorrow. Maybe there could be a ceremony in their future where he could use that quote.

Thump! The RV shuddered, followed by a yell: "Bitch!" and the squeal of tires.

Brilliant flickering light flooded through the window of the only door on the rig, illuminating the RV's interior.

Jake bolted up onto his elbows, dazed.

Crash! The window shattered from the heat. Flames and fumes gushed through.

"Jake, what happened?"

"I don't know! But, the RV's on fire, get up, get up, we have to get out!"

Jake sprung out of bed and ran forward toward the door to grab the handle. Angry flames pushed him back. Fumes from burning plastic filled his coughing lungs.

"Jake, we can't get out that way! Use the emergency exit!" She was curled in one corner of the bed, as far away from the flames and fumes as she could get.

Jake jumped back on the bed, and with his back braced on one wall bordering the bed, started smashing his bare feet against the window on the other side. One, two, three kicks, and the plastic glass broke away, gashing his legs in the process.

A new supply of oxygen raced in, feeding the fire to an even higher level of intensity. Black smoke choked both of them, blotting out any light created by the fire.

"Jake, not that window! This is the emergency exit, behind me!" Just Nell found the red handles, yanked them up, and forced the window out.

A pair of hands reached through the emergency opening, grabbing Just Nell by her bare shoulders and pulled her out, her legs whipping around to kick Jake in the face.

Fiercely burning, the fire feeding on all the plastics used in the manufacture of lightweight RVs, climbed walls and across the ceiling toward Jake, consuming all the oxygen. Jake collapsed on the bed, barely feeling a hand grab him by a fistful of hair and pull.

More fingers curled under his shoulders and pulled. Jake fell to the ground, where he was quickly picked up and pulled a long away from the now fully fire-consumed RV.

"Get away, get away before the fire reaches the fuel tanks!"

Tears streamed from his smoke-burned eyes, but he could see the fully naked Just Nell safe beside him, helping him get away. He turned to see who was on his other side — who had rescued them.

"Daniel? What are you doing here?"

"Saving you two, it looks like. Can you stand by yourself? I can get some blankets." The lean, white-haired man Jake had met briefly and who said he was a long-haul trucker months ago at this campsite ran off toward his rig.

"Just Nell, are you OK?"

"Yes. But you have blood running down your legs." Both looked down at his legs, and at the same time, both realized as they were naked in bed, they were now naked outside.

More campers came up to see flames shoot towards the surrounding Ponderosa Pine trees.

"Everybody, move your rigs! This whole campground could go up if the fire gets into those trees!" someone shouted. The bystanders ran off to get away from the growing fire.

Daniel was back with a fluffy blanket for each of them. "Come over to my RV where I can look at those cuts on your legs, Jake."

Sirens announced fire trucks turning into the campgrounds. Soon, streams of water played over the smoldering RV and onto surrounding trees.

As Daniel cleaned dirt and soot off Jake's legs and then applied ointment and bandages, Jake again asked how he came to be there.

"That's a story for another time, Jake. Let's get you two settled down. I can make up the table into a bed, because obviously, you won't be sleeping in your rig tonight, nor will be you retrieving any clothes."

Jake and Just Nell first had to talk to the volunteer firefighters, and then explain to the sheriff's deputies he believed his RV was firebombed, all the while draped in blankets.

Other RV'ers offered spare clothes. Soon they were dressed — in mismatched pants and shirts, true, but at least warm and feeling more human.

When they were alone again, Jake tried to figure out what exactly happened, and why.

"I don't get it. The gold treasure has already been found and taken away. What's the point of attacking me now?" Jake was thinking of Dumb and Dumber and others in town who might have wanted him off the trail of the treasure.

"Attacking you, Jake?" Just Nell spoke quietly.

"Yeah, I mean, Dumb and Dumber had threatened the RV at the bar, but now, why?" Jake hitched up the belt on the donated oversized pants one more notch.

"Jake, Jake, Jake." Just Nell took a deep breath.

When he looked questioning at her, she added: "You said something was said just as the firebomb hit the RV. Do you recall what it was?"

"I heard the smash of the bottle against the door, the whoosh of flames, the sound of a vehicle squealing off, and I thought I heard a yell."

"And what was that yell?"

"Well, it sounded like 'Bitch,' but I can't be sure."

Running her palms over the flowered drapery dress a senior camper woman had given her, she said, "Maybe the attack wasn't against you but against me. Maybe I was the target."

Chapter 54

"You're the target? You had nothing to do with the gold."

"Jake, get your mind off the gold." Just Nell turned to look deep into the desert night, now dark once again that the fire was out.

"Who was shot the first time we went out into the desert?"

"You were."

"And, who was the passenger in your truck when some asshole tried to run us off the road?"

"You were." Damn it. A familiar feeling of a lamb being led down the path to slaughter crept over Jake.

"And which one of us in the RV might the word 'Bitch' refer to?"

"Ok, not thinking about the gold, but why would a person want to kill you? Is there a spurned lover I don't know about?"

Just Nell looked at Jake for a moment. "I have men in my past, naturally. But, it might not be a lover... it might be my husband."

"Your husband? You're married?"

"The husband I told you about, in Florida. When I talked to my mom after I was shot, she said he had been around a few times over the years, asking about me. The last time, he got so aggressive, that my mom's boyfriend had to chase him off with a baseball bat. By the way, my mom said that's when she realized he was the guy to marry."

Jake reflected back on the story Just Nell had shared when he first met her at the caverns when he was there to report on Suzanne's murder.

"I guess I thought after all this time, and the way

you left, he would have probably divorced you. I think you can do that even if the other party has left the state."

"It's the way I left."

Raising his hands out in a "so-what" gesture, Jake said, "You left with a guy. Lots of married people leave with someone new. It's the plot of half the romance books written."

She slowly drew out the word, "Yeah," then added, "I told you about seeing the guy changing the tire behind the county club, and I told you about asking for a ride in exchange for … services… but I didn't tell you when I went back into the club's cloakroom to get my coat and purse, my husband, Junior, was there. He knew something was up and started shouting at me, calling me a bitch. He cornered me, hiked up my dress, and pulled down my panties."

Jake wrapped an arm around her shaking shoulders. "Just Nell, you don't have to tell me he raped you."

"It's not rape. In Florida, a husband can't be denied. No, it wasn't what he did, it's what I did.

"I was desperate, thrashing around, and somehow my hand fell on scissors left on the end of the counter. I grabbed them and swiped at Junior. I only wanted him to stop, well, that's what I tell myself. I only wanted him to stop, but the scissors caught him across the face, slicing open a huge cut.

"I destroyed the face he was so proud of — 'this face gets me more pussy than you'll ever know' he bragged to me."

"I left him bleeding in the cloakroom, grabbed my

purse, ran outside, hopped in the VW van, and told Marv, 'Drive, just drive as fast as you can!'"

"But," objected Jake. "That was 20 years ago. Why would he be after you now?"

Just Nell explained that the last owners of the caverns wouldn't let her slide using Just Nell. The new accountant demanded a last name. She had figured then what happened in Florida was so far in the past there would be no harm in using her true name.

"Junior and his family were rich. Are rich. Maybe he had somebody checking records now and then. When my name came up, it came up with a location.

"He has found me, and he has not forgotten."

* * * * *

Jake was back at Lester's waiting for a burger, a cold beer in his hand.

Today, Bonny's t-shirt read: "Where there's smoke, there's BBQ."

"Is that shirt for me, Bonny?" asked Jake, referencing his rig that burned the night before.

"No, but this is." She slid a plate full of fries and a BBQ Cowboy burger his way.

A man drinking alone is a man prone to thought — to rummaging through his life, looking for signs and tendencies.

Today, Jake was that man, trying to sort out recent events by looking over his past.

Shortly after starting work in the sports department, the editor assigned Jake college games to cover. This was one of the best jobs in the world — he got to watch a game, and then write a dozen or so paragraphs about it. Since the lead paragraph was about who the teams were and who won and by how much, and the last three or four paragraphs were generally statistics about scoring, Jake only had to write five or six paragraphs about the action.

Those five or six paragraphs, though, were extremely challenging. A hack reporter would type out the usual clichés, or try to focus on one play that turned the match. Jake tried to recreate the flavor of the game, the ebb and flow, the heroes and goats.

While he certainly never lacked self-confidence in his ability to write, he also realized what he wrote was a pale echo of the real game.

After a while, he began interviewing players and coaches after games, seeking insight. Instead, the game they described seemed even further removed from the game he watched. They were caught up in a moment — a catch, a clutch basket, a third-down run — but missed the flavor of the whole experience. It was like reading a single page and believing you experienced "Gone with the Wind."

When he moved over to general news assignment and the cops and fires beat, he seldom actually witnessed the crime or blaze. Rather, he reported on what he was told. The gnawing feeling of his stories floating away from real life grew and grew.

When he was made a section editor, he not only didn't get to witness the stories, he didn't talk to first-hand sources. Now, he depended on reporters for the full story.

At every step, "the real" was another doorway

away.

When he became editor of the *Gazette*, and once again started interviewing people and writing stories, he delighted in being so much closer to real lives.

And sure, people might fool themselves or might misconstrue their actions, but for the most part, people were honest in telling their own stories. It was the story they knew best, after all. And Jake cherished catching a glimpse of the little bit of life's flame in their stories.

Now, however, he had been thrown.

Was everything he knew about local events wrong? Was the dead mayor Suzanne a hero or a villain? Hell, was she even dead? True, he had seen an orange tennis shoe attached to a leg on the gurney brought up from the caverns, but was that her?

Could he believe the sheriff? This sheriff showed no progress in finding three local murderers, and when a murderer was caught in New Mexico, the sheriff sent the one honest — likely honest, anyway — deputy to fetch him, and then the deputy died in a suspicious crash. Only the sheriff knew about the errand the deputy was on.

And what about Jimmy Daggett and, maybe, his Brazilian wife? What was she doing in town? How did she find Gus's body? Did she and Jimmy have something to do with Gus's death? Were they after the gold, or diamonds, or what?

And Jamie — Jake so much enjoyed the eager young reporter, but now, could he trust him? Was he telling lies about the pollution of a local well? And, why would he? Could he rely on Jamie now?

And finally, Just Nell. His heart told him one thing, but as Just Nell kept pointing out, his heart — his intuition — had been misleading his head. She admitted to telling big lies to others, was she being honest with him?

Too much. Too much indeed. There was just one thing to do.

"Another one here, Bonny, if you please."

Chapter 55

"We have these mysteries in town I can't figure out how to get to the bottom of, especially since I don't trust Sheriff Highkok. He could be involved."

"You should talk to Daniel."

"What?"

Jake wiped his hands on a wet dishtowel he had been using to dry the freshly washed breakfast dishes. Since the fire destroyed his RV, he had been living at Just Nell's full-time. Not that it wasn't a pleasure.

In exchange, he sometimes made a favorite dish, such as this Saturday morning when he made his own version of eggs Benedict. And this time, they got to eat the ham steak and eggs on toasted English muffins, topped with a creamy cheese sauce.

After the late breakfast, he planned to run to the office. The New York Times had contacted him for a story on the gold treasure discovery and he needed to get something written and sent off.

He figured the Times reporter would write his own story, only using Jake's article for background and quotes. But, this way, Jake would be able to say he "once wrote for the New York Times." Quite a bragging point for any newspaper journalist.

Pausing in his post-breakfast chores, Jake was puzzled by Just Nell's suggestion, "Why should I talk to a retired long-haul truck driver about a couple of murders in town?"

"He's neither retired nor a truck driver," said Just Nell. She put down the business magazine she had been thumbing through.

Jake exhaled loudly. "Why am I not surprised? Does no one in this town tell me the truth? They should rename this place 'Liars' Junction.'"

"They can't do that, silly. There is already a town named Liars' Junction."

"Really?" said Jake, sarcastically. "Really? And you are telling me the truth?"

Just Nell giggled, which led to Jake chasing her, lightly snapping the dish towel, which led to her allowing herself to be caught after one loop around the kitchen table. Which led to Jake getting to the *Gazette's* office an hour later than he had planned.

* * * * *

"Daniel, it's me, Jake."

After he had sent off his story to the Times, Jake had driven out to the campground where Daniel was still camped. Jake winced when he drove past the burned asphalt where his RV had been sitting.

Seeing a car parked next to the rented Cruise America RV, Jake knocked on the door.

When Daniel answered in bare feet, dressed in

worn jeans but a warm wool shirt over a white tee, Jake offered — again — his sincere thanks for the rescue a few nights ago.

"It's lucky I don't sleep that well at night. I happened to be up, looking out the window at the stars and nearly full moon when I saw the pickup scream into the campground. Then the driver jumped out, threw something at your RV, and tore off. I told the sheriff all of this. But, too bad I didn't see a license plate.

"When the fire exploded at your front door, I ran over, just in time to pull you guys out. I'm so glad neither of you was injured."

Jake related how the fire was just one of several mysteries in town, including the murders of the newspaper's editor and publisher.

"I want to solve these puzzles," said Jake, "but I'm just a newspaperman. I'm not some hard-drinking, two-fisted movie hero."

And then he added, with a smile, "OK, maybe a little hard drinking... Anyway, Just Nell suggested I talk to you, but she didn't tell me why."

Daniel didn't say anything for a moment. Jake started to think Just Nell was kidding him. An apology was on his lips when Daniel opened the RV's door wider.

"You had better come in."

In the next half hour, Daniel explained how he was an investigator for a large environmental fund that sought out polluters to turn over to the EPA. The government didn't have enough agents to follow up on every lead, so offered a bounty on information that led to convictions. Daniel's environment fund used the bounties to fund more investigations.

"We're like a shark," explained Daniel. "We feed on one polluter to go after the next. We've been quite successful at putting bad people in jail, or at least making them pay hefty fines."

Daniel's group got a lead — he wouldn't divulge who from — that the Cowboy Caverns were a site for illegal chemical dumping. He and a couple of other agents visited the town last fall for an initial assessment, now he was back on his own for a thorough follow-up.

"You may be able to help me a great deal," Daniel told Jake, "and in turn, I could help you unravel what is going on."

The environmental fund had investigators and attorneys but didn't have the legal authority to demand cooperation from those under suspicion. Daniel had gathered quite a few facts and developed theories, but now he needed people to talk to him. And so far, they had been evasive.

"Just a minute," interjected Jake. "Just Nell suggested the current owners of the caverns seem shady. But how can a tourist attraction get caught up in something illegal?"

"Jake, the owners have ties to the New York mob. The caverns are large holes in the ground. There could be lots of reasons gangsters would like a large hole in the ground far removed from any population center."

Jake acquiesced by nodding his head. "Ok, what do you want from me?"

"You could begin interviewing people for a series

of newspaper stories. Maybe something will shake out.

"And, the first person I suggest you interview is Jamie's mom."

Chapter 56

"Jamie, I need to know the truth about what's going on with your mom."

"Well, she seems to be recovering just fine, the doctors..."

"Jamie, the truth."

Jake had waited until it was just he and Jamie in the *Gazette's* office on Monday morning. Now, he was standing over Jamie's desk as the young reporter squirmed in his chair, not looking at Jake.

After a few minutes of silence, Jake tried another approach. "Ok, how about the truth on the well water test and the substance we found in the caverns. Did you actually have the samples tested by a friendly chemistry professor you know from your college days?"

"Err... well, I was going to have them tested, but as I thought I already knew the answer, I just took a shortcut to the results."

"A shortcut? So, we have no actual evidence the well is contaminated or that toxins residue is in the caverns? You were with me when we questioned mayor Cheese, and you let me grill him about pollutants when you knew my information could have been wrong? How could you do that?"

After starting merely curious, Jake was now getting hot. "Journalists are supposed to deal in facts, not assumptions. The *Gazette* might be a small newspaper, but that doesn't mean we have to be fools."

Jamie sank lower and lower in his chair. "I was trying to protect my mom," he barely whispered.

Jake started to say one thing, and then he started to say something else, until seeing Jamie almost in tears, he softened his voice and drew up a chair to sit beside him. "Ok, I get that I'm totally in the dark here. Tell me, honestly, what is going on. Maybe I, or the paper, can help."

Straightening in his chair, Jamie said, "I think my mom better tell you."

* * * * *

Twenty minutes later, Jake and Jamie were sitting in the kitchen of Marilyn Vetter's neat-as-a-pin rambler. After fussing around for several minutes starting a new pot of coffee, she poured three cups and set them on the table.

"Do you take anything?" she asked.

"I'm fine," said Jake. "Look, Jamie says you have a story to tell, but he hasn't told me anything. I'm not trying to put anyone in jeopardy, but we've had three murders in this town recently — Suzanne's, Gus's, and the woman at the RV campground — and I'm trying to get to the bottom of them."

"Four murders. I think there could have been four murders."

Jake sat back, looking astonished. "Four murders? What! Who's the fourth?"

"You don't have to say anything, mom," Jamie interjected. "You're not accused of anything, and we're not the police."

Marilyn looked once at Jamie, held up the palm of her hand to quiet him, and looked straight at Jake.

"Ok, let me start at the beginning. Or even before the beginning."

Over the next several minutes, she told how 20-some years before, she went to work at Schmidt Bros. Farms when Ray needed summer office help.

"I was young, Ray was younger then too, and, you know, things happened when it was just the two of us in that trailer office."

"Mom..."

"It's all right, honey. It's part of the story.

"I told Jamie a few months ago that Ray is his father so it's all on the table. We never got married, in fact, after that first summer, we never were romantically involved again.

"I know a lot of women would have made demands or caused a fuss, or at least left town in shame. But it was more my fault than Ray's, and the result of our involvement was the most beautiful baby in the world.

"Ray left it up to me if I wanted to share the information he was the father. He was a bachelor farmer, so no harm one way or another for him. For me, though, I guess I just got stubborn. Who was the father of my baby was my business and no one else's."

A tear formed at the edge of Marilyn's eye she wiped it away with a finger.

"I continued to work for Schmidt Bros. Farms, as there are not a lot of jobs in this town. Ray has always paid me well, I can pretty much come and go as I want, and we have a friendly, but professional relationship. When I hear stories from other working women in this town, I am grateful for what I have."

Jake was dumbfounded remembering how he once thought diamond hunter Jimmy Daggett was Jamie's father through a long-ago hook-up with Marilyn.

Wishing to veer away from a painful subject for Jamie, he offered, "So… the fourth murder?"

"Yes, that. Ray has always run an honest, straight-up operation. I know because I'm the bookkeeper and general manager when he is not there.

"He has been savaged and unfairly criticized by many in this town for operating a poop farm. Actually, he is doing a good thing by recycling human waste, and is making a nice profit from it.

"Anyway, you know he has a brother, right?"

Jake recalled from his first visit to the poop farm Ray had told him about the brother and that the brother turned over his interest in the then failing farm and moved to Phoenix.

"Well, about a year ago, the brother started coming around, asking about the farm, asking how the poop was processed after being dumped on the fields, asking whether environmental inspectors ever came by.

"At first, Ray was overjoyed to tour his brother around in his pickup, showing how the operation worked. Ray would say, 'I've fallen into a shit property, mixed in human shit, and have come out smelling like a rose.' Ray was very proud of what he had accomplished.

"I never liked the brother, though. He would leer at me when Ray wasn't present and a few times tried to look down my blouse when he asked me to show him the farm's books."

Marilyn paused, swishing her cooled coffee around in her cup.

"Then one day, I was in the office and heard a terrible argument between Ray and his brother out in the yard. The brother was calling Ray a 'damn fool for turning his back on easy money.' Ray called his brother a worse fool for letting gambling debts get him into the pocket of gangsters.

"Then Ray shouted, 'What have you done, what have you done? You let these bastards dump their poison on my property! Just so you can make a few dollars!'"

"The brother then shouted, 'We're both in this now, we can't quit! Others around here haven't taken your high and mighty attitude.'

"Then Ray grabbed a wrench from his toolbox in the back of the pickup and swung at his brother's head. He must have made contact because I saw the brother stagger. Ray shoved him into the pickup's front seat and then roared off towards the back of the property.

"When Ray came back in half an hour or so, he came back alone."

When Marilyn asked Ray what had happened, he said his brother had to leave. "And he's never welcome back!"

The next day, Ray suggested to Marilyn she take some time off. Call it a medical leave. He would continue to pay her but she should stay away from the farm for a while.

A couple of months later, Ray called and suggested she leave town for a bit. She could say she was going to Phoenix for special treatments. "There are people around who I just don't want you to have any contact with," Ray told her.

Recently, he phoned her in Phoenix and said she could come back. "The bad actors have left town," he informed her.

"Have you told the police any of this?" Jake asked.

"No, because, really, I don't know anything for sure, other than Ray has proven over the years to be the most decent man I know."

And now Jake was left with a journalist's worst dilemma — whether to publish material harmful to the people you know for the sake of a good story.

Chapter 57

"Jake, I'd like to keep my mom — and my dad — out of any newspaper stories you write."

"OK, I get that." Jake was at his computer, inputting notes from the interview with Marilyn about the suspicious happenings at Schmidt Bros. Farm. He hadn't told Marilyn he would be writing a story about what she told him, however, anyone who talks to a reporter should expect to see their words in print.

"Let's do this," Jake continued. "For the first stories, let's concentrate on the bankrupt owners of the caverns. Let's see if they have any ties to organized crime and let's learn more about the bankruptcy itself. They have to file tons of records, we need to dig through those."

While he was saying this for Jamie's benefit, Jake already knew the owners were tied to mobsters in New York. Daniel had used the resources of his environmental fund to run deep background checks and had come up with plenty.

Just Nell had also helped. Before she had left the employ of the caverns company, she made copies of various records, including the payroll list. She didn't know why she had done it, but it felt at the time like the lists might be useful in the future. When Daniel ran the names at the top of the list, he found all had popped for past illegal activity.

On Wednesday, the *Gazette* had its second-biggest news scoop since Jake had arrived:

"Cavern owners linked to N.Y. mob"

Using records supplied by Daniel, Jake's story detailed how all the top management of the caverns were felons with a history of illegal dumping of raw, toxic wastes. Daniel also supplied mug shots of the top officials.

And then in a bombshell secondary story, Jake wrote how a criminal investigation in another state tied these same figures to a front company running illegal dumping. Also indicted were the town's water superintendent, the town's waste management manager, and two members of the town council.

"Town officials were taking bribes to look the other way?" asked Just Nell, who was reading the story for the first time when it was already printed. Jake had decided he didn't want anyone seeing the story before being printed. Just to be safe from troublemakers eager to stop the news.

"Yes. A similar town to this one, small, out of the way, where a little bribe money goes a long way."

"This story is going to get people talking, and maybe not all friendly talk," cautioned Just Nell.

"Then you should see this list I was just sent. Daniel fished it out of the bankruptcy court proceedings. Several local people are owed large sums of money. It looks like they were investors in the caverns."

"Investors?" Just Nell rose from her desk and came to look over Jake's shoulder at his monitor.

"Some of them are local business people. When we name them in next week's issue, you might need a flak jacket to make your ad calls."

Just Nell ran her finger down the list on Jake's monitor. "$25,000 from Ed at the hardware store, $50,000 each from the two local dentists. Oh, and $75,000 from the Flanagan Foundation — the family used to own the furniture factory. $25,000 from Donny Rucker, he had the waterpark. Oh my goodness, there's $50,000 from the Hurst brothers, they own the clothing store."

"As I say, maybe you don't want to call on business people after this story comes out. They could be really upset with us."

"Hmmm... Jake, you need to look at the ads in your own paper a little more." Just Nell kept moving her finger lower on the list.

"What do you mean? I look at the ads. I love the ads. I especially love the woman who sells the ads." Jake instantly realized he hadn't meant for that last sentence to slip out, but it had. No taking it back now.

Ignoring Jake's comment, she turned toward him and started ticking off points on her fingers.

"The Flanagans closed their business, the two dentists suffered when the town voted in fluoridation five years ago, Donny blamed the lawsuit from parents whose son drowned in the park for closing, but everyone figured he was covered by insurance. He likely used the suit as a way to close without admitting his business was failing. Ed at the hardware store laid off his longtime employee Linda just after Christmas and his shelves are increasingly bare, and the Hurst brothers claim they don't advertise because ads don't work, but their clothing store still owes subcontractors for the remodel three years ago.

"All the businesses on this list are struggling or dead. And, none of them are advertisers. There are no ads for them to pull."

Thinking for a moment, she added: "Maybe this investment was a moonshot, one last chance before going down the drain."

"Just Nell, look at this last name and amount on the list."

She turned back and bent lower toward the screen. Right above Jake's finger was: Patrick and Suzanne McPhee, $100,000.

Chapter 58

On the Wednesday afternoon when the story about the local investors in the Cowboy Caverns came out, the phones at the *Gazette* lit up with angry calls.

It caused Jake to appreciate the frugal newspaper only paid for two phone lines. That slow callers were further annoyed by a busy signal gave him a rueful chuckle.

Before publishing the story, Jake had tried to contact each name on the list to ask why they invested money and how the investment scheme came about.

In each case, he was told "no comment," along with the request of "don't print my name." And, in each case, Jake explained the list was a matter of public record, filed with the bankruptcy court.

Now, when callers did get through, they had plenty to say, mostly along the lines of, "I'm suing you and the paper." Usually, this was sandwiched between profanities.

Jake patiently explained — patiently when he had the chance to talk — the paper couldn't be sued for printing public information that was true. Truth was always a newspaper's best defense.

The one call he didn't get was from the one person who could actually retaliate — Patrick McPhee, who as publisher could fire Jake. Of course, it was late in the afternoon when the paper was distributed, maybe Patrick was already deep in his bottle of whiskey, thought Jake.

"That's probably a call for tomorrow," figured Jake as he turned out the lights at 6 p.m. and left the office.

He had taken so much abuse he felt half the town was mad at him and the paper. Even the moms of the paperboys and papergirls, once they had glanced at the page one headline, avoided him.

And now, sitting at the bar at Lester's for his usual post-publication drink, it seemed as if Bonny was slow bringing him a cold one. If he had any visions of a local parade cheering his investigative work, they were turning to dust.

* * * * *

"Sam Murphy down at the tractor store wants to see you," said Just Nell, back from her Thursday morning ad calls. "He said he has something for you."

"What, a punch in the nose?" As much as he tried to portray himself as a hard-shelled newsman, Jake was typical of the breed — as thin-shelled as a robin's egg. Along with all the abuse he had taken on the phone yesterday, he was still on edge awaiting the call from the paper's owner.

If Patrick fired him now, all the work up to this point to uncover who was responsible for Suzanne's murder would have been wasted.

"I don't know, he didn't say. But, he is continuing the half-page ads for Murphy's Farm Implements. So, it can't be too bad."

Too antsy to hang around the *Gazette's* office anyway, Jake walked the half dozen blocks to the tractor store. While it was true that no one threw a brick at him along the way, no one in a passing car waved at him either.

"Come to the back," said Sam when Jake found him at the service counter.

With increasing dread, Jake followed Sam to his office. After holding the door open for Jake, Sam lowered the mini-blinds on both big windows facing the retail area.

Now Jake's dread ratcheted up a notch. While stories the past two weeks called out the owners of the caverns for being connected to mobsters, it never occurred to him that real mobsters have a way of doing away with their problems. Permanently.

"I don't have too long," Jake fibbed. "I told the office I was coming here but would be right back for an appointment."

Sam was seated at his desk, his back to Jake while spinning the knob on a floor safe. He shot Jake a glance over his shoulder as if to say, "What BS," then went back to turning the knob. Opening the safe, he pulled out a computer memory stick.

"You'll want to see this." Sam slid the stick into the computer on his desk.

Holding his finger over the enter button, he paused. "I saw your story, of course. And I know every name on that list. It connected some dots for me."

When Sam hit enter, a video started playing. Shot from over Sam's shoulder, it showed a ghost walking into the same office Jake and Sam were now in.

She has on her orange shoes, thought Jake.

Suzanne wasn't a ghost but was once there in real life. She came to convince Sam to join local business people in re-imagining the Cowboy Caverns attraction.

"A New York group plans on spending millions to make it first class, rather than the rinky-dink affair that is there now," Suzanne told Sam. "They'll replace the rickety elevator with a larger, modern, high-speed elevator, will repave and reroute the walking path so to better show off the wonder of the caverns, will expand and upgrade the restaurant, and will modernize the RV campgrounds to turn it into a money maker.

"All they want from us is a local commitment to show we support this revitalization. They are spending millions, they are asking us for a few hundred thousand... and as investors, we will share in the profits.

"Plus," said Suzanne in the video, leaning forward toward Sam, "as a town, we need this development. Look around you, you can see the life slowly ebbing away as the big cities attract more and more of our youth. The caverns will be an employer, and just as importantly, more tourists coming through will mean more business for our local stores and restaurants, creating more local jobs."

Sam hit pause on the video.

"She went on like that for another 10 minutes or so," he told Jake. She told Sam she knew more tourists wouldn't necessarily benefit his farm store, but as a good citizen, he had a duty to his town, and now the town was calling on him to step up.

"I'll give you a copy of this video, and you can see she tried to strong-arm me.

"And, finally, she shared a list of the other business people investing, as if I would want to jump aboard the save-the-town team."

Jake took a minute to absorb what he just saw, then asked, "A little off the subject, but how is it you have this recording?"

"This is farm country," replied Sam, "where a man's handshake seals his commitment. For the big deals I conclude in this office, I have found video helps everyone recall the handshakes. I now habitually record everything."

"So, Suzanne was going up and down the street, rounding up financing for the new owners of the caverns," Jake mused. "Looking at the list of people who signed up, though, I'm a little surprised. Some of them are rumored to be a little hard-pressed."

Sam laughed. "Surprised, are you? That's because you haven't heard the best part."

Chapter 59

Saturday afternoon Jake was to meet with Daniel to go over strategy for future newspaper stories in the search for murderers and polluters.

Jake figured the best place to do that was Lester's, since his scare — unfounded, to be sure, but still — with Sam at the tractor store, he liked to stay in a public place as much as possible.

Today, Bonny was wearing a tee-shirt reading: "Live life to the emptiest — Lester's" and displaying a tilted beer glass with just a sip left.

"Hey Bonny, what's the story behind Lester's anyway?"

"What's the story behind Lester's?" came a booming voice behind him. "Buy me a beer and I'll tell you the story. It's a gripper."

"Oh, hi Rodney." Jake held up a finger for Bonny to see. "Have a seat. I like stories."

Rodney slid onto the stool next to Jake, satisfied he had scored a free beer.

Taking his first sip, and exhaling an "ahhh," he started.

"It all began more than 150 years ago when there was no 'here' here.

"Legend has it that Lester — Sam Lester was his full name — came from the South, maybe Appalachia, but hill country in any case. Some say there was trouble at home that Lester was running from. Or, maybe, he was just run out.

"He was part of a wagon train heading to the Oregon Territory when there was a split caused by the hardships of the journey. Some people wanted to go on, others said this was far enough.

"Lester was one of those who, some stories say, decided to stay. Other stories say he was left behind. Anyway, he was here."

Rodney abruptly stopped to stare at the empty glass in his hand, as though startled by its appearance.

Jake held up two fingers to Bonny.

"The others who stayed immediately got to work, staking out their claims, digging shallow wells, building cabins before winter.

"Lester, though, didn't have any of those skills. He was also a drunk. The others couldn't figure out where he was getting the alcohol until they discovered Lester's one and true skill: he was a superb moonshiner. With just a little bit of corn, some water, and a contraption he rigged up, he produced a smooth, high potency 'shine.

"This being the West, a place with no doctors and no diversions from hard work, moonshine was greatly appreciated as a pain reliever and a pleasure.

"The problem, though, was Lester was his own best customer. He'd often get drunk and would wander around, either in his skivvies or bare-ass naked. This was not appreciated by the womenfolk, and the shout would go around, 'Lester has got his ding-dong out again.'"

Rodney pointed to a sign posted on the back wall. "Have you noticed? Other bars have their happy hour, Lester's has its ding-dong time."

Jake looked at the sign, thinking he had wondered what ding-dong time was. Maybe it was good he hadn't inquired before.

"Anyway, back to the story.

"There were only a handful of people here and life was tough and the soil was poor. Being a farmer was for the shits. Then someone had a bright idea: What if they sold Lester's 'shine to other wagon trains and wanderers passing through?

"There were only two problems: Lester drank up most of what he brewed, and then he walked around with his ding-dong out.

"To solve the first problem, the men began helping Lester with the distilling process, and then confiscating most of what he produced to sell... and to limit Lester's drinking.

"To solve the second problem..." Rodney looked down at his again empty glass and then up at Jake, who again held up two fingers to Bonny.

"For the second problem, they looked around to find him a woman. The West was desperately short of available women, so finding a woman was tough. The woman they found, well, she was reputed to be the ugliest woman around. She was so ugly a passing wagon train left her behind, as she was scaring the animals.

"Her name was Bonny. By the way, all the women who have tended bar here at Lester's are called Bonny in her honor, because she did give Lester what he needed to keep him at home, and keep him in pants when he did go out."

Jake was laughing as Rodney told the story, the weight of the past couple of weeks lifted momentarily.

"So moonshine became this town's first industry?" Jake asked. "And, the bar is the result?"

"Yep. But that was not Lester's biggest contribution.

"Producing moonshine can only employ so many people. And the territorial government was sniffing around with thoughts of levying taxes on the booze. Plus, moonshine takes water, and there was not much water here for expansion.

"The future did not look bright. Until, one day, sitting around the still, one of the farmers mentioned it was too bad they weren't a county seat like the town up the trail. Being a county seat when Arizona was admitted to the Union would be a boon for government money.

"After a couple more rounds of tasting Lester's product, another guy suggested, 'Why hell, let's all ride up to the county seat, grab them records and bring them back here. That way, we can be the county seat.'

"And that's exactly what happened," said Rodney. "Surprisingly, there was little opposition. The other town also had water problems and was about to blow away. And, it had a terrible name for a county seat."

"Terrible name?" asked Jake. "What was it?"

"Liar's Junction," replied Rodney, shocking Jake. Maybe Just Nell was telling the truth.

And fortunately, a modern — for those times — well drilling operation came through and found dependable water 100 feet down.

"Now, we had water and the county seat. Our future was assured." Rodney tipped back his head to empty his glass.

"So, this town was founded on moonshine and thievery?" said Jake.

"Yep. Ain't America great?" Rodney stood up and left for the other end of the bar, where he offered to roll a visiting fisherman for pool.

Chapter 61

The poop didn't smell bad today.

Maybe I'm getting used to it, or like at Lester's, maybe I'm a 'regular' around here and it is just part of the background smell thought Jake.

He was about a mile away from the office of Schmidt Bros. Farms, recyclers of human biosolids. He knew owner Ray would be in as Jake called ahead to set up an appointment for mid-Sunday.

I'm working seven days a week at a once-a-week paper, he berated himself, whereas I used to work five days a week at a seven-day-a-week paper. And, where I used to be paid Newspaper Guild wages, now I'm making minimum wage, with nothing for overtime. Oh Jake boy, you have not come up in the world!

The trip to the poop farm was his idea, though. After two weeks of blockbuster stories about the felons who owned Cowboy Caverns and their ties to environmental pollution, he had nothing for the coming week.

He had talked with Just Nell last night about whether to reveal the video of Suzanne putting pressure on the tractor store owner to invest in the caverns. But, Just Nell suggested holding off until Jake learned more. The video wasn't going anywhere.

So now, Jake wanted to talk with Ray about what Marilyn — Jamie's mom and office manager of Schmidt's — saw and heard and whether Ray's brother might have been involved in dumping toxic wastes.

Ray was waiting, sitting on the tailgate of his pickup in the office yard, dressed in his usual brown Carhartts.

After saying hi, Jake got right to it. He said he had heard about Ray's brother, about the dumping, about Ray's angry fit at his brother, and about how the brother disappeared.

"Yeah, I know who you heard it from," responded Ray, standing up. "I guess you had better come with me. I have something to show you. Hop in."

Damn it! thought Jake, closing the pickup's passenger door. Just Nell said I'm too trusting, and here I am again — going with a possibly dangerous guy to who knows where.

Ray pointed the pickup straight back from the office, not following a road, but bouncing over desert ruts and rocks and dodging cactus.

"Where are we going?" Jake tried to keep the

nervousness out of his voice.

"You'll see." Ray didn't slow down as he steered through a hole in a barbed-wire fence.

"Some big Eastern concern came along 10 years ago and bought up thousands of acres of this dry country. Maybe their in-house scientists predicted global warming would turn this desert into a Garden of Eden. I don't know. But they put up this fence that the javelina pigs and wild burros knocked down almost immediately. Still, nobody goes here so I guess it's like a Garden of Eden before man and rain were invented."

"How about those tracks?" Jake pointed to a small rise in the distance with tire marks worn into the desert bed.

"Yeah. Those are new."

After a few minutes, Ray came to a low spot and braked hard, tossing up red dust. Jake caught himself on the dash with one hand and grabbed the paper's camera that was on the bench seat with the other.

"We're here." Ray slammed his door on his way out.

Jake wrapped the strap of the camera around his right hand, allowing just a little slack. Usually, he took notes with his right hand but remembered a story a photographer told years ago about defending himself by swinging his camera at the head of a guy being an asshole.

"Those Nikons are unbreakable," the photographer had bragged.

Jake hoped he wouldn't need to verify that claim.

"Here." Ray was standing beside a 40-foot across hole. When Jake gingerly stepped forward, he couldn't see the bottom. But he did see streaks of slime along the sides, some green slime, some yellow, some red, some dull, and some fluorescent.

"This is where the illegal dumping has been taking place. I believe my brother set it all up."

Keeping the camera low at his side, his arm ready and his distance from Ray, Jake said, "I'm a little confused. I heard you verbally attacked your brother for poisoning your land, not somebody else's land."

Nodding his head, Ray responded: "You heard right. When he told me the spot, he thought it was my land. That's when I lost it. And yes, I winged him with a heavy wrench, and yes, I drove him out here because I wanted to see for myself."

Spitting on the ground, Ray added, "The dumbass didn't even remember where our family land stopped."

"What is this hole anyway," wondered Jake.

"It's part of the caverns system," replied Ray. "There are tunnels and holes to the surface like this one all over this sandstone."

"Next question: What happened to your brother?"

"Let me get something out of my toolbox." Ray turned towards the pickup.

"You're not going to wing me with a wrench and leave me for dead, are you?"

"You? Why would I harm you? You had nothing to do with the dumping."

Ray retrieved a large flashlight by the handle. "You'll need this."

Jake tensed and stepped back a foot or two when Ray approached, handing the flashlight over by the barrel.

Jake took a couple more steps back but stayed near the edge. The powerful light shot a beam along the walls, showing hues of slime flowing together as the light went deeper into the hole. At the bottom, was a muddy pothole, broken barrels — and a body.

Hands in his Carhartt's, Ray studied where Jake was pointing the light. "My brother was OK by the time we got out here, but mad as a bull. He had always been a bully and now was cussing and threatening me with his 'friends' if I blew the whistle.

"My brother was also a man who seldom pushed himself away from the table. As he was carrying on, he stepped a little too close to the edge and the sandstone — which is not stone at all but hardened clumps of sand — couldn't hold his weight, and down he went."

Both men stared down the hole for a few minutes, the story having been told.

On the way back to Jake's car, Ray said he didn't report the accident. The brother had been through three wives, had no family except for Ray, and wasn't working. No one contacted Ray about his missing brother.

Except, about a month after the fall, two men came to the Schmidt Bros. Farms office to ask Ray about his brother. They appeared to believe him when he said he hadn't seen his brother in years, since the two became estranged over the inheritance of the farm.

"They didn't look like policemen, and they didn't say their names. I had already told Marilyn to take some time off to get away from the office. That's when I told her to leave town for a while, and take our son Jamie with her."

Back at the office parking lot, Jake had started his car when Ray leaned in.

"What are you going to do with this information? Should I expect to be arrested? Or, on the front page of the newspaper?"

"I am reporting on the illegal dumping. So, yeah, I'll report on the site here. That could shed light on the other murders in town.

"I don't know what to do about your involvement with your brother. However, questions will be asked. You need to think about how you will answer them. Tell me how to locate the back way into the dumping site, and for the time being, I won't mention your property adjoins the hole."

On his way back to town, Jake laid out the story in his head about finding the illegal dumpsite. He could get the EPA and state officials involved and have a gripping front-page story for this week's edition. All the while keeping the heat on whoever was behind it all.

He believed Ray and his account of the accident. And yes, he should have reported it to the police, but considering how competent the police were on the actual murders in town, maybe it was best not to get the police involved.

What a bizarre town thought Jake. Bodies keep piling up, but the mystery is no closer to being solved.

Chapter 62

"Jake, my old boss from the caverns is on the phone for you."

Jake quickly called up a blank screen on his

computer so he could type notes. These days, his scribbles were harder and harder for even him to read and this was one interview he wanted to get exactly right.

The voice on the phone offered no preamble. "You've been smearing me in your little paper, and me and the fellas don't like that."

"Reporting the truth is not smearing," Jake shot back. "You guys are felons with ties to organized crime and dumping illegal wastes. And, you collected half a million dollars from local people to fund your operation. Money you never paid back."

The phone went quiet. And stayed quiet for a minute or longer. Jake wondered if he had been hung up on.

"Ok," finally came the voice. "Some of what you say is the truth. Most of us have made mistakes in our past. But, we paid for those mistakes.

"We did get to know each other through our past activities, but we saw the caverns as a fresh start. Whatever you say about our pasts, we do know how to run an organization, how to make money, and how to find financing.

"Don't people in America have a right to own up to their mistakes and then make a fresh start?"

Jake was astonished. His fingers were typing but his brain was in turmoil. Should he believe the caverns' owner, or should he laugh at his audacity?

An investigative reporter can go down one of two paths. On one, he can toss out flamboyantly challenging questions, hoping the person being interviewed becomes angry and says what he is trying not to say.

Or, the reporter can sidle up to the source, almost as a friend, again hoping more gets told as the source tries to make the friend understand.

Jake dropped his combative tone. "Walk me through it," he suggested. "Let's start with the local investors, to who I understand you made a unique offer."

"Having local investors wasn't our idea."

"What? Do you mean you didn't raise half a million dollars locally? I heard you wanted locals to show a commitment before you bought the caverns and launched grandiose plans on revitalizing."

Following another long pause on the phone, and the sound of tired exhaling, the voice said the mayor, Suzanne McPhee, approached the buyers with the idea of local financing.

"But there was a catch. She would raise half a million for us, but she wanted a personal loan from us for $500,000."

"What? She got local investors to pony up half a million, but then had you return it to only her? But keep the investors' money on your books? That seems fishy. Why would you do that?"

"We have had experience working with local officials before. You want to keep them on your side. Sometimes, it's the cost of doing business."

Jake next wondered about the plans for the caverns that Suzanne used to reel in investors. He hadn't noticed any improvements to the caverns or the campgrounds. He knew from Just Nell that other promises, like upgrading the gift shop and expanding the restaurant, never happened.

"Those were all blue sky promises," said the voice on the phone. "Sure, if cash started flowing as we hoped, we would have made those improvements."

"I have also heard," said Jake, going out on a limb, remembering what Just Nell had said about gift shop sales being wildly inflated, "that the actual cash flow and the real cash flow weren't always a match."

Another sigh. "Yes, near the end, we may have inflated the numbers a bit to keep our New York backers on board. But show me any business that runs a completely clean set of books. There isn't one out there."

Jake turned to toxic waste dumping.

The response was quick and strong. "I want to state categorically and clearly, that we never allowed any toxic wastes to be dumped on land we owned or in the caverns.

"I know our past, we learned toxic dumping is a bad business, and we paid for that knowledge with time in prison. We left the caverns and all the grounds around as pristine as we found them. You can put that in the paper in capital letters."

"Ok. Oh, I almost forgot. The unique offer for investors. I understand from what Suzanne was saying, a few investors were told they only had to put up half the money they promised. The caverns owners would match the other half, and then interest would be paid on the full amount, and the full amount paid back. Plus, they would get shares of profits in the future. That seems generous of you."

"I don't know what Suzanne was saying. We did hear stories, but I do know she delivered half a million dollars and we loaned her back half a million, off the books. No shares were involved. We intended to repay the investors, plus high-yield interest, but collect back from Suzanne, plus the same interest. For us, it was a wash."

Jake thanked the voice for the call and for filling in details on what went on. It's usually a good idea to end such a call on a friendly basis in case another call needs to be made.

"Oh, one other thing. You seemed to have what is needed to run a successful business, why is the business in bankruptcy now?"

"You know what we learned from the cavern business? It's a hole in the ground you throw money into."

Chapter 63

"Well, damn. This is not good news for my environmental fund. But, it will be great for the environment when the toxic dump is cleaned up.

"That's a win."

Daniel was conferring with Jake at the *Gazette's* office on Tuesday afternoon as Jake prepared the front-page story on finding illegal dumping behind Ray Schmidt's property.

State officials had already cordoned off the site, and the sheriff's office had requested FBI help to extract the body from the pit's pond of poisoned chemicals. An EPA team with hazmat suits was on the way.

So far, no one had tied Ray of Schmidt Bros'

Farms — or his brother — to the unidentified body or the dumpsite. That likely would be next week's front-page story, figured Jake.

Ownership of the dumpsite belonged to a Wall Street investment firm. The firm — a real estate investment trust — owned a million acres of farmland across the West and Midwest. Investors in the REIT were paid dividends earned either from leasing the land to working farmers or through sales when the land value appreciated.

"America's not making any more farmland," went the slogan of the firm. However, officials probably didn't figure on the farmland depreciating when toxic chemicals were pumped onto a site.

The REIT naturally feigned ignorance about the illegal activity. And since, along with wide swaths of farmlands, it also had bushels of attorneys, it could defeat any attempt at being tagged with blame.

This meant unless the actual dumpers were found, the EPA would have no one to levy fines against. And, without fines, the environmental firm Daniel worked for wouldn't earn a bounty for discovering an environmental disaster.

"I was so sure it was the mobsters who owned the caverns," said Daniel. "I thought we could go after the New York backers."

Sharing the front page was a story quoting the caverns' owner. It was only fair that after two weeks of pummeling the owners for their past sins, the *Gazette* give them space to defend themselves.

Fair and honest, because now, it looked like the caverns were not the source of the poison into the town well. If the well was even poisoned, which Jake was no longer sure of.

"My job is done here, on to the next environmental disaster. It's been a pleasure knowing you, Jake." Daniel held out his hand, and after Jake shook it, was out the door.

"It's funny." Jake turned towards Just Nell, who was waiting to proof the pages. "When I met Daniel almost a year ago at the campground, he offered me a clue to nirvana. He left before I could ask him again. I guess I'll never know how to get there now."

"Maybe your nirvana is here, Jake."

"You mean here, this community? A place that stole its future from a town named Liar's Junction?"

*****

"I still don't get the math, Jake. Tell me again."

Just Nell was riding with Jake to the press early Wednesday morning. Jamie had a morning interview for next week's paper and Just Nell didn't want Jake to do all the work himself.

She had sold an insert to this week's edition to Scott's Appliance Store advertising his truckload sale. When the printed papers came off the press, someone — and today that meant Jake and Just Nell — had to open each paper and stuff in the flyer. The *Gazette* was paid a nickel for each insert, or a little more than $80 for the entire press run.

Then, they would tie the papers into bundles of 100, light enough to be toted to the car.

"Ok. Suzanne went around town raising a pool of investment money to loan to the caverns' new owners. In some, maybe several, cases, she added an incentive by saying the caverns were matching the individual investment.

"Say you were Ed from the hardware store. If he put up $12,500, the caverns would credit him with $25,000. They would pay him a high rate of interest on the full $25,000, plus repay the entire sum at the end of the investment period, which was three years. In effect, Ed would double his money in three years while earning far better interest than he would have gotten from the bank."

"Yes, yes, I get that part. Although, pretty amazing. I can see why a struggling business would take a moonshot like that. But, I don't get how Suzanne made out."

"Without telling the cavern people, Suzanne was the one adding to the investment kitty. She matched Ed's investment of $12,500. All the cavern folks saw was $25,000 from Ed. They would have thought he put up the entire amount, which they promised to eventually repay.

"Yes, I get that. But, how did Suzanne benefit?"

"She delivered $500,000 to the caverns — much of it actual investors' money but some of it hers — and then arranged to have the caverns loan her back $500,000.

"For the caverns folks, it was money in, money out. But for Suzanne, she turned $100,000 to $250,000 of her own money, depending on how much she had to match, into an instant $500,000. In effect, the investors were loaning money to Suzanne, but they didn't know that."

"But she would have owed all that money to the caverns' owners. When that note came due, she would have had to repay it. She would not have gained anything," she said.

"That's the stumbling block in my mind, Just Nell. I am thinking she was desperate for the money when the deal went down and had expectations of being able to repay it later. The note was for three years. Two of those years had already passed. Maybe she was feeling the heat in the last few months."

"If Suzanne had $100,000 to $250,000 now — or two years ago when all of this happened — why did she need more? She and Patrick lived in a nice home, but it was not new. It should be paid for. They didn't display a lavish lifestyle. And while the paper was losing money, it wasn't a lot — just a few hundred a month."

"Another stumbling block."

"And after all of this, how and why did she wind up dead?"

"You just named a third stumbling block."

Jake turned into the back parking lot of the press. "Here we are, the exciting life of small-town newspapering. Ready to get your hands dirty — or more accurately, inky?"

Chapter 64

Thursday morning is Monday morning at a weekly newspaper.

With this week's issue out and delivered to

subscribers, Jake could relax and enjoy his second cup of coffee.

Now was the time to respond to emails he skipped over the last few days, to update computer software if needed, and jot down ideas for feature stories.

Now was the time to consider how the high school games would be covered this weekend, whether he should raise or lower the price on classified ads, and how to find a diplomatic way of telling Robbie she needs to leave crows out of her column.

Thursday morning was a time for editors to dream big. Maybe next week's front page will be one to hang on the wall.

"Jake, you'd better look at this." Just Nell had been opening the morning mail and was coming his way with several sheets of paper.

And so it begins… thought Jake

Taking the papers, he said, "Trustee sale? Why am I looking at a trustee sale? We run them all the time. For big money, I am told."

"Look at who is being foreclosed on." Just Nell pointed to a section where names and an address had been added to the boilerplate legalese.

"Patrick and Suzanne McPhee? What the hell…?"

Jake read over the foreclosure document carefully. "It looks like I can't put it off any longer. I better go see Patrick. It's morning, still pre-whiskey time."

* * * * *

Several minutes later, Jake's knock was answered by Patrick, who swung open the front door and then turned away towards the kitchen.

"If you see anything you like, take it," said Patrick, dressed, as last time, in a falling open bathrobe, well-worn fluffy slippers, and tighty-whities that Jake saw too much of. His hair had been washed sometime last week.

He had a coffee cup in his hand that Jake hoped was full of actual coffee.

"Patrick, we just got the trustee sale notice on the house. What is going on?"

"What is going on is what has been going on. I'm on a sinking ship, going down, down, down."

Jake poured himself a cup of coffee from the half-filled carafe, found milk in the fridge and sugar above the stove, and joined Patrick at the kitchen table.

"The trustee sale documents say you are more than six months behind in your mortgage payments. Did you forget to pay?"

"Forget? Like I 'forgot' I had a pile of money under the mattress? I mailed in checks, and they mailed them back to me. Apparently, the bank likes you to have money in your account before they will make good on a check."

Using his most "I'm your best buddy" voice, Jake asked again what was going on.

Patrick rambled on for a while, but it came out he had lost his frozen chicken accounts four and five years ago to an internet broker. At first, he and Suzanne lived on savings, then refinanced their house.

It all looked bleak and the hard times the

economy was going through didn't make it better. Renters stopped paying on investment properties the couple owned and the newspaper took a hit in advertising.

"Then one day, Suzie came home all aglow. I mean really, she was lit up. She said she had found a way out and it was under our noses all the time."

Again Patrick rambled along, Suzanne had discovered Gus's hobby of looking for the lost gold. Gus must have said something to her like he was getting close to finding the exact site.

Shortly after, Suzanne worked the investment deal with the new owners of the caverns to buy time, expecting to pay off the loan with proceeds from the treasure.

But over the next couple of years, Gus didn't find the treasure, and the clock was ticking on the loan.

Then the cavern owners started bankruptcy proceedings. It looked like the investors around town — all of who were Patrick's and Suzanne's personal friends — were going to lose all their money they had put up, and the McPhee phone started ringing day and night.

"People were in a panic," said Patrick, "and demanded we make good on their investments. Of course, we had no money, but couldn't tell them that. So, Suzie stalled people along."

And then, a ray of hope.

Flying his drone over the empty desert, Gus found what looked like an ancient trail leading into a hillside, maybe into a cave. "This could be it!" Gus had told Suzanne.

The property, though, was part of an old military training grounds about a dozen miles out of town. No one went there, even though the military didn't use the site anymore, as big warning signs promised swift and harsh government response to trespassers.

"Suzie had an in, though." The town 15 years ago had received permission to drill a deep well in a small valley just within the grounds. The water was piped down to the town. A grant for towns adjacent to military bases paid most of the cost of drilling and piping.

"Suzie told the town water superintendent to stop using the well while she investigated possible contamination. She made up the story about contamination. She wanted to keep city crews away from the area while she, Gus, and another couple scoured the valley for the treasure.

"She was so sure of finding gold she dreamed of dollar signs."

Jake knew exactly what Patrick was talking about, remembering the gold fever he had experienced for a while.

Patrick rose, went over to the kitchen sink, and poured out his half-cup of cold coffee. He reached into an overhead cabinet and brought down a bottle of the good stuff.

"The last night she came home crushed. All of the life had gone out of her. She barely said a word to me, and instead locked herself in the bathroom. I heard her draw a bath, and then cry.

"She was a broken woman."

"The next day, I left on a wing-and-prayer sales

trip to Japan, to try to recoup a few lost accounts. I never saw my little Suzie alive again."

Patrick took one long drink straight from the bottle and then poured more into his coffee cup.

Jake let him have a moment before saying, "I am so sorry, Patrick, I am so sorry.

"However, you don't have to lose your home to the trustee sale. This is a great house, large, with a view overlooking the town. I bet you could sell it pretty quickly. And, there's always the other half of the duplex you own where Just Nell is living. You could move in there.

"Get a realtor up here."

"Yeah," said Patrick. "Self-pity is not a plan, is it? The Daggett boy is an agent there now, isn't he? He owes us a favor, I'll call him in the morning."

Chapter 65

Driving back to the office, Jake saw flashing lights from an ambulance and fire department aid car on main street.

This calls for a reporter, he thought, quickly parking.

Slipping his reporter's notebook into his back pocket and holding a camera discreetly at his side, he walked fast into the block of office buildings.

Recognizing an EMT — and who better yet recognized him — Jake asked what happened.

"It's old man Daggett." As the EMT was walking without haste to the ambulance, Jake figured it was for the worst.

And the worst is what he found. Betty Daggett was crying into the shoulder of another woman, who from her nametag, Jake realized worked in the real estate office with the deceased Jim Daggett and his daughter, Betty.

"I'm so sorry, Betty," he said, edging over beside her. "I didn't know Jim well, but I do know he was well spoken of and a pillar in this community."

Jake didn't know Jim Daggett at all, as the old man had been housebound with an illness since Jake arrived. However, sympathy eases the path toward an interview with survivors.

"He was a pillar and he loved his work. He loved the buyers and sellers, he loved working with people. He was so kind and everyone loved him."

"Had he been back at work long?"

"He just came back this week. Like he knew the end was near. He died at his desk. That's just the way he would have wanted it." She started crying again, repeating the refrain of "he died at his desk."

Jake followed Betty's eyes towards a glassed-in office at the back. A white sheet covered a figure slumped onto the desk. Jim Daggett had indeed died at his desk.

Jake made a show of writing in his reporter's notebook. Likely, the funeral home would supply a story created with the help of survivors of Jim's life for the paper, however, Jake had learned in a small town, it's nice to appear interested.

The funny thing was, he was interested. The vast number of people in a big city numb a reporter to life and death issues. But in a small town, where everyone is someone connected to everyone else, the simple passages of life mean more.

"Hey, buddy, haven't seen you in a while." Jimmy Daggett had silently come up behind Jake and put his hand on his shoulder and whispered into his ear.

"Hi, Jimmy. I'm sorry about your father. And yes, we should catch up. Care to step out into the hallway?"

"Jake, I owe you an explanation and an apology. And, probably a few beers." Jimmy still had the smooth touch of BS'er even at a moment like this.

Noise from the back office by EMTs prepping a gurney drew the two men's attention.

"Honestly, seeing my dad these last few months and coming to realize what was going to happen," he tilted his head toward Jim's desk, "made me reexamine my own life.

"I never got along with the old man, that's one reason for leaving town and never returning until now. But the older I got, the more I realized maybe I wasn't the perfect son, either. I was a jerk in so many ways. I didn't have to be, I just was.

"These last few months, sitting with him, I came to see he had a life, too. While on the surface, he was usually upbeat and smiling, I realized he had knockdowns in his life. He just chose to get back up. And, get back up with a smile."

Jimmy tried a smile on his face. It came off sad. "You know, I think he was a better man than I am.

"I always told myself I was running to adventure, but maybe I was just running away from responsibilities. I was always in such a hurry to get to the next place, I never really made a place for myself anywhere.

"So, I'm going to try to be a better man. And that kinda starts with telling you everything."

"Let's go down to the *Gazette* now," suggested Jake.

"How about tomorrow? I have some things to take care of here."

"Tomorrow" is a profanity to a newspaperman. Stories need to be written today to get into the upcoming issue. "Tomorrow" has a way of slipping into next week and then to never.

Jake was about to object when the EMT wheeled the gurney past with Jim's body. "Sure, I'm around all day. Come on down tomorrow."

* * * * *

Between speaking with the "sinking ship" of Patrick McPhee, seeing the dead body of Jim Daggett, and then having the long-sought Jimmy Daggett reappear in his life, Jake was pretty much wrung out for the day.

When everything he tried to do on his computer just turned to crap, he looked across the room.

"Hey, Just Nell, it's Thursday. Let's cut out a little early for a beer at Lester's."

Jake could see a "no" start to form on her lips when Just Nell looked at him, saw the tiredness on his face, and changed her mind. "You bet. And, the first round is on me."

The walk to Lester's was quiet, Jake using the physical motion to relax his brain. Just Nell slid her arm through his as Lester's front door came within sight.

"Bitch! Whore!"

Jake jerked his head around to see an enraged man charging at them with a raised fist and yelling. Or, more accurately, charging at Just Nell.

Startled, Jake froze for the briefest second. But quickly regained his senses and lunged to block the attack on Just Nell.

The attacker hammered his fist down on Jake's face, knocking him to the sidewalk, where he banged his head on Lester's doorway on the way down.

Unable to make his body move, Jake saw the man push Just Nell against the building, strangling her. She vigorously fought back, clawing at his face, twisted in anger.

Then, in the slow-motion that can occur when all hell breaks loose, Jake saw a pair of hooves jump over his prone body, followed by a huge horse's belly and then another pair of hooves.

Smack! The rider swung something at the attacker, knocking him away from Just Nell and to the ground.

"Rodney!" Jake's daze lifting, he recognized the rider.

Just Nell recognized Rodney, too. She leaned into the horse, lifted a hand to grab Rodney by the shirt, brought him low, and kissed him on the lips. "My prince," she said.

She then helped Jake to his feet.

"It was nothing. We regulars at Lester's look out for each other. Good thing I had a roadie with me." Rodney held up a bottle of Bud by the neck.

"You two go inside. I'll deal with the police. There's probably a deputy in the bar."

After they ordered, when Jake asked Just Nell why she was smiling, she explained the attacker was her husband from Florida. But now that he had shown his face in an assault, he would likely be jailed and out of her life... at least for a while. That makes this day a reason to celebrate.

When their cold drafts came, Jake said, "You know, I was about ready to leap up and save you."

"I know, Jake."

"My head had hit hard against the door. I was in a daze."

"I know, Jake."

"I can protect you when I'm not blindsided."

"I know, Jake."

"So, the kiss...

Her smile widened. "It's not every day a girl is saved by a man on a horse. The white knight deserves a kiss from the damsel."

Chapter 66

"Who murdered Gus?"

"Who murdered Gus? Technically, no one."

"Technically...?"

True to his word, Jimmy Daggett had come by the *Gazette* office Friday morning to tell all to Jake.

Grande coffee in hand in a carry cup from Sweet Williams, Jimmy sat upright in the hard chair next to the editor's desk. The desk used to belong to Gus until Jake and a mystery woman found him dead.

Jake made no pretense this was anything other than an interview on the record. Along with opening a new screen on his computer to type notes, he asked and received Jimmy's permission to record the conversation.

Jake flashed a "get real" look at Jimmy. "I found Gus's smashed head buried under rocks — I don't think he put his head under there himself."

"Ok, I probably need to start at the beginning."

"Wait, before you do." Jake turned away from his keyboard to face Jimmy. "I woke up at 2 a.m. this morning, and several pieces clicked together.

"I realized the woman who called for help and was with Gus when I found him was your wife from Brazil. And she wasn't in running gear, but a sports bra and Spanx — her underwear.

"And I puzzled over why Patrick McPhee said you 'owed him a favor.' It was Suzanne who paid to bring you and your wife up from Brazil, wasn't it?

"And why would she do that? Because she had teamed up with Gus to find the missing treasure, and she needed help because she was getting desperate for quick money. Maybe hearing of your father's illness, and knowing you might want to come home, she contacted you, an experienced treasure hunter.

"And, all the time you were friendly with Jamie and with me, you were trying to learn what we knew about the gold."

Jimmy swirled the coffee in his cup, looked down, then back at Jake.

"I do like you and Jamie. This town can be dull, you guys are a couple of sparks. But the rest, you have right. Now, can I start at the beginning?"

Jake nodded and poised his hands over the keyboard. He had to type fast because when Jimmy started, the words flew.

Jimmy told that with his research and the aerial surveys from the drone, Gus felt he was getting close. His meticulous plotting of the possible routes of U.S. Army Major Pat Moser and the gold miners led him to two prime locations where the party might have sought protected shelter during the Indian troubles that broke out.

Since they were packing quite a bit of gold, they were paranoid, Gus figured. Rather than come to any settled community, they hid out in the hills.

Maybe while hiding, Major Moser came up with the idea of taking all the gold for himself, or maybe he encouraged the paranoia in the miners to get them remote and alone. In any event, the key to his plan was finding the perfect, remote spot for his double-cross.

Gus figured of his two best locations, the most likely was centered on a small valley protected by cliffs not too far from town. But, the location came with a problem. It was on the military property with strict no trespassing rules and a locked gate. However, by luck, the town had permission for a well there, and Suzanne, as mayor, had access to the gate key.

She told the town's water superintendent she suspected the well was contaminated by illegal waste dumping, and to stop using water from the well and keep all the town employees away until she could do an investigation.

"And, she told him to keep quiet, because rumors

of contamination in the water could kill the town."

So, with a remote location and no interference, Gus, Suzanne, and the Daggetts walked and rewalked the floors and cliffs bordering the valley.

"Shit, we about kicked over every rock, and peered in every hole in the cliffs, dug up dimples in the floor of the valley thinking the sink holes could reveal buried treasure.

"Nothing."

This went on for several weekends, as Suzanne and Gus had regular duties they had to be seen at, and Jimmy needed to spend time with his bedridden dad.

"Then, one Saturday morning, Isabella — that's my wife's name — ducked behind a bush and lo and behold, found a small slot in the cliff. Gus and I enlarged the hole with our shovels, and Suzanne shined a bright beam inside. We could see a narrow tunnel that looked to open to a large cavern.

"Oh boy, we were excited! Finally, this was it! Suzanne was practically jumping out of her skin. I knew from my days of diamond hunting not to get excited until you saw the gleam of the stone, but those two were shouting and high-fiving."

They shoveled some more to enlarge the cave's entrance and then all bent low to get inside. The tunnel was a dozen feet long leading to a cavern as large as a small bedroom in a house.

"Now, they really got excited," continued Jimmy, "and started digging everywhere, tossing up a shovel full of dirt here, and then a shovel full from the next spot.

"Again from my diamond hunting days, I

cautioned them to be more precise, to carefully dig deep in one spot, and then the next."

This went on for several hours until the floor of the cavern had been completely excavated a couple of feet deep.

"Suzanne's endurance frankly surprised me," remembered Jimmy. "But she was driven by greed and desperation."

Still nothing. No bones, no saddlebags, no gold.

The four dejected treasure hunters gave up, and with Gus leading, started out of the cave.

"And then, turning his head over his shoulder to Suzanne, said his last words. 'That's it for me. That was my best idea.'

"That enraged Suzanne. She shoved him in the back, he tripped on a rock, whacked his head on a protrusion in the cave wall then fell, striking his head on a stone on the floor.

"Isabella pushed past me to get at Gus. She had experience with terrible accidents in the diamond fields. Kneeling, she lifted his head onto her lap and ran her fingers over his skull. She came up with dripping goo. Her fingers on his neck revealed no pulse.

"It all happened in seconds — an unfortunate chain reaction, and Gus was dead."

When the realization of what had happened set in, Suzanne panicked. It wouldn't be right to leave Gus's body in the cave, but she couldn't take him to town either and be exposed for what she had been doing.

She came up with the idea of moving him to the buttes next to the campground and trying to make the death look like an accident.

Jake stopped typing to look up. "When I saw your wife, Isabella, in the crack in the cliffs, she wasn't in her running clothes, but her underwear because she had stripped off her bloody blouse and pants. That took some nerve."

Jimmy smiled. "You should see what Brazilian women wear in public. They are proud of their bodies."

After Jake came to the calls for help from Isabella, she left to phone the police and then disappeared. They thought by placing the body near the campground, the person who came to help would be a tourist passing through, but since Jake hung around, Isabella had to go into hiding. Jimmy told his family she had returned to Brazil.

Jimmy tilted his cup high, taking the last drink. "Unfortunately, when I told her I wanted to stay here — 'make my place' as I told you yesterday — she did leave for Brazil. I think she found the people here too drab."

Jake had been typing furiously to keep up with Jimmy's story. After a moment, he took a breath. "Patrick told me Suzanne came home that day 'a broken woman.' And then, she was dead in a few days."

Jake looked directly at Jimmy. "Did you kill her?"

Jimmy sighed. "A natural question. But, with Gus — the mastermind to finding the treasure — dead and leaving no leads, there would have been no reason for me to kill Suzanne.

"Besides, the one thing hunting for diamonds in the Amazon teaches you is to be prepared for disappointment. I didn't have the gold fever Suzanne and Gus did. That had been burned out of me years ago.

"If you want to know who killed Suzanne, you

should review that list of investors in the caverns. Sex and money, one or the other, is behind most murders."

Jake nodded, then saved his notes. "What are you going to do next?"

"I need to go to Sheriff Highkok and tell him my story. Maybe the worst that can happen is I'll get charged with moving the body."

"It pays to be an optimist," replied Jake. "But, if I could ask, how about waiting for early next week? That way, the *Gazette* would have the story of the editor's death first. Seems only right."

Jimmy laughed out loud. "For you, my friend, I can do that. And then maybe — if I'm still free — we can toast your scoop with a beer at Lester's."

Chapter 67

"Jake, did you know the woman you deal with at the bank is the twin sister of Greg's administrative assistant at the chocolate company?"

"No, but I need to know this because...?"

"I'm saying relationships in a small town spider every which way. If you were in the bank, complaining about the chocolate company, or at the chocolate company saying something bad about the bank, boom! It would get right back to whoever you were talking about instantly. And you, a newcomer, wouldn't have a clue how it happened."

Jake looked over at Just Nell, who was reading the front page from two weeks ago at the *Gazette's* front counter. "Well, I'm not saying anything bad about the chocolate company or the bank."

"I'm saying there are relationships in the small town hidden in plain sight.

"I think what I see is you are about to tell me something."

"You know about Flanagan's furniture company, right?"

"Yeah, they closed a year or two ago, and the town lost tax revenue."

"Old man Flanagan was a great guy, a real sweetheart, and a classic schmoozer. Everybody loved to see him coming.

"He'd visit the caverns, even when it was obvious we weren't doing well, and make sale pitches. Now, I know a lot of guys look at me as the older sister to the mud flap girl. I know what I have and I've used that to my advantage at times.

"Frank Flanagan would come by, and while he saw what every other guy saw, he had a way of making me feel pretty and smart, rather than just someone to toss in bed. He was the sexiest man I met — until I met you, naturally."

"Naturally."

"Frank died about five years ago, and his daughter, Francine took over. She was the opposite of Frank, and I don't mean just her sex. She was cold, brittle, and condescending. What's that old saying? 'She was born on third base and thought she hit a triple.' That's her.

"She ran the business into the ground, blamed everyone else, and then closed about two years ago."

Just Nell folded the paper she had been looking at and dropped it on a pile of back issues under the counter. "As far as I can tell, she has had one accomplishment in her life — her second marriage is to Sheriff Highkok."

"Whoa!" Coming over to pick up the paper Just Nell had put away, Jake reviewed the story on page one about local investors.

"You mean the Flanagan Foundation that put $75,000 into the caverns and is now likely to lose all that money in bankruptcy, is Sheriff Highkok's wife, Francine?"

Just Nell nodded.

"Maybe I better go see the sheriff." Jake slipped his reporter's notebook into his back pocket, threw on a jacket, and was out the door.

Turned out he didn't have to go far. The sheriff had parked his patrol car just outside the *Gazette's* front door and was stepping out.

"Sheriff."

"Jake."

Both men at the same time said, "I want to talk to you."

"The public street is no place for it," said the sheriff. "Hop in the car, there's something I want to show you anyway."

When Jake went to open the passenger door, the sheriff said, "Not the front. I have a bunch of files on the seat. Get in the back. Riding in the back of a police car, it's always an experience to talk about, right?"

Jake wasn't so sure, but when the sheriff opened the back door, he slid in without complaint. At least, he wasn't handcuffed.

"Where are we going?"

"It's just up here a little way." The sheriff backed out of the diagonal parking space into the street and then pulled away.

"My wife, Francine, wasn't very happy with the story about the investors in the caverns. She felt you were revealing private information people don't need to know. It's nobody's business but ours. I trust you don't have any more stories in mind."

"The bankruptcy court made it public information," said Jake, twisting around to draw out his reporter's notebook. "I tried to call most of the people on that list, but I didn't realize Francine was a Flanagan. I'm sorry I didn't contact her, but that list may have some connection to Suzanne's death. I can't say there will not be more stories."

The sheriff drove on in silence for a moment, a little under the town's speed limit, Jake noticed. He also noticed they were now heading out of town.

"I thought we were going to your office."

"No, what I want to show you is a few miles out of town. I wish you wouldn't do any more stories on the investors, or frankly, Suzanne. We are awaiting information from the state crime lab that could have some bearing on the case, and I don't want anyone involved to be spooked."

"Maybe a little heat from the newspaper might speed up that report," suggested Jake.

"A little heat is the last thing we need. I just want peace and quiet."

The sheriff drove on silently, picking up speed when he hit the state highway.

An idea exploded in Jake's mind. "Sheriff, was

Francine involved in Suzanne's death?"

Another minute of silence passed. "Francine tried so hard to run the furniture factory, but she wasn't her father and didn't have his silver tongue for sales. Then competition from China heated up, and nobody wanted quality U.S.-made furniture anymore. They all wanted that cheap, throw-away junk."

The police car jumped up in speed. "When she was forced to close, she came away with less than $100,000. She put it all into a foundation for her children's education. My salary paid our day-to-day bills, so we didn't need it.

"It was earning next to nothing in the bank. So when Suzanne came around with promises of high returns through a simple loan to the new owners of the caverns, plus a share in future profits, Francine bit."

The police car picked up more speed, worrying Jake.

"When the cavern owners declared bankruptcy, making the investment worthless, Francine was devastated. And then when she learned from other investors some of them only put up half the money they were credited for, she went ballistic.

"The failure in running the factory her father started combined with the failure to properly safeguard what little was left for her children had her seething in rage. She felt Suzanne had stolen her kids' money, and their future.

Suzanne evaded Francine's calls for weeks, continued the sheriff. Finally, Francine demanded her husband pick up Suzanne and bring her to the house. "There must be something you can do to get our money back," Francine told the mayor when the sheriff delivered her.

But, there wasn't. Suzanne said she had lost money, too. They all just had to wait for the bankruptcy to play out. Maybe investors would get a piece of the caverns as part of the bankruptcy settlement.

That inflamed Francine. Saying "Get a piece of this!" Francine swung a brass candlestick at Suzanne's head, knocking her to the floor before the sheriff could react.

"It was a piece from the furniture factory. Turns out, American-made is very solid."

But, by then, it was too late to save Suzanne. When their emotions settled, they decided to save themselves by making Suzanne disappear.

Jake realized where the sheriff was driving. "Why the caverns?"

"It was closed for the winter, and as I have a key to all the businesses in town as sheriff, we thought it was a good place to store the body until we could think of a better idea. And, the way the dry caverns suck all the moisture out of a body, maybe any evidence would be compromised. We never counted on a pair of kids looking for a place to screw."

"So sheriff, there is nothing to show me at the caverns. Probably we should just turn around, and head back to town. I'm sure a good lawyer can get you and Francine off lightly. You were conned by Suzanne."

"A good lawyer? Do you know how much one of those cost? No, I think this needs to be settled without going to trial."

Coming to a bend in the road, the sheriff slowed

when he saw a van coming from the opposite direction riding the yellow line.

"Damn kid on a phone," said the sheriff. "I ought to pull him over."

Looking over the sheriff's shoulder, Jake saw a pink pizza delivery van. Aaron O'Dell was driving and talking on the phone.

"Help me! Help me!" Jake screamed and pounded on the window as the van tore past. A startled Aaron just looked at him.

"Nobody's going to help you, Jake. I don't think the town likes you all that much, anyway. All this investigative crap in the paper. People want nice stories."

Jake looked back to see the van brake, then turn around.

"What the hell is that kid doing?" Sheriff Highkok jerked the wheel to the left as the police car had drifted into the gravel shoulder while he was staring intensely into his rear view mirror.

Jake braced himself. The van was catching up, coming fast.

Then Aaron zoomed around, getting in front, where he slowed, zigzagging wildly in the middle of the road.

Drawing his service Glock, the sheriff powered down his window, switched the gun to his left hand, and fired twice.

The van pulled right. Oh no, Aaron's been shot... or is giving up! thought Jake.

Then an arm came out of the van's window, tossing something at the sheriff's car. Splat! "What the hell, a pizza!"

The pizza hit right in the center of the sheriff's vision, stunning him. His reflexes instantly reacted to get out of the way by jerking the car right.

Gravel grabbed the front tire, yanking the car farther right, and the speeding vehicle left the road, colliding with a large Ponderosa Pine tree.

Branches smashed through the front window, puncturing the airbag that had inflated on impact.

Jake was tossed all over the unprotected back seat, but the screen between the front and back — designed to protect officers in front from criminals in back — had prevented him from flying through the windshield. Unfortunately for the sheriff, with the airbag deflated by a limb, he was thrown into the windshield.

When Jake looked up from the back seat footwell when he landed, Aaron was working the automatic door locks on the driver's armrest.

"Get out, Jake!" And Jake did.

In a fast-flowing torrent of words, Jake explained to Aaron what had happened, and what the sheriff had told him.

"But, why did you come back, Aaron? Why help me?"

"My uncle, deputy Verne, had been saying something was rotten in the sheriff's office... rotten at the top. He was talking about bringing in state inspectors.

"And when we heard his accident in New Mexico may not have been an accident, well, many in the family were feeling the sheriff may have engineered it.

"So, when I saw you, and you yelled for help, knowing that you were a good guy — a good guy for an editor anyway — I came back to help. When the sheriff shot at me, I used the only way to retaliate I could — a cheesy pepperoni pizza."

Aaron and Jake watched the settling dust around the accident scene. A check of the sheriff showed no pulse.

Now the seriousness sunk in. "Maybe, though, it would be best if I just said I came upon the crash scene. Do you suppose we could leave out of the newspaper story the pizza toss?"

"That's the best part, Aaron. But, sure, since you likely saved my life, I could omit that from the story. Make sure to clean up the cheesy remains."

"Cool! Besides, I could use it in my next book. Did I tell you my Vampire in Mexico series has been downloaded more than 20,000 times on Amazon?"

The relief of surviving the accident and near-death made Jake giddy and he laughed and laughed.

"' Newspaper editor saved by a best-selling novelist!'" What a headline that could have been!

Chapter 68

"Last beer on your way out of town?"

Bonny slid a cold one Jake's way. It was a little before noon on Saturday. Early for a beer but Bonny was right. It was his goodbye beer.

How did she know? Probably somebody saw Jake load his few possessions into the bed of his pickup at Just Nell's duplex. That somebody told somebody else, and word got to Lester's before Jake did.

The morning had started with Jake fixing his second favorite Saturday breakfast, a Joe's special.

Sauté half of a Walla Walla sweet onion, add Jimmy Dean's hot sausage, remember a large handful of sliced morel mushrooms, add a few green onions late to keep their snap, mix in scrambled eggs, stir in fresh spinach near the end just until it wilts then top with parmesan cheese once on the plates.

Toast a couple of English muffins so crisp they crunch to the bite and it was a perfect breakfast to start the weekend. Along with coffee made from freshly ground beans, naturally.

Jake delighted in making breakfast for Just Nell on the weekends. They usually ate slowly and talked in the warm comfort of this simple domestic life.

"I've decided what to do with my half of the money," Just Nell announced, spreading raspberry jam on one half of a muffin.

The 10 percent finder's fee payment had come through a few weeks before from Arizona State University for leading Prof. Dusty Rhodes and her team to the legendary lost gold treasure. Jake and Just Nell each received a little more than $75,000.

"Really, what?"

"I'm going to buy the *Gazette* from Patrick. He has no interest in owning the newspaper, and he needs the money. He said he would make me a good deal for all cash."

Jake put down the buttered muffin he was using to help scoop up a fork-load of breakfast from his plate. "So, you are going to be my boss? That will be fantastic!"

Just Nell looked off to the side. "Yeah. Jake, I can't thank you enough for hiring me at the *Gazette*. My life was in a hole at the caverns, and when I celebrated my last birthday by serving myself a piece of defrosted pie at the caverns' closed restaurant, I felt all the joy of life was ebbing away.

"I love working at the *Gazette* and I love my connection to the people in this town. Knowing what is going on, being in on the news, I feel I'm at the heart of a town. I even love making ad calls and talking with business owners up and down the street.

"Even the silly features that sometimes Jamie does — the man who raised the biggest pumpkin or the woman with a thousand salt and pepper shakers — and Robbie's column, the rants and raves in the letters column, all of it, really has me so excited to go to work every day."

Jake's brain tried to catch up to Just Nell. What is this? Is there a "but" coming? he wondered. In a serious conversation, everything before the "but" was meaningless compared to what came after.

"But..." And there it was.

"Jake, I've watched you these last few weeks when you were chasing down the stories on the illegal dumping and the murders. You were in your element, drawing together sources, badgering state officials, and writing on deadline.

"This is who you are. When the *Gazette* goes back to being just another small-town newspaper, you would not be happy. Even Gus, who was no great shakes as a newsman, had to have his hunt for the gold treasure to keep him interested here."

Now, with the cooling breakfast all but forgotten, Jake asked in an almost whisper, "And us?"

"Oh, Jake, this has been one of the happiest times of my life. I was so full of self-pity, and as Patrick McPhee said, 'self-pity is not a plan.' You rescued me from that."

Another "but" was coming, Jake knew.

"But..."

Damn it! And there it was.

"I'm the type of woman who walks away from a man. Sorry, but that is just the way it is."

Just Nell looked like she wanted to say more, but what more was there to say?

After talking a little more about logistics, such as who would edit the paper after he was gone — Just Nell had already talked to the husband of a new deputy who moved to town to replace Verne who had worked at a weekly newspaper in Oregon — and how soon should he leave — now was the answer they both decided on — Jake loaded up and was gone.

It didn't take him long. He had few possessions after the fire in his RV.

And now, he was looking at his last beer at Lester's.

Today's Bonny's t-shirt read, "Game over. You lost." That pretty much nailed it, thought Jake, taking the last sip of his last beer.

"Hey, Bonny. I just realized I've been coming here for almost a year, and I still don't know your name. In fact, I don't know much about you at all."

"Then you're not much of a reporter, are you?"

Her smile took away the sting.

"Since you're leaving, I'll tell you. My name actually is Bonny. I was named after my great-great-grandmother, the original Bonny Lester."

"You're Bonny Lester? You are Lester's bar? Wow!"

"Watering drunks. That's been the family business for the past 150 years."

She turned towards the taps, filling a fresh glass. "Speaking of family, let me get you another beer... on the house. My family owes you one."

"The Lesters? Other than the fact I've spent too much time here, why do the Lesters owe me a beer?"

Placing the filled glass in front of Jake, she said, "My aunts owned the pie shop. People laughed at them and their gold treasure placemats. You showed everyone it was all real."

Jake was about to say most of what was on the placemats was wrong, but a free beer was a free beer.

Instead, he said, "Your aunts ran the famous pie shop and you own Lester's? I had no idea."

Bonny leaned in from her side of the bar. "You know nothing, Jake Stewart."

Author's notes:

While there are small towns, deserts, and caverns in Arizona, all persons, businesses, and events in this book live only in the author's imagination. Any resemblance in this story to actual persons, living or dead, is purely coincidental.

This is the first Jake Stewart novel about his adventures as an editor of a small newspaper in danger of dying. It used to be said a community needed three things to be a community: a bank to show local financial wherewithal, a school as a belief in the future, and a newspaper to knit people together. Banks and schools seem to be doing OK, but newspapers...

Made in the USA
Las Vegas, NV
21 November 2023

81305397R00154